KT-452-451

22.

JACK AND THE BEANSTALK

By Ed McBain
THE 87th PRECINCT NOVELS

Cop Hater • The Mugger • The Pusher • The
Con Man • Killer's Choice • Killer's Payoff •
Lady Killer • Killer's Wedge • 'Til Death •
King's Ransom • Give the Boys a Great Big
Hand • The Heckler • See Them Die • The
Empty Hours • Lady, Lady, I Did It! • Like
Love • Ten Plus One • He Who Hesitates •
Eighty Million Eyes • Hail, Hail, the
Gang's All Here! • Sadie When She Died •
Let's Hear It for the Deaf Man • Hail to the
Chief • Blood Relatives • So Long As You
Both Shall Live • Long Time No See

AND

Ax • Bread • Calypso • Doll • Fuzz • Ghosts •
Heat • Ice • Jigsaw • Shotgun

THE MATTHEW HOPE NOVELS

Goldilocks • Rumpelstiltskin • Beauty and
the Beast • Jack and the Beanstalk

OTHER NOVELS

The Sentries • Where There's Smoke • Guns

JACK
and the
BEAN-STALK

—

by
ED McBAIN

—

HAMISH HAMILTON

LONDON

GLOUCESTERSHIRE

Class F

Copy 009

COUNTY LIBRARY

First published in Great Britain 1984
by Hamish Hamilton Ltd
Garden House 57–59 Long Acre London WC2E 9JZ

Copyright © 1984 by Hui Corporation

British Library Cataloguing in Publication Data

McBain, Ed
  Jack and the beanstalk.
  Rn: Evan Hunter   I. Title
  813′.54 [F]   PS3515.U585
  ISBN 1–241–11270–2

Printed and bound in Great Britain by
Richard Clay (The Chaucer Press) Ltd, Bungay, Suffolk

This is for Elaine Perry

1

Japanese lanterns festooned the outdoor gardens of the Ca D'Ped. Their glow only seemed to add to the suffocatingly moist heat of the August night. The Ca D'Ped was Calusa's art museum, a vast hacienda back when Florida was still a Spanish possession, renovated and refurbished in 1927 when its original name—Casa Don Pedro—was abbreviated to its present form. Calusa natives called it "The Ped." My partner Frank called it "The Carport."

The party on that eighth night of August was a formal affair in honor of Calusa's resident artists. "Formal" in Calusa, at least during the summer months, meant white dinner jackets and black ties for the men, and long gowns for the women. Frank's wife was wearing a slinky black creation slit to her waist, the better to expose what Frank proudly called "the family jewels." Like a juggler defying an expectant crowd, Leona kept daring one or the other of her precocious treasures to spill from the front of the gown, seemingly unaware of how dangerously close they were to indecent exposure.

Frank was holding forth on his favorite topic. Frank is a lawyer, like myself, but he is also a transplanted New Yorker, than which there is nothing worse in the entire world. When a New Yorker moves to California, he will eventually stop reading *The New York Times*, and after a brief period of mourning he will begin referring to New York as "Back East," as if it were a remote province somewhere in China. Most migrants to Florida will refer to New York (or Chicago or Detroit or Pittsburgh or wherever they've come from) as "Up North," but not my partner Frank. New York is New York is New York, and there is no place like it in the world, and any other city, country, or even *continent* is but a pale reflection of that glittering city Frank still thinks of as home. The Sunday *New York Times* costs him two and a half bucks down here. He would gladly pay a full month's draw for it. He is an impossible chauvinist, but he has been my partner for many years now, and he is a good lawyer and an endearing man when he is not comparing Calusa to the Big Apple. He was doing just that tonight, within earshot of the museum's curator, who, I was certain, did not enjoy hearing the Ca D'Ped compared unfavorably to MOMA. I tried to hush him when he got on the topic of Calusa's pretensions to culture, but once Frank boarded the Lexington Avenue Express, there was no stopping him.

"If Calusa was a fat banker . . ."

"Were," Leona corrected.

"*Were* a fat banker," Frank said, and glanced into the open front of his wife's gown as though discovering an enticing stranger, "and if all its various writers, sculptors, and painters were the banker's mistresses, they would all pack their frilly underwear and leave tomorrow morning. Nowhere in America is the local talent so taken for granted as it is in this sad excuse for a real city."

"Frank's a New Yorker," Leona said to Dale, as though the obvious needed explanation and amplification.

I should explain that Dale O'Brien is a woman. There are still many telephone callers to her office who ask for *Mister* O'Brien, assuming that any lawyer named Dale O'Brien must also and perforce be a male. She is a female. Very much so. She is a

2

female who is five feet nine inches tall, and she has red hair she prefers to call russet, and glade-green eyes, and a beautifully proportioned figure that was draped tonight in a shimmering green gown that matched her eyes. Those eyes seemed vacant and bored just now. Perhaps she had heard Frank sounding off once too often. Perhaps she was disenchanted with the insipid white wine the museum was serving in tribute to its "honored" artists. Or perhaps the heat and humidity had got to her. It is easy for the heat and humidity to get to you in Calusa during the month of August.

"I know a playwright down here," Frank went on, ". . . I believe you know him, too, Matthew . . . who won the Drama Critics Circle Award back in his heyday, and who can't get a house seat at the Helen Gottlieb, can you believe it? This is a man who can call any theater in New York, and get sixth-row-center seats to the biggest hit, but he can't get a choice seat down here for any of the moth-eaten road shows that pass through. At the same time, of course, anytime there's a charity benefit, no one'll think twice about calling him and asking him to speak. The same applies to artists. The Carport decides to honor the local painters and sculptors, right? Okay, so *when* does it throw its munificent party? On a Monday night in August! You won't find a goddamn *iguana* down here in August! Have Motherwell passing through in *January*, however, or Warhol, or anybody who doesn't *live* here, and out comes the red carpet. And you can bet they won't be serving warm white wine, either. Do you know what I think it is? Do you know what I *really* think it is?"

"It's that it isn't New York," Leona said.

"Well, of *course* it isn't New York," Frank said. "But that's not it. What it is, deep down in its heart of hearts, Calusa *knows* that most of the artists down here are dilettantes. Uproot a cactus plant, and you'll find a self-proclaimed writer, painter, or sculptor sitting there in a hole in the sand. My friend says he's afraid of identifying himself as a playwright down here because the dentist he's talking to at a party will say, 'Are you? Gee, *I'm* a playwright, too!' The cultural pretensions of this city—*imagine* calling itself the Athens of Florida!—are simply unimaginable in terms of what the *real* world considers . . ."

"Matthew, let's go," Dale said.

I blinked at her.

"Please," she said.

Her abrupt request seemed not to faze Frank at all. He turned to Leona and continued with his premise as though trying to impress a new girl in town, his eyes continually flicking to breasts he surely knew as well as he did the Florida Statutes. We said our good nights, thanked the curator for a wonderful show, and went out to where I'd parked the Karmann Ghia. Dale was unusually quiet.

"Frank get on your nerves?" I asked.

"No," she said.

A Karmann Ghia, for all its recent status as a "classic," is perhaps not the best vehicle for transporting a leggy woman in a long gown. Dale was fidgeting on the seat beside me, trying to make herself comfortable. The air conditioner wasn't working. When my former wife and I were divorced, *she* got the Mercedes-Benz with the air conditioner that worked. *I* got the Karmann Ghia. She also got custody of my daughter, whom I saw every other weekend and on alternating holidays. My daughter absolutely *adored* Dale, and was constantly asking me when we were going to get married; for all their hip attitudes about sex, today's teenagers nonetheless seemed a bit uneasy about grownups sharing the same bed without benefit of clergy. The bed Dale and I shared was actually *two* beds, hers on Whisper Key or mine on the mainland, whichever way the wind blew. The wind tonight seemed to be blowing out of the south: Dale's house on the Gulf would be cooler than mine on the mainland. I made the right turn onto U.S. 41, and immediately found myself in a traffic jam as monumental as anything conceived by Fellini.

"Shit," Dale said.

It was unusual to find heavy traffic on the Tamiami Trail at 10:00 P.M. on a sweltering night in August. In August, the snowbirds and their automobiles and campers were up north, where

4

they *belonged*, with not a thought of migration in their heads. The roads were normally empty, the restaurants uncrowded, the lines outside the movie theaters nonexistent. Year-round residents like Dale and myself were grateful for the respite, while at the same time mindful of the *reason* for the peace and quiet: as Frank had put it, almost, only an iguana would find Calusa habitable during the summer months. Despite what the calendar said, summer in Calusa began at the beginning of May and often lingered through October, though many of the full-timers insisted that those two bracketing months were the nicest ones of the year. Native Calusans tended to forget that May and October were lovely *anywhere* in the United States. They also conveniently forgot that in May down here, you could have your brain parboiled if you didn't wear a hat. August was worse. August was impossible. But a *traffic jam* in August? On a Monday night?

"What *now*?" Dale said impatiently.

It occurred to me, belatedly, that she had been somewhat impatient all night long. She had been impatient, first, with the gown she'd originally planned on wearing, telling me the moment I entered her house that it had come back from the cleaners with a spot on it. She had next been impatient with the green gown she finally chose to wear, the one she was in fact now wearing, telling me that it was too tight and that the line of her panties would show. When I suggested that she forsake the panties altogether—an idea she might normally have found interesting if not particularly inventive—she had turned away and stomped off into her bedroom, leaving me waiting in the living room for the better part of a half hour, after which she'd emerged triumphantly resplendent, but complaining that she looked like a stuffed sausage. She had seemed impatient to get to the Ca D'Ped, and then impatient to *leave* it. As I got out of the car now to see what the trouble was up ahead, she was impatiently jiggling one sequin-slippered foot.

The trouble up ahead was a trailer truck that had jackknifed across the road, smashing into two automobiles in the process. The state trooper I spoke to said it might take an hour or more before the ambulances and the wreckers were out of the way. He suggested that I go back to the car and listen to some good music on the radio. Dale suggested instead that we pull off onto the dead-end street on our right, and then walk over to a place called Captain Blood's, glaring its neon just up the road. Neither of us had ever been to this particular watering hole before, but a tall cold drink was a tall cold drink. In Calusa, it should be mentioned, there are more lounges called Captain Something-or-Other than there are orange trees. The town is nautically oriented, situated as it is on both the Gulf of Mexico and Calusa Bay. Captain Blood's seemed from the outside like any one of the other Captains sailing U.S. 41. A blue pickup truck was parked close to the front entrance. Orange and then blue neon blinked onto the barrel of a shotgun resting on a rack just inside the rear window.

The decor inside the place was exactly what one might have expected. Timbers and ropes, fishing nets and running lights in red and green, a huge brass engine-room telegraph just inside the entrance door. An old man wearing a yachting cap was sitting alone at the bar on the right. A waitress turned from the bar at the sound of the bell tinkling over the entrance door, and came over to us with a smile on her face.

"Just the two of you?" she asked, and then led us into a vacant back room with a jukebox. There were a dozen or more booths fashioned of high-backed wooden benches and varnished hatch-cover tables. We settled in a booth farthest from the juke, which was blaring a country-western ballad. Dale sat on one side of the table, I sat on the other. She ordered a gin and tonic. I ordered a Dewar's on the rocks.

I think I should mention right now that the last time I'd had a fistfight was when I was fourteen years old. An important point, perhaps, since I am now thirty-eight and presumably wiser, and certainly bigger, and possibly stronger than I was back then when a high-school jock named Hank advised me to keep away from his cheerleader girlfriend, whose name was Bunny Kaplowitz. Until then, I had always thought only the *good* guys were named

6

Hank. What Hank said was, "Keep away from her, dig?" or jock words to that effect. I told Hank he was a moronic turd. I remember the words clearly and distinctly. They are etched in acid on the restoration Dr. Mordecai Simon put into my mouth in the city of Chicago, where I was living at the time. No sooner had I uttered those memorable words than Hank blackened both my eyes, dislocated my jaw, and knocked out one of my molars. Under anesthesia in Dr. Simon's office, I vowed eternal fidelity to the policies of a man named Gandhi, since immortalized for a whole new generation in a film of the same name.

The fight back then had to do with protecting one's disputed turf, a masculine prerogative in this land of the free and home of the brave, where macho males strut about in Calvin Klein designer jeans. The turf in that long-ago instance was a nubile cheerleader. The turn tonight, as I was about to discover, was a thirty-two-year-old woman named Dale O'Brien. We are both sensible, mature attorneys, Dale and I, officers of the court sworn to uphold the laws of the state and the nation. Together, and considering the vast sums of money our respective parents had invested in the pursuit of our separate law degrees, we should have known better than to allow ourselves to become a "turf" and a "defender of the turf," which was most certainly what we *did* become at precisely ten-fifteen. I remember looking up at the clock—set into a ship's wheel on the other side of the room—a moment before disaster loomed.

It loomed in the shape of two young cowboys—both in their mid-twenties, I guessed—who came sauntering out of the men's room. They were not wearing designer jeans. Their jeans were faded and their boots were scuffed, and they wore cowboy shirts with embroidered pocket flaps and little pearl snap buttons on the flaps and at the cuffs, and they wore great big ten-gallon hats tilted over their sunburned faces and they wore kerchiefs around their necks, a blue one for the blond guy with the mustache, and a red one for the guy with the black beard. It was not unusual to see an occasional cowboy in Calusa. You do not have to ride very far out of town before you come into cattle country. The state of

Florida, in fact, counts cattle-breeding as among its chief sources of revenue, ranking it fifth after narcotics, tourism, manufacturing, and farming.

The two cowboys, who went directly to the jukebox, looked as if they might be quite at home tossing thousand-pound steers over their respective shoulders. The blond one had to be at least six-four, with the awesome bulk of a wrestler, and the one with the black beard was just as tall, with the hard, lean, muscular body of someone who'd begun lifting weights at an early age, probably in a correctional center someplace. I was willing to bet he had tattoos on both arms. The first thing they did was pour what appeared to be a hundred dollars in coins into the jukebox. The next thing they did was push a multitude of buttons—every button in sight, it seemed—after which the first of their selections flooded the room: the same country-western ballad that had been playing when we walked in. Dale rolled her eyes and said, under her breath, "Oh, no, not again," and the blond cowboy immediately said, "What's that, lady?" qualifying him at once as a recipient of the Better Hearing Award, since the din of the jukebox should have drowned out anything but a shout.

Dale, of course, did not answer him.

From the jukebox, smiling, his hands on his hips now, he said again, "What's that, lady?"

And again, she did not answer him.

He came over to the table. His friend with the black beard was still standing at the jukebox. Dale, as I know I've mentioned, was wearing a long green gown she felt was too tight for her. I don't remember whether she'd decided to put on panties or not. I *do* remember that she wasn't wearing a bra, and that whereas the scoop neck of her gown could in no way compete with the outrageous open slash of Leona's, it nonetheless revealed more of her than might have been appropriate in a tacky little roadside joint. I was wearing a white dinner jacket and a black bow tie, which I had tied myself with great difficulty before leaving the house that night.

I should add that before the fight I had brown eyes and dark hair, and I possessed a face my partner Frank classifies in the "fox" category. (He himself, by his own system, has a "pig" face.) I weighed a hundred and ninety pounds soaking wet, which I was close to being on that humid night. I was an even six feet tall. *After* the fight, my eyes were black and blue, my hair was as red as Dale's (or at least a patch of it was, where my head was banged repeatedly against the hatch-cover tabletop), my face looked rather more piggish than it had earlier—and I was *short*.

"Don't you like the music, lady?" the blond cowboy said, grinning. His teeth were very white. His eyes were blue.

"The music's fine," Dale said without looking at him.

"You don't seem to like it much, though," he said, almost apologetically.

"It's fine," Dale said.

"Hey, Charlie!" he called over to the jukebox. "The lady *likes* the music we picked!"

Charlie came over.

"That right?" he said. He, too, was grinning, his teeth flashing brightly against his black beard. "Well, I'm right pleased, ma'am. You like the music, too?" he asked, turning suddenly to me, the same lopsided grin on his face. I realized all at once that they had both been drinking heavily. And I reasoned that the best thing to do with a pair of happy drunks was humor them.

Smiling, I said, "It's okay, you did all right."

"Only *okay*?" Charlie said, and opened his eyes very wide. "He only thinks it's *okay*, Jeff."

"Lady thinks it's *fine*," Jeff said, sounding hurt.

"Lady must be right, then," I said, still smiling. "Why don't you go sit down and listen to it?"

"You asking us to *leave*?" Charlie said, seemingly surprised.

"We'd like to be alone, if you don't mind," I said.

"He'd like to be alone," Charlie said, grinning again.

"Yeah, I heard him," Jeff said, grinning back.

"Can't say I blame him, though," Charlie said.

"Don't blame him a'tall," Jeff said, and glanced into the front of Dale's gown, still grinning.

Like a grownup scolding two naughty youngsters—which, from my elderly advanced age of thirty-eight, they actually seemed to be—I said, "Come on, fellas, behave yourselves. Go on back to your own table, huh?"

It became immediately apparent that this was exactly the wrong thing to say. The grins dropped from both faces at the same time. Jeff put his hands flat on the tabletop and leaned into me. The reek of alcohol when he spoke was overpowering. A scrap of potato chip clung to his blond mustache.

"We ain't *got* a table," he said.

"We been standin' at the bar," Charlie said.

"Then go on back to the bar," I said.

"We like it here," Charlie said.

"Look," I said, "let's not create a problem, okay? My friend and I . . ."

"Who's got a *problem*?" Charlie said. "*You* got a problem, Jeff?"

"No problem a'tall," Jeff said. "Maybe the man in the monkey suit here's got the problem."

"You been to the senior prom?" Charlie said.

Dale sighed. "Let's go, Matthew," she said, and started to rise.

"Stay put, lady," Charlie said, and placed his hand on her shoulder.

Dale shrugged it off at once, her eyes flashing. "Let's go," she said again.

"You talking to me, lady?" Jeff said. "Where you wanna go?"

"Take you anyplace you wanna go," Charlie said.

"Matthew . . ." she said.

"Matthew don't wanna go just yet," Charlie said. "Ain't that right, Matthew? Matthew's enjoyin' this here conversation."

"Matthew likes talkin'," Jeff said.

"Matthew's a big talker," Charlie said.

"Okay, fellas," I said, "that's enough, okay?"

"What's enough?" Charlie said.

10

"Lady tells us she likes our music," Jeff said, "Matthew tells us that's enough."

"How was the prom?" Charlie said. He was proud of his little metaphor, eager to trot it out again. "Have a nice time at the prom?"

"What kinda music was they playin' at the prom?" Jeff asked.

"Did you do a lotta dancin'?" Charlie asked.

"How would you like to dance, lady?" Jeff asked.

"How would you like me to call the police?" I said.

"If you can get to the phone, that might be a good idea," Jeff said. "Meanwhile, me and the lady's gonna dance."

He grabbed her wrist and started pulling her out of the booth. Charlie stepped aside to give them room. I started to get up, but Charlie, with his weight lifter's muscles, slapped out at me effortlessly, backhanded, and I sat down again on the high-backed wooden bench. I thought, *This isn't happening.* This encounter with two redneck cowboys in a shitty little lounge was as far removed from the ordered reality of my life as would have been an elephant hunt in darkest Africa. But Jeff, the one with the potato-chip mustache, was dragging Dale out onto the postage-stamp dance floor near the jukebox, and Dale was calling him a son of a bitch and struggling to release her wrist from his grip, and Charlie—the black-bearded weight lifter—was standing with his back to me and the booth, his hands disdainfully on his hips, throwing his head back to laugh as Jeff pulled Dale in against him, and I thought, *It's happening, all right.* I lunged out of the booth and shoved myself past Charlie, trying to get to where Jeff, the ballroom wrestler, was sliding his beefy hand onto Dale's behind, Dale yelling and trying to shove him away, and that was when Charlie hit me on the back of the head with both hands clenched together like a mallet.

I staggered forward, my arms wide, my eyes wide, my mouth open, and Jeff released his grip on Dale only long enough to punch me full in the face as I came lurching toward him. I wish I could say that, in the brief massacre that followed, I got in even one solid shot, but I didn't. As I fell to the floor, I saw Dale lift her knee and take off one of her sequined slippers. I wish I could say that the heel of it connected with Charlie's head, because that's where she was aiming it, but he simply brushed her arm aside, and then decided it would be gentlemanly to punch her as hard as he could over the left breast. Dale was screaming as they dragged me over to the booth again and began pounding my head against the tabletop. The waitress was screaming, too. The bartender ran into the back room and started shouting. Somebody— the old man in the yachting cap, I think—was running for the wall telephone.

When the Calusa police officer finally arrived, I was mopping the back of my head with a handkerchief monogrammed with the letters *M.H.*, and Charlie and Jeff were long gone. I told the officer I didn't know their last names. I told him there had been a blue pickup truck out front, but I hadn't noticed either the make or the license plate number. I also told him I personally knew Detective Morris Bloom of the Calusa P.D., but he seemed singularly unimpressed by this piece of information. The bartender thought he should call for an ambulance. I said, No, no ambulance. The cop insisted that I be taken to a hospital. Dale said she would drive me to Good Samaritan. Somebody else— the old man in the yachting cap again, I think—remarked that there was blood all over my nice white jacket. The last thing I heard before leaving the appropriately named scene of the crime was the waitress sadly saying, "Have a nice day." I guess she was referring to tomorrow, because the night wasn't over yet, and it was going to get a hell of a lot worse in the next little while.

It took the intern in the emergency room at Good Samaritan almost a full hour to anoint me and bandage me and assure me repeatedly that nothing was broken. Dale and I left the hospital at close to midnight. She got behind the wheel, pulled her long gown up over her knees, started the car, and drove out onto U.S. 41, utterly deserted now. We sat side by side in complete silence.

I felt totally inadequate. I felt like a dope. I felt like a sissy. I felt everything I had been taught to feel as a boy growing up on the wild and woolly streets of Chicago, Illinois. Boys weren't supposed to cry, but I felt like crying. My head hurt, and my eyes hurt, and my mouth hurt, and I was only grateful that I hadn't lost any teeth this time around. I wanted to say "I'm sorry," but I didn't know what I was sorry for. My mind kept circling the same labyrinth of dead-end thoughts. Should I apologize for being a civilized human being in a world populated by occasional barbarians? Should I apologize for not carrying a deadly weapon, the way so many people in America do? Should I apologize for not being the heavyweight champion of the world?

When I was a boy, whenever my Aunt Nora said anything nasty to my mother, my mother would reply, "Excuse me for living." Should I apologize for living? What if the reverse had happened? What if I had mopped up the floor with those two goons? Would I be a better man for it than I was now, sitting here in abject silence, nursing my wounds while a woman drove me home? And what was *that*, huh? Dale had driven me home on more occasions than I could count. Why should it matter *now* that she was a woman?

They had really reached me, those bastards.

I wanted to kill them.

We passed Marina Lou's, and we passed Calusa's red brick high-school building, and then Dale took a left at the light on Parsons, and we headed inland for my house. We still had not said a word to each other. I kept thinking *Dale* was thinking I was as inadequate as I myself thought I was. I kept remembering her yanking off that sequined high-heeled slipper and going for Charlie's head with it. I should have grabbed a knife from the cutlery tray. I should have broken a beer bottle or something. I should have gone straight for the jugular. But I didn't know how to do such things.

She pulled the car into my driveway.

"It's on the visor," I said.

"What is?"

"The clicker."

"The *what?*"

"The thing that opens the garage door."

"Oh," she said.

She fumbled for it, found it, pressed both buttons in the wrong order, then pressed them again in reverse, and the garage door went up. She pulled the car in, cut the engine, and handed me the keys. I got out, unlocked the door leading into the kitchen, and snapped on the lights.

"I can use a drink," she said.

"Me, too."

"I'll make them," she said, and somehow even that innocuous comment seemed a reflection on my manhood.

"Sons of bitches," I said.

"Yeah," she said.

"People like that in the world," I said.

"Yeah," she said.

She brought me my Dewar's on the rocks. She was drinking a gin and tonic. Just like the one she'd ordered in Captain Blood's before the universe started spinning crazily.

"Cheers," she said.

"Cheers," I said.

I got up to turn on the pool lights. The pool glowed blue and bright in the darkness.

"Feel like a swim?" I said.

"No," she said.

"Want to go straight to bed?"

"No," she said, but I didn't detect anything ominous in her voice at that moment. I thought, instead, that she was saying she wanted to finish her drink first. We'd been heading for her house before the traffic jam had changed our plans, to put it mildly. I hadn't questioned her when she'd driven directly here from the hospital. I figured she'd assumed that a defeated gladiator might appreciate the comfort of his own bed. Besides, my house was closer, and we were both still shaky after what had happened. It was tacitly understood, I thought, that she would spend the night here with me, as she had so many other nights. "Your place or mine?" was a meaningless question as far as it concerned Dale and me.

"Matthew," she said, "there's something I have to tell you."

Here it comes, I thought.

"I know," I said. "It's a hell of a thing when a grown man can't defend . . ."

"Don't be ridiculous," she said at once. "You don't think I *admire* that kind of macho bullshit, do you? God!"

"Then . . . what . . . ?"

"Maybe this isn't the right time for it," she said.

"Maybe not," I said. "Can it wait till morning?"

"I won't be here in the morning, Matthew."

I looked at her. Her eyes would not meet mine. I might just as well have been Jeff back there at Captain Blood's, asking her how she liked the music.

"What do you mean?" I said.

She didn't immediately answer.

"Dale?" I said. "What is it?"

"I want to end it," she said.

The taxi didn't come for her until a quarter past two, by which time we had gone over it, and gone over it again, and gone over it yet another time. When the driver honked his horn outside, she went to the front door, opened it, waved to him, and then kissed me. On the cheek. I watched her as she ran up the front walk. I watched the flash of her long legs as she hiked up her gown to slide in onto the back seat. I watched the taxi as it pulled away from the curb. Dale did not look back. I listened to the sound of the taxi's engine until it faded on the sodden night.

I went back into the living room then and mixed myself a very strong, very dry martini. I did not put an olive in it. I mixed another one the moment I'd finished the first. I sat drinking in my empty living room, watching the lighted pool outside, replaying in my mind everything she'd said and everything I'd said.

First she'd told me she'd met someone else. When I asked her how she *possibly* could have met someone else when we'd been seeing each other virtually every night of the week, she'd said, "But not *every* night, Matthew." I asked her where she'd met this *person*. I couldn't bring myself to call him a man. He was still a faceless *person*, someone she'd met, someone she'd been seeing on the nights she wasn't seeing me. She said she'd met him at her office, Blackstone, Harris, Gerstein, Garfield, and Pollock, repeating the name of the law firm as if she were a receptionist answering the phone. She said he was a client. She said she was handling a collection case for him. She said he was forty-two years old, a recent widower. She said he'd asked her to marry him. She said she was going to marry him.

I asked her how long this had been going on. I felt stupid as hell asking the question. I felt like a husband whose wife had been cheating on him. She told me she'd met him a month ago. I made some snide remark about him being a fast worker, or something equally inane, I still didn't know the guy's *name*, she hadn't told me his *name*—"What's his name?" I asked. She said that didn't matter. What mattered was that she loved him and wanted to marry him, and that she felt cheap and shoddy being with me when she felt so committed to him. I think I was beginning to get angry by then, and I said something cruel, which I apologized for a moment later, I said I could certainly understand how shuttling back and forth between two beds *might* make a woman feel cheap and shoddy, and then I immediately told her I was sorry, and she kept watching me with those glade-green eyes looking a trifle sad and she said something like, "So that's it, Matthew," and I told her we couldn't just *end* something that had been going on for such a long time, if all she wanted to do was get *married*, why hadn't she *said* so? I'd marry her in a minute if that was what she wanted. She said, "Yes, that's what I want," and then she said something as cruel as what I'd said only a few moments earlier, she said, "But it's not *you* I want to marry."

So we sat in silence for what seemed a very long time, and then I asked her to please tell me what I had done *wrong*. I sup-

16

pose I was still thinking of my ineffectualness with the two goons at Captain Blood's, was thinking that if only I had behaved in a more manly fashion, this might not be happening now, I would not now be sitting in an air-conditioned living room listening to a woman telling me she no longer wanted or needed me while outside the pool rippled a sparkling blue under a starless night. She told me I hadn't done anything wrong, it was just that she'd fallen in love, and I interrupted immediately to say, "I thought you loved me," and she said, quietly and calmly, "I never told you that, Matthew," which was the truth; we had never exchanged the words "I love you."

This seemed in retrospect a serious oversight, so I told her at once that she *knew* I loved her, and that I *thought* she loved me, otherwise what had it all been *about* these past seventeen months, eighteen months, however the hell long it had been? She said it had all been about sex. I denied that. She repeated it. "*Sex*, Matthew." And then she went into a sort of rhapsodic reverie about this new man she'd found, whose name I still didn't know, and possibly didn't *want* to know, telling me about all his virtues and even his faults, of which she was well aware, but they didn't matter, the faults. She was in love with him, and he'd asked her to marry him, and she'd accepted, and that was that.

I fell back on the cheap male strategy of trying to work her into bed, figuring that if I could get her in bed just one more time, hold her in my arms, kiss her, make love to her, she would realize what an important relationship she was throwing away. I reminded her of all the good times we'd shared, and of how passionate our lovemaking had been—didn't she remember that first time at her house on Whisper Key, didn't she remember all the other times, didn't she remember Mexico and the few ecstatic days we'd spent down there, didn't *any* of it mean anything at *all* to her? She was very quiet for a very long time, and then she said, "It meant a lot to me, Matthew. I'll never forget it. But I'm marrying Jim."

And with his name out in the open, with his name falling leadenly into my own air-conditioned living room, it all became a reality, and I knew that indeed she had done what she had planned to do from the very start of the night, she had effectively and irrevocably ended it. When the taxi driver honked his horn outside, I was thinking about her taking off that sequined slipper and coming to my defense earlier, when all we had to worry about was assault and battery. She said, "There's my taxi," or something like that, and she just shook her head sadly, and went to the door and opened it, and waved out at the driver, and I followed her to the door, and she touched my bruised cheek with her hand and said, "Goodbye, Matthew," and kissed me on the cheek and said, "I'm sorry," and then turned swiftly and went running up the walk to the waiting taxi, and I didn't know whether she'd meant she was sorry I'd been beaten up or sorry she was ending it this way.

I sat there drinking. I guess I fell asleep right where I was sitting. I feel certain I didn't pass out, I simply fell asleep.

The phone woke me up.

I blinked at the sunlight outside the sliding glass door. It was Tuesday morning, the ninth day of August. I looked at the clock on the wall over the stereo equipment. A few minutes past seven. The phone kept ringing. *Dale!* I thought. *She's changed her mind!*

I stood up abruptly and felt a sharp pain at the base of my skull. For an instant I didn't move. The room swam dizzily and then came into sharp focus again. The phone was still ringing insistently. I went into the kitchen and yanked the receiver from the wall hook.

"Hello?" I said.

"Matthew?" A man's voice. "I didn't wake you, did I?"

"Who's this?" I said.

"Morrie Bloom."

Detective Morris Bloom of the Calusa Police Department. I figured he had come into work early this morning and seen the uniformed cop's report, and seen my name on it, and was calling now to find out how I was.

"How are you?" he said.

"Okay," I said. I did not feel okay.

"I'm sorry to be calling you so early," he said, "but I've been working on this all night, and I waited till what I thought was a respectable hour."

"Uh-huh," I said. Seven A.M. did not seem like a respectable hour.

"Matthew, we caught a homicide at a little past ten o'clock last night," he said. "Condo out on Stone Crab, multiple stab wounds, kid named Jack McKinney, does the name ring a bell?"

"Yes," I said. "A *homicide*, did you say?"

"Yeah. Reason I'm calling, we found your business card in his wallet. Was he a client, Matthew?"

"Yes, he was."

"What were you handling for him?"

"A real-estate transaction."

"Here in Calusa?"

"Yes."

"Matthew, I know this is an imposition, but I wonder if you could come down here and fill me in on the details? We want to get a fast start on this one, maybe get a few steps ahead of whoever did it."

"I just woke up," I said.

"How long will it take you to wash and dress?" Bloom asked.

"Morrie, I'm not feeling too hot this morning . . ."

"Jack McKinney feels even worse," Bloom said. "Can you do me the favor, Matthew?"

"Give me an hour or so," I said.

"I'll see you," Bloom said, and hung up.

His eyes opened wide the moment he saw my face.

My own eyes had opened just as wide when I'd seen myself in the shaving mirror forty minutes earlier. Or at least as wide as I *could* open them, considering that they were puffed and discolored and looked a lot like the poisonous man-of-wars that sometimes washed up on Calusa's beaches.

"What the hell happened to *you?*" he said.

I told him all about Charlie and Jeff.

"Did you report it?" he said. He meant to the police. Since he *was* the police, it hadn't been necessary for him to elaborate.

I told him I'd reported it.

"What was the responding officer's name?" he asked.

I told him I didn't remember.

"I'll check the Activity Report spindle," he said, "make sure it's followed up."

I thanked him.

"Fucking Wild West down here, huh?" he said, and shook his head.

I hadn't seen him since November, when our separate professions had thrown us together on a case he still referred to as "the Beauty and the Beast mess," but which I always thought of as "the George Harper tragedy." He seemed to have lost a great deal of weight. Bloom was six feet three inches tall, a heavyset man with the oversized knuckles of a street fighter and a fox face with a nose that had been broken more than once. He had shaggy black eyebrows and dark brown eyes that almost always seemed on the imminent edge of tears—a bad failing for a cop. But the last time I'd seen him, he had to have weighed a least two hundred and thirty pounds, and he didn't look anywhere near that now.

"So how are you?" he said. "Otherwise."

"Fine," I said. "Otherwise. And you?"

"Much better now," he said.

"Now?"

"I got hepatitis just before Passover," he said. "Jews aren't supposed to eat shellfish, am I right? It's in the dietary laws. So what does the good Jew, Morris Bloom, do? He eats shellfish. Clams on the half-shell, to be exact. I been eating them all my life, don't tell my rabbi. Only this time, bingo—hepatitis. Type A. I was sick as a dog. I wanted to die. Fever every goddamn day for a full month. I lost *thirty pounds,* can you believe it? I'm thinking of writing a book called *The Hepatitis Diet,* you think it might sell? How do I look? I look better, don't I? I weigh an even two hundred now, I could be a fashion model. Who makes more money, fashion models or guys who write diet books? *Cops* sure don't," he said, and grinned. "It's good to see you, Matthew. I'm sorry I called so early . . ."

"That's all right," I said.

"I wouldn'ta called at *all* if I'd known about your trouble last night. I'll have all the blues looking for those punks, we'll find them, don't worry. Charlie and Jeff, huh? Sounds like a pair of vaudeville comics. Some comics. They did a nice job on you, Matthew. I'll have to teach you to fight dirty."

"I'd love to learn," I said.

"Are you serious? Come down the gym one night, I'll kick you in the balls a few times. Are you serious?"

"I'm very serious."

"Good, we'll make a date. About McKinney," he said. "I just got a call from the coroner's office, they'll be sending the written report up later. McKinney was stabbed or slashed fourteen times, somebody did a very nice job on him, I can tell you that. What do you know about him, Matthew? I'd appreciate anything you can tell me. When did you last see him? Because in police work, when we catch a homicide, there's a rule we follow, we call it the Twenty-four P-and-P . . . does this sort of stuff interest you?"

"It does."

"'Cause some people it doesn't," Bloom said. "What it is, P-and-P stands for past and present. The first thing we try to do is track down the past twenty-four hours in the victim's life, because that way we can work up a timetable on where he went and who he saw and what he did and maybe get a lead that way. That's the twenty-four *past*. At the same time, we try to work as fast as we can in the twenty-four hours *following* the murder—that's the twenty-four *present*—because that's the only time we've got a slight edge. The killer hasn't had time to cover too many tracks, he doesn't know how much we already know, or even if we've found the *body* yet. Like that. Very important time, those first twenty-four hours. After that, it can get mighty cold mighty fast, Matthew, even down here where you can melt like a snowman. The Twenty-four P-and-P, live and learn, am I right? Did you see McKinney anytime during the past twenty-four hours?".

"I saw him last Friday at two o'clock."

"Okay, tell me about it," Bloom said. "You won't mind if I make a few notes, will you?"

I told him about it.

Jack McKinney had come into my office sometime in July, recommended by a friend for whom we'd handled a disability claim. McKinney was twenty years old; I'd specifically asked him because he looked much younger, and I wanted to make certain he was legally of age to make a binding contract. In the state of Florida, you're considered legally capable of making an enforceable contract once you reach the age of eighteen. McKinney showed me his driver's license to prove that he was indeed twenty, and then he explained that he'd made a handshake deal with a farmer out on Timucuan Point Road to purchase fifteen acres of land midway between Calusa and Ananburg. The farmer's name was Avery Burrill, and his crop was snapbeans; young Jack McKinney wanted to become a snapbean farmer.

He told me what the purchase price was—forty thousand dollars—and said he wanted to close the deal as soon as possible, before Burrill changed his mind. Because of the boy's extreme youth, and because I'd never heard of snapbean farming in this part of the state, I called a man named John Porter, the County Extension Agent, to get his opinion. Porter informed me that snapbeans were grown mostly on the East Coast, in Palm Beach County, and also in South Dade County, in the Homestead area. On the Central West Coast, here in Calusa, the truck crops were tomatoes, strawberries, escarole, chicory, beets, and some Chinese cabbage—but *not* snapbeans. He then surprised me by asking if this had anything to do with a man named Avery Burrill.

It seemed that Burrill had come to him some three years back, asking pretty much the same questions I was asking now. Burrill's idea had been to start small, planting his fifteen acres in snapbean bushes, and then selling his product only to local markets. Porter had told him that snapbeans *could* be grown here, but that they did better in organic soil. Moreover, the reason they were grown primarily on the East Coast was that the technology for harvesting and marketing was there, and here in Calusa he'd have no access to machines and his harvesting costs would double because he'd have to hand-harvest.

He'd gone on to break down for Burrill what the actual pre-harvesting costs—feed, fertilizer, spraying and dusting, repairs and maintenance, licenses and insurance, and so on—would be, and these came to something like $450 per acre per year. Added to these would be his harvesting and marketing costs—picking and packing, containers, handling, brokerage fees, and so on—which would come to $228 per acre per year, for a total operating cost of $678 a year. Burrill could expect a yield of eighty-five bushels per acre, and he could expect to realize gross receipts of $804 per acre. When he deducted his operating costs of $678 per acre, this would leave only $126 per acre, from which he would have to subtract return to capital, management fees, interest, and whatnot. In short, a snapbean farm in this part of Florida would be a losing proposition, and Porter had told that to Burrill as clearly and succinctly as he knew how. Burrill had gone ahead anyway, and—as predicted—had gone under. And now he was trying to sell his losing proposition to a twenty-year-old kid who didn't know snapbeans from snapdragons.

I called McKinney as soon as I had this information.

I told him exactly what I'd learned, and I advised him against making the purchase. McKinney told me the same thing Burrill had told Porter three years ago: he knew how to make snapbean farming profitable in this part of the country. I gave him the facts and figures. I told him there was no way he could make it work. But he insisted that I call Burrill's lawyer to confirm the details of the deal, and there was nothing I could do to persuade him otherwise. McKinney had come to my office to sign the contract last Friday. At that time, he brought with him four thousand dollars in cash, the ten-percent deposit required by Burrill. I asked him at that time if he would need a mortgage or other financial assistance to meet the balance due on the closing date. He told me he had the $36,000 in cash and that he would bring it with him to the closing. I suggested that he bring instead either a certified check or a cashier's check. When I told him we should insist on a week or ten days to inspect the plumbing, heating, and electrical systems in the farmhouse, he told me he would waive such inspection. I'd insisted, however, on an exterminator's inspection for termites and other pests. Pending the customary title examination and tax search, the closing had been set for the second day of September.

That was it.

"Four thousand in cash, huh?" Bloom said.

"Yes," I said.

"Against a forty-thousand-dollar purchase price."

"Yes."

"And he said he was going to pay the *balance* in cash, too?"

"That's what he said."

"On my block, that's a lot of money, Matthew."

"On my block, too."

"Where'd a twenty-year-old kid get forty thousand dollars to spend on a farm?"

"I have no idea."

"Big money," Bloom said thoughtfully. "What's the first thing that comes to your mind, Matthew?"

"Inheritance," I said.

"That's the difference between a lawyer and a cop," Bloom said. "First thing comes to *my* mind is narcotics."

"Well," I said.

"Only because this is Florida, and the kid was murdered. He didn't say where he got that kind of money, huh?"

"He didn't say, and I didn't ask."

"Twenty years old," Bloom said, "he's got forty thousand dollars in cash. You know what *I* had when *I* was twenty? A suit with two pair of pants, and one pair had a hole in them. Who knows nowadays? How'd he strike you, this kid? What was your impression of him?"

"He was well dressed, both times I saw him. Jacket and tie, looked very preppy, in fact. Dark hair, brown eyes, well built . . . looked like an athlete. Or at least someone who used his body a lot and took good care of it."

"What address did he give you? Did he give you a home address?"

"I don't remember it offhand. It was out on Stone Crab Key. He said he was living in a condo out on Stone Crab."

"You know how much that condo was costing him, Matthew? The one where we found him dead last night? He was renting it for twelve hundred clams a—God forgive me, I'll never mention clams again as long as I live. Twelve hundred a month. The resident manager said he'd been living there since the beginning of June, renting from a guy up in Pittsburgh. That's already thirty-six hundred he's laid out since June, not to mention the security deposit. He was pretty rich, this kid, huh?"

"I would guess so."

"I wonder how he got so rich," Bloom said. "Maybe that's what the killer was after. The apartment was a shambles, clothes thrown all over the floor, upholstery slashed, bed tossed—looks to me like somebody was searching for something. Maybe it was the thirty-six K, huh? And maybe he found it. The cash McKinney would have needed at the closing. You said it was set for next month sometime, didn't you?"

"Yes. September second."

"Mm," Bloom said, and nodded. "Well, I'll be going out to talk to his mother in just a little while, her name was in his address book. I'll let you know if the kid came into any big money recently." He smiled and said, "You think he won the sweepstakes, maybe?"

My partner Frank said it served me right. My partner Frank said it did not pay to get into fights over women. My partner Frank also said Dale was probably asking for it, the way she was dressed, which almost got my partner Frank into a fight with *me*, and over a woman at that.

I told him Dale and I had ended our relationship.

"You're a born loser with women," Frank said. "It's written all over your face. You have a Second City mentality when it comes to women. I happen to have liked Susan very much," he said. Susan was my former wife. "Why you took off after that coozy blonde is beyond me," he said. He was referring to a lady named Agatha Hemmings, who had been the cause of the breakup between Susan and me, and who had since divorced her former husband, remarried, and moved to Tampa. "Not that I don't like Dale, too," Frank said. "Very smart lady, Dale, very pretty. But I could see this coming, Matthew, you do not know how to relate to women. One of the things I learned very early on in New York was how to relate to women. You see how beautifully I get along with Leona? That's because when I was seventeen I wrote down these ten rules on how to get along with women. I still follow those rules, Matthew, they outline how a man is supposed to treat a woman if he expects to enjoy a good relationship with her. How did you treat Dale, Matthew?"

"That's none of your business," I said.

"Is it my business that you come to work looking like somebody ran you through a meat grinder? Because you got into a fight over a woman you didn't know how to treat properly?"

"No, that's not your business, either."

"I thought we were partners," Frank said.

"Not in everything," I said.

"You look terrible," he said.

"I *feel* terrible."

"Why don't you go home?"

"I have work to do."

"You'll scare away all our clients. Would you like me to write down my rules for you?"

"No, I don't think so."

"I realize the horse is already gone, and there's no sense locking the barn door," Frank said, "but there'll be other women, I'm sure, and it wouldn't hurt if you knew how to treat them."

"I don't want to see your rules," I said.

"I'll write them down for you," Frank said. "Leona and I have a perfect marriage because of those rules. We've been married for fifteen years, you think all it takes is luck?"

"I don't know what it takes. That's your business, Frank."

"I'll write them down," Frank said. "I'll have Cynthia type them up for you."

"No, don't bother," I said.

"It won't be any trouble," Frank said, and that was when Cynthia buzzed to say a Mr. Burrill was calling on six. As I picked up the phone, Frank mouthed the words, "I'll write them down," and then left my office.

"Matthew Hope." I said into the phone.

"Mr. Hope?" he said. "This here is Avery Burrill."

Redneck farmer voice, Southern accent you could cut with a machete.

"Yes, Mr. Burrill," I said.

"I'm the man sellin' that farm to your client."

"Yes, sir, I know."

"I just heard it on the radio," he said. I assumed he was talking about the death of Jack McKinney. "My lawyer's up in Maine fishing, out on a goddamn lake someplace, can't be reached. What do we do now?"

"About the closing, do you mean?"

"Damn right, about the closing. Your client's dead, somebody killed him. I got a signed piece of paper sayin' he's buyin' my farm. I coulda had a dozen other buyers for that property, turned them all away 'cause Jack had his heart set on snapbean farming. I want to know who's responsible, now, Mr. Hope. Who's gonna be there at that closin'?"

"I have no idea."

"I thought you was Jack's lawyer."

"I am. But I have no idea whether or not he left a will, or who . . ."

"Well, you damn well better find *out*, Mr. Hope. The way I

look at it, he owes me thirty-six thousand dollars. I made plans of my own, you know. Punctuated on this deal going *through*. It ain't my fault he went and got hisself stabbed. I want my money."

"Mr. Burrill," I said, "I suggest that you contact your own lawyer regarding . . ."

"I jus' tole you he's out on a boat. How'm I supposed to get to him?"

"I'm sure someone in his office . . ."

"I already *called* his office, how you think I know about him bein' on a boat? Ain't nobody there but the girl answers the phone. Us farmers can't afford big-shot lawyers with assistants runnin' aroun' all over the place. Harry Loomis runs a one-man operation, just him an' the girl answers the phone. An' *he's* out on a boat till the end of the week, won't be back in his office till the fifteenth."

"I suggest you wait till he gets back," I said. "The closing wouldn't have taken place before the beginning of next month, anyway."

"I was plannin' on bein' out of here by the second."

"I'm sorry about that."

"All of it punctuated on this deal goin' through. See what you can find out for me, would you, please? I really would appreciate it. And seein' as Harry's away, I wouldn't mind throwin' a few dollars in your direction if you can help speed this thing along."

"That won't be necessary, Mr. Burrill."

I didn't mention that it would also be unethical.

"Have you got my number there?" he asked.

"No," I said.

"Well, you ought to have it. Have you got a pencil?"

I wrote down the number he gave me. He advised me to keep trying if the line was busy, since it was a party line and the lady who shared it with him was a big talker.

"Call me, Mr. Hope. Soon as you fine out anythin'," he said, and hung up.

I had no intention of calling him.

2

It did not seem likely to me that Jack McKinney had drawn a will. To begin with, the furthest thing from the minds of most twenty-year-olds is death. When you're twenty, you're immortal. But even assuming he *had* considered the possibility—he had, after all, been in apparent possession of at least forty thousand dollars—which attorney had he gone to? If *another* attorney had indeed drawn a will for him, then why hadn't he gone to that *same* attorney on the real-estate transaction? Why come to me instead? He could have drawn the will himself, of course; anyone can. But he'd still have needed witnesses, and no person with any knowledge of a will had yet come forward.

In the state of Florida, anyone having custody of a will is required to deposit it with the clerk of the court within ten days after receiving information of a death. The murder of Jack McKinney had made newspaper headlines and had been reported on every radio and television station in the area, but my call to Probate on the nineteenth of August revealed that no will had yet been deposited. I got this information at nine-thirty in the morning, and immediately called Harry Loomis, who had come back from his fishing trip in Maine the preceding Sunday, and who had been calling me daily since his return to the office on the fifteenth. I told him I was fairly certain now that McKinney hadn't left a will, and that I would be checking with any close surviving relatives to see if they knew anything about what sort of estate he'd left. Loomis told me there *had* to be an estate of at least $36,000 because that's what McKinney had agreed to pay in cash at the closing. I told him I would have to discuss that with McKinney's heirs. Loomis told me his client expected to close the deal, and if he had to sue the estate to get the balance due, he would damn well do it. I promised I'd get back to him and hung up thinking I had needed Jack McKinney like a hole in the head.

The *real* hole in my head had healed. There was still a scab, but I considered it healed nonetheless; at least there was no longer an adhesive patch back there. My eyes looked okay, too, if you like lingering sunsets. It had been eleven days since Charlie and Jeff had waltzed me to near oblivion, and I had not heard a word from Dale. I had tried to call her once, but when a man answered the phone at her Whisper Key house, I told him I had the wrong number, and hung up. I had not spoken to Bloom, either, since the morning after the beating (*and* the murder, of course; the beating had left a more indelible impression on me), but I figured he might now be able to tell me what I needed to know about next of kin. I dialed the number at Calusa Public Safety, as the police department is formally known here in genteel Calusa, asked for Detective Bloom, and was put through to his office at once.

"How's it going?" he said. "When're we getting together for that lesson in street fighting?"

"Anytime you say," I told him.

"You're really serious, huh? How about sometime next week?"

"Just let me know when," I said.

"Bring a sweat suit and sneakers to the office, I'll keep in touch. We can walk from here to the gym, it's right next door, in the basement of the jailhouse. Maybe we can get some of the cons in there to give us a few pointers, huh? They know all about gouging out eyes. What can I do for you, Matthew?"

"I just called Probate again to check on whether or not they've received a will for McKinney. They've got nothing yet, Morrie, and yesterday was the deadline for deposit. I know you've been investigating the case . . ."

"Cold as a mackerel," Bloom said.

"I'm sorry to hear that."

"But we're still working on it. Also on those punks who did the boiler-room number on you. They'll turn up sooner or later, don't worry, how many Charlies and Jeffs can there be in Calusa County? By the way, we still haven't found that big chunk of money McKinney was supposed to have for the closing. Went through his apartment with a fine comb—nothing. Checked every bank here in Calusa and also in Bradenton and Sarasota to see if he had a savings account, checking account, or safety deposit box—nothing. You think he buried the money on the beach someplace? Like a pirate or something? Who knows?" Bloom said. "So what do you want to know? Who his next of kin are?"

"Exactly."

"His father died two years ago, right after the Fourth of July. Man named Drew McKinney. Incidentally, he didn't leave a cent to the kid, so that rules out inheritance as a source of the forty K. McKinney's mother is still alive—lady named Veronica, has a cattle ranch on the road to Ananburg, lives there with the kid's sister, twenty-three years old, a real beauty. Well, *both* of them, in fact. I forget the sister's name, Patty or something. I can look it up, if you like."

"No, the mother would most likely be appointed personal representative of the estate."

"We talked both her and the sister blue in the face. They've got alibis a mile long. We look for family, you know. Never mind what you read in mystery novels, the way they make all these murders look like things planned a hundred years in advance and pulled off with the skill of a hit man. Bullshit. Most of your murders, it's a family situation. Kid kills his father or vice versa. Guy takes a hatchet to his wife. Or her lover. Or the wife kills the old man's girlfriend. Like that. Anyway, they both seem clean. The mother . . . does this sort of stuff interest you?"

"You know it does," I said.

"Yeah, well, you never know. The mother was home watching television with a veterinarian who'd come to dinner that night. He was out there looking at a sick cow, and she asked him to stay to dinner, and they sat around later watching television. The vet says he was with her at nine o'clock—that's about when McKinney was getting himself stabbed. So that lets out the old lady."

"Where was the sister?"

"'n the sack with her boyfriend. We got this out of her after a lot of hemming and hawing. Nobody likes to admit something like that until they realize we're *really* talking about murder here. Her boyfriend's name is Jackie Crowell—another Jack, common name. Except in *my* family. In *my* family, the common names are Sidney, Bernie, Marvin, Irving, and Abe. Anyway, Crowell confirmed he was with her that night, in his apartment. Took her to dinner at McDonald's . . ."

"Big spender," I said.

"Yeah, well, he's only eighteen years old. The sister is twenty-three, and positively gorgeous. So she's making it with an eighteen-year-old twerp who's got pimples all over his face. Anyway, they went right back to his place—you should see it, it's a regular dump, the kid works stacking oranges in a supermarket here in town. Got back there around eight, he said, spent the rest of the night together. So that lets out Patty or Sally or whatever the hell her name is. It's never easy, is it, Matthew?"

"Never," I said. "Have you got an address for that ranch?"

"It's called the M.K. Ranch, I guess that stands for McKinney, don't you think? Anyway, you go south on Forty-One and then east on Timucuan Point, it's about midway between here and Manakawa. Big sign on the right-hand side of the road, you can't miss it."

"Would you have Mrs. McKinney's phone number?"

"Yeah, just a second, let me get the file."

I waited.. He was back on the line almost immediately. I wrote down the number he gave me, and was about to thank him when he said, "Yeah, here's the sister's name, too. Where'd I get Patty from? It's Sunny, with a *u*, like in sunshine. Sunny McKinney. I didn't ask her whether that's a nickname or not. Let me know how it goes, huh?" he said, and hung up abruptly.

I did not particularly wish to talk to my former wife, Susan, but today was Friday, and it had been two weeks since I'd seen my daughter, and Joanna was scheduled to spend this weekend with me, as specified in the divorce agreement. I simply wanted to know what time she'd be ready for pickup. I don't know why so many divorced women drift into selling real estate, but it seems to be an immutable fact of nature, and that was what Susan was doing these days, so I called her at Ridley and Nelson, and asked for Susan Hope, please, the name sticking in my throat as it always did; her maiden name had been Susan Fitch, a perfectly respectable Midwestern WASP name; I could not understand why she hadn't gone back to it after the divorce. Neither could I understand why I never called her "Sue" anymore. It was always "Susan" now. "Sue" did not seem an inappropriate familiarity for someone who'd lived with a woman for fourteen years—and yet I could never get the diminutive past my lips.

The reason I did not enjoy talking to Susan Fitch Hope on the telephone was that I never knew who might be greeting me on any given day. I certainly would never accuse my former wife of being schizophrenic, a contention I'm sure she could successfully refute in any court of law in the land—*maybe*. She did, however, assume many different roles in her conversations with me, and two of these were clearly—if not clinically—identifiable as personalities at opposite ends of the psychological spectrum. As I waited for her to come to the phone, I wondered whether I'd be talking to Susan the Witch or Susan the Waif this morning.

"Matthew!" she said, as though delighted by the very sound of my Biblical name. "I'm *so* glad you called!" The Waif. "How *are* you, Matthew?"

"Fine, thanks," I said, which was more or less true. "And you?"

"Oh, you know," she said.

This last, delivered with the self-pitying tone of someone for whom the travails of the world are simply too much to bear, meant she was going to tell me about one of her various allergies. Susan had discovered, almost the moment we'd moved to Florida, that she was allergic to virtually everything that grew down here. Whenever Susan started talking about her allergies—and she often did when she assumed the role of the Waif—she sounded like someone who was terminally ill. I did not want to hear about her allergies. *Or* her sex life, which I didn't think I'd be hearing about today; usually, only the Witch talked about her sex life.

"Matthew, I know you must be very busy," she said, "and I promise I won't take up a minute more of your time than I have to."

The old Butter-Wouldn't-Melt Waif. But at least she wasn't telling me about the way punk trees made her sneeze. Not *yet*, anyway.

"That's okay, Susan," I said, "take all the time you need." I had learned over the years since the divorce that the only way to deal with Little Orphan Annie was to assume the role of a tolerant Daddy Warbucks. Better the Waif than the Witch. The Witch was impossible to talk to on any human level.

"I have a serious problem," she said.

I waited.

"It has to do with Joanna," she said.

"What's the matter?" I said, instantly alarmed. Both the Waif *and* the Witch knew exactly which buttons to push to get a paternal rise out of me.

"Nothing, nothing, she's fine," Susan said. "But she's supposed to see you this weekend . . ."

"In fact, that's why I'm call . . ."

"It's been two weeks, I know," Susan said sweetly, "and the agreement calls for every other weekend."

"Yes, it does," I said, becoming vaguely suspicious.

"Matthew," she said, "do you remember my brother?"

"Of *course* I remember your brother," I said.

Susan seemed to think that divorce, as it affected the male of the species, brought on premature senility and the subsequent loss of memory. She was always asking me if I knew people we'd known together for years. I expected her to ask me one day if I remembered my own daughter. I did indeed remember Jerry Fitch. Jerry Fitch was the son of a bitch who'd refused to tell my mother-in-law that she was dying of cancer. I had loved that woman a great deal. She'd never known she was dying, because all the doctors, on Jerry's instructions, kept the information from her and therefore robbed her of whatever dignity she might have mustered at the end. Instead, she died in agonized surprise. I kept thinking of her that way—as dying in surprise. I had not liked Jerry then, and I did not like him now, and I was enormously grateful that he was no longer a part of my life.

"He's here," Susan said. "In Calusa."

"That's nice," I said. I was hoping he'd get eaten by an alligator.

"He always loved Joanna so much," Susan said sweetly.

I waited.

"He'll only be here for the weekend," she said.

I kept waiting.

"I realize you haven't seen Joanna since the seventh," she said, "and I know this is supposed to be *your* weekend, Matthew, but I was wondering—you've always been such a generous man—I was wondering if you'd let Joanna stay with me this weekend, so she can see her uncle. He came all the way from Chicago, Matthew, he'd be *so* disappointed if he didn't see . . ."

"Sure," I said.

I don't know why I agreed so readily. I think I didn't want to explain to Joanna the lingering shiners around both my eyes. I think, too, that I didn't want to tell her Dale and I had split up. *That* was going to be a tough one, telling her about Dale and me.

"Provided I can see her for the next *two* weekends," I said.

"Oh, of *course*," Susan said. "You don't think I'd want to deprive you of any time with her, do you?"

I said nothing. The Waif would not deny me the world; the Witch would deny me a sip of water in the middle of the Sahara.

"Is it all right, then?" Susan asked. "For her to stay home this weekend?"

I resented Susan calling *her* place "home," even though it was my daughter's legal residence. I liked to think that when Joanna was with me, *that* was home as well.

"I get the next week and the week after that," I said.

"Agreed," Susan said. "Oh, Matthew, I can't tell you how appreciative I am. I'll give Jerry your regards."

Which I hadn't offered.

"Tell Joanna I'll talk to her next week," I said.

"I will. And, Matthew . . ." Her voice dropped almost seductively. "Thank you, Matthew. Really. Thank you."

I visualized her replacing the receiver delicately on its cradle, even though the click sounded as abrupt as if she'd slammed it down. I sighed—I seemed always to sigh after a conversation with Susan—and then I dialed the number Bloom had given me for the McKinney ranch.

If you do not know U.S. 41, then you do not live in the United States of America, and you are unfamiliar with any red-line highway that crisscrosses the nation and spreads blight upon the countryside. The Tamiami *Trail* may once have been just that, a dirt road hacked out through the palmettos and palms, but them days is gone forever, Gertie. Today, U.S. 41 is a four- (and sometimes six-) lane concrete thoroughfare lined for miles and miles with fast-food emporiums, gift shops, car washes, gasoline stations, pizzerias, furniture stores, nurseries, carpet salesrooms, automobile dealers, shopping malls, movie theater complexes, and a variety of one-story cinderblock shops selling plaster figurines, citrus fruit, discount clothing, rattan pool and garden furniture, cigarettes and beer (free ice if you buy a case), stereo equipment, lamps, vacuum cleaners, typewriters, burglar alarms, swimming pools, and (the only such shop in all Calusa) adult marital aids, games, and reading material. In short, U.S. 41 is your typical American highway bazaar, ugly and blaring and tasteless. In the wintertime is is thronged with automobiles bearing out-of-state license plates; they only add to the sense of clutter and confusion and cause most native Floridians (a native is anyone who lives here year-round) to pray desperately for Easter. In August, U.S. 41 is, by comparison, abandoned. I made the trip from downtown Calusa to the Timucuan Point Road in ten minutes.

The landscape changes abruptly as you head eastward off 41. The road leading to Ananburg is a black-topped two-lane thoroughfare that runs past a scattering of housing developments with modest homes on small plots, and then past what used to be farmland but are now "country estates," meaning that a developer has come in, dredged a big lake, sold land around it for $5000 an acre, and put up luxury homes starting at $250,000. Beyond these—and this was only six miles east of 41—you run into real country, a reminder of what Calusa must have been like only thirty or forty years ago.

I drove past citrus groves only eight miles from the hustle and bustle of U.S. 41. I drove past open farmland not fifteen miles from downtown Calusa. And suddenly there were cows grazing in pastures on either side of the road, and the grass beyond the palmettos seemed to stretch endlessly to blend with an eternal sky already turning gray in preparation for the rain that would come sometime later in the day. I almost passed the wooden posts and lintel from which hung a red sign lettered in black with the words THE M.K. RANCH. I braked sharply, glanced belatedly in the rear-view mirror, and drove the Ghia in through the open gate and onto a single-lane dirt road. I had come about half a mile up the road when I saw a red pickup truck coming from the opposite direction. I stopped the Ghia. The pickup truck slowed and then stopped. The door behind the driver's seat opened. The letters M.K. were painted in black on the side of the door. A man with a shotgun in his hands stepped down onto the dirt road. He looked like a cross between Charlie and Jeff. A bit over six feet tall, I guessed, wearing faded jeans and a red plaid shirt and dusty brown boots. Wide shoulders and a narrow waist. Big ornate brass buckle on his belt. String from a bag of cigarette tobacco hanging from his left-hand shirt pocket, little round tag on its end. Straw hat tilted back on his head to show a forelock of dark hair that clung damply to his forehead. Black mustache under his nose. Dark eyes to match it. Black eyebrows. Skin burned by the sun to a leathery brown.

"Help you, mister?" he said, and turned the shotgun on me.

"My name's Matthew Hope," I said. "I have an appointment with Mrs. McKinney."

He said nothing.

"I phoned her this morning, I'm supposed to see her at one o'clock." I looked at my watch. "It's almost that now."

He still said nothing.

"So put up the shotgun, okay?" I said.

He did not put up the shotgun.

"I'm a lawyer," I said. "I'm here to see her about her son."

He still did not put up the shotgun.

"Jack McKinney," I said.

He kept watching me. He was chewing gum, I noticed. His jaws worked and his eyes worked, but the shotgun remained level and steady in his hands.

"I was handling a real-estate transaction for him," I said.

Without answering me, he went into the pickup again, took a walkie-talkie from where it was lying on the dash, said something into it, listened, said something else, and listened again. I was suddenly aware of the flies everywhere around me. Cattle meant flies; it went without saying. He came down out of the truck again, the shotgun dangling loosely at his side now.

"Missus McKinney's out on Crooked Tree just now," he said, "but Sunny says it's okay to send you up."

"Thanks," I said.

"Got to be careful these days," he said, by way of apology for the shotgun greeting.

I simply nodded and put the car into gear again.

"She's at the main house," he said. "Sunny is. Big white building on your left, top of the road."

I drove up the rutted dirt road to where a large white clapboard house dominated a compound that included a smaller house also painted white, a barn painted red, and a mobile trailer home that hadn't been painted since the year of the great flood. The big house nestled in a copse of tall old oaks. The other structures sat on land running wild with palmettos and cabbage palms. There was no tropical bloom anywhere in sight, no stray African tulip tree to delight the eye with its creamy, fuzzy flowers, no pink or purple bougainvillea, no oleander or trailing lantana. Except for the scruffy cabbage palms and palmettos, this could have been a ranch in Texas or Colorado. I parked the car near a pair of rusting gas tanks, one marked LEADED, the other UNLEADED, and walked toward the largest of the houses. A short flight of steps led up to a porticoed entrance. I knocked on the frame of the screen door; the wooden door behind it was open. I knocked again.

"Come in," a voice called.

I opened the screen door.

"I'm in here," she said.

"In here" was a greenhouse tacked onto the back of the building. What the grounds outside lacked by way of indigenous growth, the greenhouse made up for. Everywhere I looked, there was a riotous bloom of color, pink orchids competing with African violets, red gloxinias crowding out yellow mums, yellow-and-white spinning-wheel daisies banked against the sunset hues of flame violets. A blonde girl wearing cutoff jeans and a purple tanktop shirt was spraying one of the orchids, her back to me as I entered. Without turning, she said, "Hi," and went right on squeezing the red rubber bulb.

"Miss McKinney?" I said.

"Yeah," she said, absorbed in her task.

"Your mother's expecting me," I said.

"Yeah, I know," she said, and tossed her long blonde hair, and turned to look at me.

She was, I guessed, five feet ten or eleven inches tall, a rangy suntanned girl, braless in the purple tanktop shirt, her long legs beginning where the short cutoffs ended raggedly on her thighs, and tapering eternally to narrow ankles and sockless feet encased in dusty jogging shoes. She had the kind of face any New York model would have pillaged and killed for, high cheekbones and a generous mouth, a haughty nose turned up slightly at the tip, eyes that looked gray in the bright sunshine that flooded through the sloping greenhouse roof.

"Who gave you the shiners?" she said.

"Some friends," I said.

Her eyebrows rose only slightly; a faint smile touched her lips. "You're a cop, right?" she said.

"No, I'm a lawyer."

"Right, right," she said. "Mom told me. We've had enough cops out here this past week," she said, and rolled her eyes heavenward. She put down the bulb-spray she'd been using, picked up the walkie-talkie that was resting on a counter near the wet sink, and said, "Would you like some iced tea or something?"

"Well . . . how long will your mother be, do you know?"

"I don't suppose too long," she said. "She's been gone almost an hour now, I don't suppose she'll be much longer. Too damn *hot* out there, isn't it?"

"Very," I said.

"Yeah," she said. "You want some tea, yes or no? Or would you like something stronger?"

"Tea will be fine," I said.

"Tea it is," she said, and nodded, and walked past me into the living room of the house. "The shade trees keep it cool," she said. "I hate air conditioning, don't you?" The question was rhetorical. Without waiting for an answer, she went into the kitchen, took two cans of iced tea from the refrigerator, pulled the tabs on each, and poured them into separate glasses. "We're out of lemons," she said, handing one of the glasses to me. "Anyway, there's supposed to *be* lemon in this, it says so on the can."

Bloom had told me on the phone that she was twenty-three; she seemed younger. Perhaps it was the uncertain timbre of her voice, and the casual pattern of her speech. Or perhaps it was the way she moved, coltishly, almost awkwardly—but maybe the jogging shoes had something to do with that. Bloom had called her "a real beauty." She was indeed, but I couldn't help feeling that I was in the presence of one of my daughter's teenybopper girlfriends.

"Who was the man with the shotgun?" I asked.

"Rafe, you mean? We can sit over here," she said. "It's always cooler in this part of the room, don't ask me why. He's our new manager. We run a thousand head here, don't need more than two hands to work them. Used to be my brother and Sam—till my brother moved out, and Sam went west. Rafe's the manager now."

She settled in a white wicker chair with a bright yellow cushion, folding her long legs under her. I sat opposite her in a chair with a lime-green cushion. The corner where we sat was decorated with ferns in huge clay pots, and it *did* seem cooler than the rest of the house.

"Why the shotgun?" I asked.

She smiled. "Make sure you weren't one of the bad guys," she said.

"Bad guys?"

"Where you've got cows, you've got people wanting to steal them," she said. She was still smiling. "Rustling," she said. "You heard of it?"

Rustling, I thought. In Florida. I suddenly felt a long, long way from Chicago, Illinois.

"Actually," she said, "we keep the main gate unlocked during the daytime, put the padlock on it only at night. Mom knew you were coming, sent Rafe down to look for you." She sipped at her tea. "So who do you think killed my brother?" she asked.

"I have no idea."

"Neither do the police. *Some* Mickey Mouse department we've got in Calusa. Straight out of Disney World."

I made no comment.

"Been how long already?" she said. "Ten, eleven days? Not a *clue*, can you believe it? Somebody walks in, stabs Jack *how* many times? Gee, looka this, the cops say. Gee, whatta we do now? So meanwhile the killer's out there maybe planning to knock off somebody else. If he hasn't already." She shook her head. "Strictly amateur night in Dixie."

"Are you from someplace else originally?" I asked.

"No. Why? Oh. That's just an expression, haven't you ever heard that expression? Amateur night in Dixie? What it means, it means . . . well, Mickey Mouse."

"Yes," I said.

"Sure," she said. "I was born right here," she said. "Well, not right here on the *ranch*, but in a hospital in Ananburg. That's the nearest hospital, Ananburg. For *people*, I mean. For the stock, Mom uses a vet about three miles down the road. What'd you want to see her about?"

"Well, I'd rather discuss that with her personally," I said.

"Sure, no problem."

"What's the Sunny for?" I said.

"You won't believe it," she said, "Sylvia!" and wrinkled her nose. "Can you imagine me as a *Sylvia*?"

"Not very easily," I said.

"No *way*! They started calling me Sunny when I was still a little kid. 'Cause I have blonde hair, of course, and also because I have a very sweet disposition, ha!" she said, and snorted.

"Don't you?" I said. "Have a sweet disposition?"

"Mister, I'm as mean as a fucking tiger," she said, and someone across the room said, "Nice language, Sunny."

42

We both turned.

"Oops," Sunny said, and immediately covered her mouth with her hand.

The woman standing just inside the screen door was an older, more elegant version of the girl who sat opposite me with her face now buried in both hands. She was not quite as tall as her daughter—assuming she *was* indeed the Mrs. McKinney I was expecting—but the tan high-heeled boots she wore added at least another two inches to her already substantial height. She was wearing white, form-fitting designer pants and a white T-shirt. In her right hand she held a cowboy hat like the ones Charlie and Jeff had worn on the night they'd tried to rearrange my features. In her left hand she held a pair of tan leather gloves. Her blonde hair was styled in a short shingle cut, and her cheeks, eyes, and mouth were Sunny's, exactly. The haughty nose with the slightly upturned tip would have been an exact replica of Sunny's, too, were it not for a faint dusting of freckles across the bridge. I supposed she was somewhere in her mid-forties. I got to my feet the instant she moved toward us.

"I'm Veronica McKinney," she said, and shifted the hat to her left hand, and then extended her right. "I'm sorry I kept you waiting, Mr. Hope. Sunny, go play with your dolls."

"Sorry, Mom," Sunny said, unfolding her long legs and getting to her feet.

"You should be," her mother said.

"Nice meeting you," Sunny said, and crossed the room and went up a flight of stairs leading to the second story of the house.

"I see she's offered you some refreshment," Mrs. McKinney said.

"Yes, she has."

"What *is* that? *Tea?*"

"Yes."

"God! Oh, well. Don't you find it hot in here? My daughter keeps turning off the air conditioning and opening every door and window. She has a theory about . . . well, never mind." She went back to the front door, closed it, and then adjusted a thermostat on the wall. Her movements, unlike her daughter's, were liquidly smooth and effortless. Her voice sounded a trifle breathless, not quite the voice of a heavy drinker (which might never have occurred to me if she hadn't expressed dismay over the tea), but husky nonetheless. She was altogether an entirely beautiful woman, and when she turned to me with a smile on her face, she quite took my breath away.

"The new hand tells me we've got a dead cow out on Buzzard's Roost Hammock," she said. "I'd like to take a look, mind if we talk while we ride out there?"

"Not at all," I said.

"Might be a bit muddy, all this rain," she said. "Too bad you didn't wear boots." She looked at my shoes. "Jeep's out front," she said, and turned and walked out of the house.

The Jeep was red and marked M.K. in black on its side panels. A .22-caliber rifle with a telescopic sight rested on the front seat between us. She started the engine, backed out of the dirt driveway, and said, "That's our horse barn there. We keep five horses, don't need more than that for a ranch this size. We usually figure at least two horses to a cowboy. The small house is where the manager lives, the mobile home is for the new hand and his wife. We're not a big operation—we run a thousand head, more or less, on four thousand acres. I know a man who runs twenty thousand head, has a ranch as big as the state of Rhode Island, out closer to Ananburg. We've got five pastures here, run a herd of two hundred cows on each of them. Buzzard's Roost is out this way."

We were driving north on a muddy road flanked with fenced-in pasture land. The Jeep bounced and jostled along the ruts. Brown water splashed up against the side panels as Mrs. McKinney maneuvered the vehicle through the puddles.

"The pastures were already named when my late husband bought the ranch. Historical names, all of them, I have no idea where they originated. Well, Buzzard's Roost is an easy one. More damn buzzards out there than you can shake a stick at. That's why I want to see that dead cow. Buzzards are a nuisance.

44

They'll swoop down to eat the afterbirth whenever one of our cows calves, and sometimes they'll attack the newborn calf as well. That dead cow out there is going to attract a lot of them. The other pastures—who knows?" she said. "One of them's called Mosquito Jam, must've been a breeding ground for them before the state started its control program. Still got plenty of them there, but that's native pasture. We've got a thousand acres of native, and three thousand improved now. Back in 1943, this was *all* native pasture. Been a long job planting it in Pensacola Bahia, and keeping it up. One of the pastures is called Sheep Run Hammock—somebody must've raised sheep there long ago. You know what a hammock is, of course."

"Sure," I said. "It's a sort of canvas bed you hang between two trees."

"That, too," she said, smiling. "But the word's Indian for a copse of trees. Here on the ranch, it's usually oak. So," she said. "From what you told me on the phone, I may have to handle whatever nonsense Jack got himself into, is that right?"

"Well, I'm not sure about that yet," I said. "I checked with Probate this morning, though, and there doesn't seem to be a will . . ."

"I wouldn't guess there was."

"And I've also made some calls around town—Calusa doesn't have that large a legal community—and none of the attorneys I contacted had drawn a will for him. I didn't speak to *all* of them, of course . . ."

"Who gave you the shiners?" she asked.

"Your daughter asked that same question."

"What answer did you give her?"

"I told her some friends did it."

She smiled. Her upper lip, I noticed, unlike her daughter's, seemed perpetually tented so that a small wedge of white teeth always showed. When she smiled, it only widened the wedge, magically and radiantly.

"What color are your eyes?" I asked.

"Is that a trick question?" she said.

"I'm curious. They look gray, but gray is for novels."

"They aren't *gray*," she said, "God, no. I don't know *anyone* who has gray eyes, do you? They're a pale blue, I suppose. A faded blue. A *washed-out* blue, actually. Is there such a thing as a *mousy* blue? I've always hated the color of my eyes. They make me look anemic. What color did Sunny say *her* eyes were?"

"I didn't ask her."

"They're the same as mine, so I guess they're blue, too," she said. "Jack's were brown. Well, you met him, so you know."

"Anyway," I said.

"Anyway," she said.

". . . getting back to this matter of a will."

"I think we can safely assume there was no will, Mr. Hope."

We were passing a row of—bathtubs?—set out in the pasture on our right, about a dozen in all, spaced some twenty feet apart from each other.

"If you're wondering whether we come out here to bathe," she said, "those are for the cows."

"You *bathe* your *cows*?" I said.

"No, no," she said, and smiled. "We supplement their feeding, especially during the winter months, when they're stressed."

"Stressed?"

"We've got plenty of good, tall grass now," she said, "but during the winter they can eat it off faster than it grows. They get what we call 'Miss-Meal Fever.' That isn't a disease, Mr. Hope, it just means they're *hungry*. We put out molasses in those tubs. A small, tractor-drawn tank comes around and fills them at least once a week, there are hundreds of them all over the place. We buy the molasses from U.S. Sugar in Clewiston. Just now there's a lot of water lying on top of it—all this rain. Rafe and the hand are kept pretty busy scooping it off."

"Where do you get the tubs?" I asked.

"Demolition company sells them to us. Do you see that other contraption out there? Over near where those black baldies are grazing?"

I looked out over the pasture. A dozen or more white-faced black cows were standing and eating grass near what looked like a large garbage bin with a cylindrical open top.

"Those are our mineral feeders. We fill them every week with salt, calcium, phosphorus, steamed bone meal, iron—all those goodies," she said, and smiled. "The cows go to them because of the salt, get their minerals while they're lapping it up."

"What kind of cows *are* they?" I asked.

"That particular bunch? A cross between Hereford, Angus, and Brahman. What we raise here in Florida is mostly Braford and Brangus. Those are crossbred cattle. The Braford is what we get when we breed a Brahman cow with a Hereford bull. The Brangus is mixed Brahman and Angus, short-haired and loose-skinned—so they can survive the heat. But you'll see all kinds out there. Your reds, which are the Santa Gertrudis—three-eighths Brahman and five-eighths Shorthorn—your brindles, your mottled, your yellows, we raise 'em all, or try to, a regular rainbow herd. Here," she said, "make yourself useful," and braked the Jeep just this side of an aluminum gate. "There's no lock on it, all you have to do is unhook the chain."

I got out of the Jeep and tried to skirt the mud puddles as I walked toward the gate. There was a simple thumb bolt holding the chain fastened. I pulled it back, loosened the chain, and swung the gate wide. Mrs. McKinney drove the Jeep through, and I closed the gate and fastened the chain again. My shoes were covered with mud. I got into the Jeep and pulled the door shut.

"This road we're turning onto is a better one," she said. "Those lines overhead are Florida Power and Light. I lease them the right-of-way, and they maintain the road. Buzzard's Roost is about half a mile east of here."

We had come into another pasture. The cows here were brown, fifty or more of them, all of them grazing contentedly. Graceful white birds were sitting on their backs.

"Your reds," she said, "Santa Gertrudis, the first true North American breed. Developed on the King Ranch."

"What are those little yellow things on their ears?" I asked.

"Fly tags. Like those strips you hang in your kitchen, only these are smaller. They keep the horn flies off. The flies suck blood, agitate the cows, make general nuisances of themselves. The tags work pretty well."

"And the white birds?"

"Cattle egrets. They eat the insects the cows disturb with their hooves, sit up on their backs to get a better view of the ground. The cows don't mind them at—damn, *look* at them!" she said suddenly and braked the Jeep and reached for the rifle between us. I looked off toward the sky, following her gaze. A dozen or more big birds were hovering on the air. One of them swooped down to the ground an instant before Mrs. McKinney brought the rifle to her shoulder. A sharp crack sounded on the air. The buzzard—I assumed it was a buzzard—toppled over and the other birds flew off at once, flapping their wings, climbing higher.

"There's the dead cow, all right," she said, putting the rifle down between us again. "Don't tell anyone I shot that buzzard, it's against the law. They look too much like eagles, and a lot of mistakes are made. Eagles are protected, you know, an endangered species. We'll have to haul that carcass away, I don't want them coming down after any new calves."

"Is this where the cows give birth?" I asked. "Right here on the pasture?"

"Oh, sure. Unassisted, it's not like with racehorses. We lose some of them when they're calving, but not many. They're pretty good at it," she said, and smiled. "You plan on going into the cattle business, Mr. Hope?"

"All my questions, do you mean?"

"Yes."

"It's another world to me, forgive me. Am I being too curious?"

"Not at all. But you'd do better in the money market, if you're looking for an investment. My *son* was going into real estate, is that right?" she asked, abruptly shifting the topic. Or perhaps the word "investment" had triggered the association.

"Yes," I said. "Tell me, first, was he actually twenty years old? He showed me his driver's license, but . . ."

"Twenty, yes," she said, "*just*. And I'm fifty-seven. Was that going to be your next question?"

I blinked.

"An elderly person," she said, and smiled.

"Hardly," I said.

"I sometimes feel like a *hundred* and fifty-seven."

"You look much younger."

"Than a hundred and fifty-seven?"

"Than . . . whatever you said you were, which I've already forgotten."

"I thank you, sir," she said, and nodded curtly.

"In any case," I said.

"In any case," she said.

"If your son was twenty, then the contract he signed is legally binding. And, I'm sorry to tell you, it's legally binding on his estate as well. I understand you're a widow . . ."

"Yes. My husband died two years ago."

"I'm sorry to hear that."

"He was very ill for a very long time. Cancer," she said flatly. "You mentioned on the phone that Jack had bought this piece of land, was in the *process* of buying this land . . ."

"Yes, a farm. Not very far from here, actually. A bit farther east, toward Ananburg."

"A farm," she said.

"Yes."

"What the hell would he want with a farm?"

"It's a snapbean farm."

"My son, the bean farmer," she said.

"Apparently he . . ."

"Apparently he was a jerk," Mrs. McKinney said. "How much was this farm costing him?"

"Forty thousand dollars."

"What!" she said.

"Yes."

"Where did he plan to . . . forty *thousand*, did you say?"

"Yes."

"That's impossible. No," she said, and shook her head. "Are you sure about that figure?"

"I drew the contract myself, Mrs. McKinney. That was the purchase price. Forty thousand dollars."

"I can't imagine it," she said.

"He put down a deposit of four thousand," I said.

"He gave you four thousand dollars?"

"For the bank to hold in escrow, yes. Until the closing."

"Then his check was no good. I know for a fact that Jack . . ."

"It wasn't a check. It was cash."

"Cash!" Her eyes opened wide again. They did, in fact, look gray, no matter what she said their actual color was. "How could Jack . . . ? This is all unbelievable. Where would he . . . ?" She was shaking her head again. "Jack simply did not have that kind of money."

"He was renting a condo on Stone Crab," I said. "And from what I understand . . ."

"*I* was paying for that condo, Mr. Hope. Mama McKinney. My son Jack barely squeaked through high school with a C-minus average. Even if any college in the United States would have been crazy enough to accept him, he wouldn't have gone. I kicked him off the ranch because he couldn't even learn to brand a calf properly, much less sit a horse. Tennis is what he loved, my son Jack. Big tennis player. Could ace you out of your mind, my Jack." She sighed heavily. "I figured it was better to have him out of my hair on Stone Crab someplace. Pay for the apartment, give him a little spending money every month . . ." She shook her head again. "But four thousand *dollars*? In *cash*? Impossible. No."

"It's what he gave me, Mrs. McKinney. It's still in escrow

50

with the Tricity Bank in Calusa. If you like, I can show you . . ."

"I believe you," she said. She was silent for several moments, and then she asked, "Where did he expect to get the balance? Had he planned on coming to Mama?"

"Apparently that was no problem. He said he'd have the thirty-six thousand at the closing."

"Mr. Hope, you are absolutely *flooring* me, do you realize that? Are you saying that a bank was willing to lend a *tennis bum* thirty six . . . ?"

"He was already in possession of the money, ma'am. He told me he had it in cash."

"In *cash*? And please don't 'ma'am' me, I'll *really* feel like an old lady. How old are *you*, anyway?"

"Thirty-eight," I said.

"Young whippersnapper," she said, and smiled. "Get into fistfights and everything, don't you? Bet your knees are all scraped up, too. Who *really* beat up on you, Mr. Hope?"

"Two cowboys in a bar."

"Leave it to cowboys," she said, and rolled her eyes the way her daughter had earlier.

"So," I said.

"So," she said.

"Mr. Burrill . . ."

"Who's Mr. Burrill?"

"The seller. The man who contracted to sell fifteen acres of farmland, together with all buildings, improvements, machinery . . ."

"To Jack's *estate*, as it turns out."

"I'm afraid so."

"For forty thousand dollars."

"Yes."

"Thirty-six of which is still due."

"At the closing," I said.

"I don't know of any estate Jack left," she said. "I'll have to talk this over with my lawyer."

"Of course. You might mention to him that Mr. Burrill's attorney has indicated he'll bring suit if the estate refuses to honor your son's contractual obligation."

"Suit against whom? *Me?*"

"No, the estate. There's no way *you* can be held personally responsible by virtue of being related to your son. I'm assuming you'd be the personal representative of his estate, but you'd best check that with your lawyer, too."

"How long do we have on this?"

"We were supposed to close early next month. As soon as the title search and the other necessary . . ."

"Why'd Jack get me into this stupid mess?"

"He wanted to be a farmer," I said.

"That's like wanting to be a *shepherd!*"

"Well, talk it over with your lawyer. Please understand, Mrs. McKinney, I'm not taking an adversary position here. I was representing your *son* in this transaction, *not* Mr. Burrill."

"Of course," she said. "I'll call Erik as soon as we get back to the house. Those are our pens over on the left, would you like to take a look?"

She pulled up the Jeep before a wooden fence that enclosed a labyrinthine maze of narrow, mud-churned passages similarly enclosed, a series of fences within fences.

"This is where we work the cows," she said. "You've come at a quiet time of the year, most of our activity is in the spring and the fall. In August, what we do mostly is mend the cross-fences between pastures, chop down the thistle, burn off the palmettos—like that. We'll work the cattle some, too—pregnancy testing, semen testing, and so on—but that's on an as-needed basis. In August it's mostly maintenance, a sort of holding action till October and November."

"Do you have one of these pens in each of the pastures?" I asked.

"No, this one serves the whole ranch. We drive the cows over and put 'em in a crevice—that's a small pasture, not a crack in a rock—the night before, and then pen 'em the next morning. Work one herd at a time that way."

"By work . . ."

"Well, unless you've got all day," she said, "it's really too complicated to explain."

I felt I had been mildly discouraged from asking any further questions. There was a short, awkward silence.

"This contraption here is the squeeze chute," she said, "holds the cows while we're working them."

I was looking at what appeared to be an instrument of torture, with sloping metal sides fashioned of three-inch-thick steel bars, and a curved metal plate that looked like the headrest on a guillotine. Above the mechanism was a row of levers with black plastic knobs on them.

"Herd them in from where we unload them," she said, and reached up for one of the black knobs. "I'm not too good at operating this thing," she said, "the cowboys usually do it." She pulled one of the levers down. The spread metal sides of the chute began closing. "It catches the cow in there and holds her fast," she said. "There's no way even a *dozen* men could hold a seven-hundred-pound cow when you're drenching her or trying to find out if she's pregnant. This one," she said, and reached up for another lever, "lowers or raises the head—I *think*." She pulled on the black knob, and the guillotine headrest at the front end of the chute began rising. "Yep," she said, "that's the one. Handy little machine," she said. "Man who invented it probably makes more money than all the cattle breeders in the world put together. Shall we head on back to the house, Mr. Hope? I'll give Erik a call, ask him how *he* thinks we should proceed. Erik Larsen," she said, "do you know him? Of the law firm of Petersen, Larsen, and Rasmussen—all of Danish extraction, I would assume."

"I know the firm," I said. "I don't know him personally."

"Nice man," she said, "and a good lawyer. Looks like I'll *need* one if this farmer plans to sue, huh?"

We got into the Jeep again. She backed it away from the fence, and then turned and drove onto another muddy side road. I realized all at once that we were making a big circle around the ranch. Drainage ditches ran alongside either side of the road. A small alligator, basking on the grassy bank, turned tail and splashed into the ditch.

"The gators'll sometimes prey on our young calves, we'll have a sickly one every now and then. But for the most part they're harmless. Buzzards are the chief predators to worry about. Unless you consider *disease* a predator. There's plenty of that," she said.

"Is there?" I asked cautiously, remembering her curt reply to my earlier question, and afraid she would tell me that *this*, too, was "complicated."

It was.

When they were working the cows—I still didn't know what "working" them meant—in the spring and the fall, they vaccinated for blackleg, pasturella, and malignant edema, the vaccine usually administered in a triple dose subcutaneously. A *must* vaccination for heifers they hoped to breed was for brucellosis or Bang's disease—"I don't know who Bang was," Mrs. McKinney said. "Probably a vet who couldn't spell brucellosis." The disease caused infertility, and since a "cow-calf lady" (as she called herself) was in the business of breeding cattle, Bang's disease was a dreaded nemesis. Cancer eye was another severe problem, especially in Herefords, who sunburned badly around the eyes because of their white faces. This was treatable with silver nitrate, she explained, but even so, the cow would eventually lose the eye. "Angus don't suffer from it," she said. "Black is beautiful." They vaccinated against leptospirosis, which could cause a cow to abort or prolapse ("That's when everything hangs out the rear end," she said, "and you lose the unborn calf.") Leptospirosis was highly infectious, as was scours, a form of diarrhea.

"And there's also mastitis," she said, "which is an udder infection, and colic, which you flush out with mineral oil, administered orally from a garden hose. I know a rancher out West who lost ninety percent of his calf crop because his cows were eating pine needles that caused them to abort. Moldy hay can do it too. We haven't had any of *that* yet, thank God; when *our* cattle are stressed, they go for the palmettos. The ranchers out West *also* have to worry about poison grasses like larkspur and senecio— pretty little blue and yellow flowers, but deadly. Locoweed too, out there, which isn't deadly, of course, but which makes the cows go bananas—they'll run right over you, go through fences, knock down posts, who needs it? It isn't an easy business, cattle breeding. Do you suppose snapbean farming is less work?"

Her mind kept circling back to the farm, I noticed, and what I was sure she considered a foolish investment on her son's part. We passed a pair of deer standing some fifty feet inside the pasture fence on our left. They stared at the Jeep in surprise for a moment, and then turned and went loping off gracefully. I unfastened the chain on another gate, and we drove into yet another pasture on yet another muddy road. We passed a grove of orange trees—"I keep two hundred acres in citrus," Mrs. McKinney said. "It's a nuisance more than anything else"—and we passed a huge, black wild hog rooting in a copse of trees she said was called "Happy Hammock," for reasons she could not fathom. And at last we drove past the small clapboard house where her manager lived, and her hand's mobile home, and the horse barn—a brown quarter horse was grazing outside now—and the two rusting gas tanks. She parked the Jeep under a huge old oak and we walked together up the porch steps and into the main house. She had set the air conditioning too low. The temperature inside was virtually subarctic.

"Ah, nice and cool," she said. "I'll just call Erik from the office, it won't take a minute. Would you like a drink? Something a bit stronger than tea?"

"No, thanks," I said.

"Well, make yourself comfortable," she said, and opened a door beyond which I could see one corner of a cluttered desk. The door closed. From upstairs in the house someplace, I heard a record player blaring a rock-and-roll tune. Sunny, I thought. I sat in one of the wicker chairs in the fern-cluttered corner nook where Sunny and I had earlier had our brief conversation, and I wondered why I felt it easier to talk to her mother, who—by strict arithmetical calculation—was far more distant in age from me than was her daughter.

I still found it hard to believe that anyone her age could be so—well, there were no other words for it—well preserved. I know divorced men of my age who won't dream of "dating" (a word I despise) anyone older than twenty-five. Thirty-eight is a dangerous age for a man. For a woman too, I suppose, but I'm not qualified to speak for the opposite sex. At thirty-eight, a man starts looking over his shoulder to see how closely the shadow of forty is following. Forty is a dread age. Forty means you'd better grow up fast if you're going to grow up at all. Forty means taking stock of where you've been and where you're going. At thirty-eight, forty is only two years away (in my case only eighteen months away) and forty means problems. You can go bald when you turn forty. Your teeth can start falling out, if they haven't already been *knocked* out by a football player in Chicago. You can hurt your knees. Your back can start troubling you. Forty is a pain in the ass. My partner Frank had turned forty in April. He said it was easy. Just like falling off Pier Eight, he said. I didn't know where Pier Eight was. I supposed it was in New York City someplace.

But Veronica McKinney was fifty-seven years old. *Fifty-seven!* Almost twenty years older than I, and looking fit and trim and healthy and vital. Veronica McKinney made a person believe that forty would indeed be a piece of cake. Veronica McKinney had found the fountain of youth that Ponce de Leon had come down here looking for, and had drunk of it deeply, and was living proof that all of us terrified men trembling on the brink of middle age had nothing at all to fear. Veronica McKinney was a glowing promise of hope for the future, and that was reason enough to feel comfortable and secure and somehow content in her presence.

The door to her private office opened. She stepped out into

the vast living room and walked briskly to where I was sitting in the corner nook. She moved like a sprightly teenager; I couldn't get over it. "Are you sure you wouldn't like a drink?" she asked.

"Work to do when I get back to the office," I said.

"I'd offer you a swim, but we haven't got a pool. Do you have a pool, Mr. Hope?"

"I have. And please call me Matthew, won't you?"

"Oh good," she said, "I *hate* formality, it seems so out of place here on the ranch. Will you call me Veronica, then?"

"Is that what your friends call you?"

"Some of them call me Ronnie, but I find that more suitable for someone my daughter's age. Veronica will do nicely, such as it is. I've never felt completely comfortable with it, I must admit. Back in the early forties, when I was a teenager, I began combing my hair like Veronica Lake—does she mean anything to you?"

"Yes, of course," I said.

"Big movie star," she said. "Used to wear her hair hanging over one eye, I forget which one now, either the right or the left—it was very sexy, actually. Made her look as if she'd just tumbled out of bed. I'd demonstrate, but my hair's too short now. Anyway, I started imitating her. She was a blonde, remember? I began wearing my hair like hers, and talking in that low breathy voice she had—my friends must have thought I was *crazy,*" she said, and suddenly began laughing. "But she was the only other Veronica I knew, and it was *such* a relief to be able to identify with *someone.* Adolescence is such a difficult time, isn't it? I can understand why my daughter clings to it so tenaciously."

I said nothing.

"Anyway," she said, "you don't want to listen to me prattling on about my green and salad days."

"I'm enjoying it," I said.

"Well, I'm glad," she said, and smiled. "What we've decided, Erik and I, is to tell this Mr. Burrill, as simply as possible, that my son left no estate that we know of—other than his personal belongings and his automobile."

"Yes, those would be part of his estate."

"Well, Mr. Burrill is certainly entitled to those if he insists on pressing the matter. The car's three years old, a Ford Mustang. But what Erik suggested—and I'd like your opinion on this as well—Erik thought Mr. Burrill might be willing to forget the entire matter if we simply forfeited the four thousand dollars you're already holding in escrow. It's Erik's opinion that if there's no estate—and in essence there isn't—then Mr. Burrill hasn't a prayer of collecting the additional thirty-six thousand. Erik said that even if I were a billionaire—and I assure you I'm not—there's no way Mr. Burrill could proceed against me directly."

"That's right."

"He can sue the estate, of course, but if there are no meaningful assets in it, what would be the point?"

"That's good reasoning," I said.

"Do you think Mr. Burrill would be willing to *keep* his damn farm and settle for the four thousand?"

"I have no idea. But I'm sure that once your attorney makes him familiar with the facts . . ."

"Which, by the way, is something *else* Erik and I talked about. He was wondering . . . since you've put in so much work on this already, and since he's really not familiar with either Mr. Burrill *or* his attorney . . . do you think you could?"

"Could what?"

"Represent me in this matter? As though you were still representing Jack?"

"Well . . . yes, I'd be happy to."

"You sound hesitant. If it presents any difficulty for you . . ."

"No, I was simply wondering whether there'd be any ethical problems, but I can't imagine any. Yes, I'd be delighted to represent you."

"Well, good," she said. "Then that's settled. I hate loose ends."

"I'll call Loomis . . ."

"Loomis?"

"Mr. Burrill's attorney. To ask whether his client might consider settling for the four thousand. In fact, if I can call him from here, maybe I can stop by to see him this afternoon."

"You can use the phone in my office," she said.

I went into her office. The large desk there was strewn with papers and back issues of a magazine called *The Florida Cattleman*. What I had learned was a Hereford cow—brown and white-faced—stared out at me from the cover of the October issue. Hanging on the wall behind the desk were framed plaques of appreciation from the Cattleman's Association, all of them looking like law degrees, their ornate Old English script citing Drew McKinney for this or that outstanding achievement or service. I dialed information and asked for Harry Loomis's number in Ananburg. I dialed the number and waited. Across the room, hanging on the wall, there was an oil painting of a brown-eyed, black-haired man who looked a lot like an older version of Jack McKinney; I assumed he was Jack's father, the late Drew McKinney. He was smiling out of the painting, his dark eyes crinkled, his black mustache overhanging a mouth tilted in a lopsided grin. He was wearing the same sort of pearl-buttoned shirt my cowboy friends Charlie and Jeff had been wearing. He looked like Clark Gable. Or, to update the version, he looked like my daughter's current movie-star flame, Tom Selleck.

"Attorney-at-law," a brisk female voice said.

I told the woman who I was and asked to talk to Mr. Loomis. When he came onto the line, I explained that I was here with Jack McKinney's mother, and was wondering if he might have a little time to see me, since I was so close to Ananburg and all. He told me to come by at three o'clock.

Veronica McKinney was standing near the huge fireplace when I came out into the living room again. In her right hand she was holding a tall drink with a lime floating in it. A young man sat in the green-cushioned wicker chair I had occupied earlier. They were not in conversation. In fact, Veronica's back was turned to him.

"This is Jackie Crowell," she said, gesturing toward him with the hand that held the glass. "My daughter's friend," she said. It seemed to me she punched home the word *friend*, as though she found it, and by extension the boy himself, distasteful. "Jackie," she said, "this is Mr. Hope."

Crowell rose from the chair and walked toward me, his hand extended. Bloom had described him as a pimply-faced "twerp," but he was in fact as tall as I was, and much huskier, with broad shoulders and a narrow waist, and bulging biceps showing where his denim vest ended. His complexion, as far as I could tell in the light streaming through the windows, was entirely free of any acne whatever. He looked, in fact, like your average, healthy, all-American boy, clean-scrubbed (and even smelling faintly of soap) with dark hair and dark eyes, and a pleasant smile.

"Nice to meet you," he said.

We shook hands.

"Sunny should be down in a minute," Veronica said, and dismissed him abruptly. "Did you reach Loomis?" she asked me.

"On my way to see him now," I said.

"Good luck," she said, and raised her glass in a dubious toast. She took a quick sip, placed the glass on the fireplace mantel, and showed me to the door. As I stepped outside, I heard Sunny's voice calling, "Jackie? Are you *here* already?"

It was blisteringly hot outside. A white Chevette was parked alongside my Ghia. I assumed it was Crowell's. I drove up the long, rutted road without passing another vehicle. The main gate to the ranch was still wide open. As I made the right turn toward Ananburg, it occurred to me that never once in my conversation with Veronica McKinney had she expressed the slightest grief over her son's death.

3

You did not have to drive very far past the Sawgrass River State Park to realize how important cows were to Florida's economy. The McKinney ranch was still within the confines of Calusa County, some twenty miles from the center of town, and only one of a handful of ranches before you crossed the border into De Soto County. No sign marked the dividing line between the two counties. Nothing said *Welcome to De Soto County*. But you knew at once that this was true cow country, and the moment you drove through Manakawa, the only town on the way to Ananburg, you felt you'd crashed through some sort of geographic time warp to find yourself in what appeared to be a mixture of Texas, Mississippi, and Louisiana—the deep South blending imperceptibly with the Southwest.

The regional dialects in Calusa were largely Midwestern tourist, harsh and flat and somewhat abrupt, with here and there an off-American dollop of Canadian English thrown in. But here in the boonies the accent was pure Dixie, and the inhabitants looked like anyone you might find on a dusty back road in Georgia. The men wore bib overalls here, and boots and straw hats, and they chewed tobacco and rolled their own cigarettes. The women wore those patterned cotton things my mother used to call house dresses. The roadside restaurants in Manakawa featured "home cooking," which invariably meant country ham and black-eyed peas, green beans and fatback, hominy and collard greens, corn bread and fried catfish. Forsaking the restaurants offering down-home fare, I found a greasy spoon across the street from what appeared to be a courthouse, ordered a hamburger, a side of fries, and a cold beer, and was on the road again at two-thirty.

Ananburg was only forty-four miles from downtown Calusa, but by comparison it looked like *The Last Picture Show*, a shabby, sunburned town with a wide main street flanked by palm-lined sidewalks and wooden two-story buildings that appeared temporary, as if they were part of a movie set that would be torn down and stored as soon as the showdown gunfight was shot at high noon. This was the heart of Central West Florida's cow country, and the home of the annual All-Florida Championship Rodeo that took place every January. There were a lot of cowboys in town. They clattered along the dusty sidewalks, bowlegged in their boots and jangling spurs, straw ten-gallon hats shading leathery brown faces, hand-rolled cigarettes dangling from sun-cracked lips. They called each other "Clem" and "Luke" and "Shorty," and they slapped each other on the back a lot, and they had pint-sized whiskey bottles in brown paper bags stuffed into the back pockets of their tight, faded jeans. This was Charlie-and-Jeff country, and I felt a certain amount of uneasiness as I walked up the main street looking for the address Harry Loomis had given me.

The wooden shingle read HARRY R. LOOMIS, ATTORNEY-AT-LAW, and a pointing dismembered hand painted onto the lower left-hand corner of the sign indicated a flight of wooden steps that led to the second story of the shingled building. The steps were narrow and many of the treads were either loose or entirely broken. I wondered if Harry Loomis was a good negligence lawyer; it seemed to me he might need one if someone fell and broke a leg on his rickety staircase. There was only one door on the second floor, the name HARRY R. LOOMIS hand-lettered in black on a frosted glass panel in its upper part. I opened the door and stepped into a small waiting room.

In the one and only telephone conversation I'd had with Avery Burrill, he'd informed me that his attorney ran "a one-man operation, just him an' the girl answers the phone." The "girl" sitting behind the desk just inside the entrance door had to be in her late fifties, approximately the same age as Veronica McKinney, but there all similarity ended. Where Veronica was tall and slender and blonde, the woman who peered at me over her rimless glasses was short and squat, with hair the color of iron. Where Veronica wore clothes that were casual and youthful, this woman wore a tailored blue pinstriped suit that looked as if its father had been a getaway car. Veronica's smile could melt a glacier. This woman's tightly set mouth could turn a desert to glass. Veronica's voice was soft and breathless and a bit ragged. This woman's voice, when at last she spoke, was fired from a secret concrete silo somewhere in Siberia.

"What is it?" she snapped.

"I'm Attorney Hope," I said. "Mr. Loomis is expecting me."

"Oh *yes*," she said, and wrinkled her nose as though mere mention of my name had recalled aromas of dead rats decomposing under attic eaves. "You're late," she said. "Sit down, if you like. I'll tell him you're here." The tone of her voice indicated that if I accepted her invitation to sit, I did so at my own peril. In any case, the only unoccupied chair in the small room seemed to have been carved from the same inhospitable oak as her face. I chose to stand. She picked up the phone and informed Mr. Loomis that "the lawyer from Calusa's here." She held the phone to her ear a moment longer, and then crashed it down on the cradle like the cutting edge of a guillotine blade. I thought suddenly of the squeeze chute on the McKinney ranch. "Go on in," she said. I almost answered, "Yes, sir."

Harry Loomis looked like a hanging judge in a fifties Western movie. He was wearing a dark winter-weight suit, a white shirt, and a black string tie, and—I will swear to this in a court of law—he was chewing tobacco. In fact, he spat a wad of it at what appeared to be a porcelain chamber pot the instant I came into the office. His face was the color of the tobacco juice that arced across the room and missed the chamber pot, adding another stain to those already on the wall. The wall was papered with what appeared to be a design of flattened locusts. Harry Loomis's college diploma, his law degree, and his license to practice in the state of Florida were hanging in black frames against the squashed-bug pattern. I did not recognize the names of either of the schools he'd attended. I *thought* that the ornate Old English script on his law degree read *University of the Virgin Islands*, but surely I was mistaken. Harry Loomis kept looking at me from behind black-rimmed spectacles that magnified his watery blue eyes. He kept chewing tobacco. I hoped he would not spit again. I hoped he was in a better mood than his "girl" had been. I hoped I would never have to see him again after today.

"Let's make this short and sweet, Mr. Hope," he said, "I'm a busy man." His voice was sassafras and molasses with a dash of castor oil thrown in for body and flavor. His eyebrows, I noticed, resembled the squashed bugs on the wallpaper. He was either growing a scraggly pepper-and-salt beard, or else he simply hadn't bothered to shave for the past several days. He cleared his throat, brought up a great dollop of gloppy brown juice, and fired at the chamber pot again. This time he scored a perfect ten, and grinned in satisfaction. His teeth were the color of cow dung. "State your case," he said.

I told him that so far as we'd been able to determine, Jack McKinney had left no will. I told him that according to Florida's intestate-succession statutes, whatever estate he'd left would go to his mother. I told him, however, that a police check in Calusa, Bradenton, and Sarasota had turned up no bank accounts and that the only assets in McKinney's estate were his personal belongings and a three-year-old Ford Mustang automobile. I started to tell him that considering the—

"What about that thirty-six thousand?" Loomis said. "The cash he was supposed to come up with at the closing?"

"Assuming he was actually in possession of that amount," I said. "It has not yet been found."

"Who looked for it?" Loomis said.

"I just told you. The police."

"Where?"

"In his apartment. And, as I told you, they ran a routine check on all the banks in . . ."

"Did they try the banks here in Ananburg? Or Manakawa? Or Venice? Or . . . ?"

"Well," I said, "how about the banks in New York, or Chicago, or Los Angeles? It doesn't seem likely that McKinney would have kept his money where it wouldn't be convenient for withdrawal. Ananburg and . . ."

"You don't know that for a fact," he said. He pronounced the word "fack."

"In any case," I said, "assuming for the moment that the only estate . . ."

"I don't assume nothin' till it's a proven fact," Loomis said. Again the word came out as "fack."

I was tempted to tell him to go fack himself. Instead, and patiently, I said, "Well, if we can show—to your satisfaction, of course—that in essence there's no estate, would you be willing . . . ?"

"I won't be satisfied till you've turned over every grain of sand in Florida," he said. "The man signed a piece of paper said he had thirty-six thousand dollars in cash waiting on the closing. That piece of paper is a *fact*, Mr. Hope, signed by both parties, and it tells me there *is* an estate of at *least* thirty-six thousand dollars. I don't know what you're tryin' to pull now, but it looks to me . . ."

"No one's trying to 'pull' anything," I said, "and I resent the accusation. We're convinced there's no substantial estate. Assuming we can convince . . ."

"Here we go *assumin*' again," Loomis said.

"Assuming we can convince *you* of that, we're prepared to make an offer in settlement . . ."

"An' what might that be, Mr. Hope?"

"Your client keeps the farm, of course, and the bank releases to him the four thousand dollars it's holding in escrow. We will also turn over the automobile and all of McKinney's personal belongings."

"How about damages?" Loomis said. "My client coulda sold that farm to any number of people. If there hadn'ta been that piece of paper he signed with McKinney . . ."

"He can *still* sell the farm. He'll still own it."

"Buyers don't wait on welshers, Mr. Hope."

"I would hardly think that getting killed is the same thing as welshing. In any case, that's our offer, and it seems to me a fair one."

"How'd you like us to sue the estate, Mr. Hope?" Loomis said. "Find out just *where* you're hidin' that thirty-six thousand?"

"That's your prerogative, of course," I said. "It might be a long and complicated action, however, and your client might end up spending more than the four thousand we're willing to forfeit."

"I don't like negotiatin' with gunslicks," Loomis said.

"Why don't you discuss it with Mr. Burrill?" I said.

"I can tell you now what his answer'll be."

"You never know."

"What school did you go to?" Loomis asked.

"Northwestern."

"Where's that?"

"Up there someplace," I said. "Talk it over with Mr. Burrill, won't you?"

"I *still* think there's more money in that estate than you're lettin' on," Loomis said.

"You're wrong," I said. "Good day, Mr. Loomis."

He was turning to spit at the chamber pot again as I left the office.

The rains came—from the novel and the movie of the same name. Torrents of water spilled from the roiling sky like silver vertical tracer bullets, riddling the road and drilling the roof of the Ghia. I drove very slowly and carefully through the spreading puddles of water on the road, braking whenever I approached what appeared to be a raging river rushing across the asphalt from one side to the other. It was going to be what down here they called a "frog-strangler."

The windshield wipers on the Ghia had never worked properly, and they weren't working well now. The glass on the *inside* was fogging up as well, and when I cranked down the window on my left, I was immediately rewarded with a great spatter of rain that caused me to crank it up again at once. The rain down here in Florida was fiercer than I'd ever seen it anywhere else. It seemed unleashed by a vengeful God determined to punish those of us who were foolish enough to linger here during the summer months. The Ghia sounded like a Caribbean band of steel drummers, huge raindrops pounding on the hood and beating against the windshield where the wipers valiantly tried to clear an arced area of visibility. I wiped condensation from the inside of the windshield and hunched tighter over the wheel in an attempt to see the road ahead more clearly than I *was* seeing it. With all the windows closed, the interior of the car was suffocatingly hot.

The seersucker suit I'd put on before leaving the house this morning was clinging limply to my frame, and my shirt was sticking to my chest and armpits. A rule at Summerville and Hope (for which Frank and I had no one to blame but ourselves) made it mandatory for all male employees to wear jackets and ties to work. The women had it a bit easier. After long debate, we had ruled out the necessity for panty hose or nylons during the summer months. Cynthia Huellen, our receptionist and general factotum, came to work barelegged as often as not. Our various secretaries, perhaps because they felt themselves higher up in the pecking order, still dressed a bit more formally except in the winter, when slacks ran rampant all over the place. Today I would have preferred shorts, sneakers, and a T-shirt. Instead, I sweltered inside my straitjacket suit and my hangman's-knot tie as I drove past the Burrill farm—the bean of contention, so to speak—marked with his name on a brown mailbox, and then the state park, and then the McKinney ranch, and finally found myself on the outskirts of civilization. It took me twenty minutes from the intersection of Timucuan Point and U.S. 41 to get to my office downtown. It was almost five o'clock when I got there.

Cynthia told me that Frank had gone to a late closing, and was planning to meet a client for a drink after that. She did not mention what was on the desk in my office. What was on the desk was a note in her handwriting. It read:

Sorry I couldn't get to this sooner, but I didn't think it was terribly urgent. How come you always treat me *like a lady, huh?*
C.

The note was clipped to a typewritten sheet. I folded the note back and read:

THE TEN RULES

1. Always treat a lady like a hooker.
2. Always treat a hooker like a lady.
3. Never send a lady anything perishable.
4. Never send a hooker anything durable.
5. Never try to buy a lady into bed.
6. Never try to talk a hooker into bed.
7. Always tell a lady you love her.
8. Never tell a hooker anything.
9. Never believe a lady who tells you she's a lady.
10. Never believe anything a hooker tells you.

I pondered this grave advice for all of thirty seconds, and then leafed through the batch of pink slips Cynthia had left in my IN basket. Sighing heavily, I began returning the calls I'd had while I was out on the prairies. I was *still* returning them when Cynthia came in at five-thirty to say good night. The rain had stopped by then, but the heat still lingered. Calusa was like no other city that I knew. The rain here did nothing to dissipate the heat. The rain came, the rain went, but the heat lingered. If anything, it seemed hotter after the rain. I was reaching for the phone again, hoping I'd still catch someone at his office, when it rang, startling me. I picked up the receiver.

"Summerville and Hope," I said.

"Matthew?"

Dale's voice. My heart leaped.

"Hey, hi," I said.

"I was hoping you'd still be there," she said.

"I'm still here."

"I've been worrying about you."

"I'm fine," I said. "Head all healed, everything almost back to . . ."

"I'm not worrying about your head," she said.

There was a long silence on the line.

"Matthew," she said, "the last thing I wanted to do was hurt you. I handled it badly, I know. Ending it the way I did. Especially after . . ."

"No, no . . ."

"Please let me say what I have to say, okay, Matthew, because I've got to get it all out in a rush before I start crying. You meant a great deal to me, Matthew, more than you'll ever know, it wasn't just sex, the way I said it was, I loved you very dearly, Matthew. And I almost didn't have the courage to end it, not after you almost got yourself killed over me, but Matthew darling, I *had* to, what happened with Jim was something out of the blue, there was no way I could avoid loving him, any more than I could have avoided breathing, but Matthew, it was so *wrong* what I was doing, seeing you and him at the same time, I *had* to end it, *had* to let you go, but not by hurting you, and I'm afraid I *did* hurt you, and I want to apologize because you'll always be someone very special to me, so please forgive me, Matthew, say you'll forgive me or I'll keep thinking of myself as some kind of whore for the rest of my life. Now I *am* going to cry, oh, Jesus," she said, and began crying.

I listened to her tears, not knowing what to say, not wanting this power of forgiveness she had conferred, not wanting to be the one who could absolve her like a parish priest in a shabby frock and cleric's collar, wanting to tell her instead that she was the finest lady I'd ever met in my life. I almost *did* say that, but I saw, right there in front of me on my desk, my partner Frank's second rule—*Always treat a hooker like a lady*—and the word *lady* suddenly assumed deprecating proportions after what Dale had said about feeling like a whore. So I listened helplessly to her sobs while I struggled to find the right words that would make it easier for her because she had, after all, called to make it easier for me. And my eye fell on Frank's seventh rule—*Always tell a lady you love her*—and I modified it a bit, changing it so that it would provide the proper ending Dale was looking for, the dignified ending that would punctuate our affair with a harmless period and not a hurtful trailing ellipsis.

"I loved you, too," I said.

Past tense.

And that seemed to do it.

She stopped crying after a while, and she wished me all the happiness in the world, and I wished her the same. And then she said, "Goodbye, Matthew," and I said, "Goodbye, Dale," and we both hung up.

I did not leave the office until almost seven o'clock. I locked up, and then drove up the street to a little Chinese joint Dale and I sometimes used to go to. I had two martinis before dinner, and then I lingered over the meal, thinking a lot about Dale, reflecting on the loneliness of eating alone, especially when it was Chinese food. A magnificent sunset was staining the sky over the Gulf of Mexico when I came out of the restaurant.

It was dark when I got home.

A red Porsche was parked outside the house next door; the widow lady who kept asking me in for fresh orange juice undoubtedly had a visitor. The blue light from her television set glowed behind her drawn living room blinds. Bloom had once told me that a good way to keep burglars away was to leave a little blue light burning whenever the house was empty; from the outside, it looks as if a television set is on. I wondered if the widow lady was entertaining her visitor by the light of a forty-watt blue bulb.

I unlocked the kitchen door, turned on the kitchen lights and then the living room lights, and then my own television set. I was walking toward the bar to mix myself another drink when I heard a sound outside at the pool—and I froze.

My mind immediately raced back to that night in Captain Blood's, and I recalled, at once and in wide-screen Technicolor, Charlie and Jeff leading me through the waltz of the toreadors. It did not help that the television set warmed up in that very instant and erupted into the room with the sound of a woman screaming. I stood rooted to the spot. The woman on the television kept screaming, and then a man's voice said, "You just keep doing that, lady," and I thought, *No, lady, please* don't *keep doing that*, but the lady kept screaming and outside I heard the sound more clearly now, and it was the sound of someone or something splashing around in my pool.

A raccoon, I thought.

And then I wondered how a raccoon could possibly have got inside the screened cage that surrounded the pool, and then wondered what I was afraid of, and I knew damn well what I was afraid of; I was afraid of having my brains scrambled yet another time. But I reasoned—correctly, I hoped—that neither Charlie nor Jeff could possibly know where I lived, even though my name and address were listed in the telephone directory, because they didn't *know* my name. Well, they knew I was *Matthew*, they had heard Dale calling me Matthew and had picked up on it, but they didn't know I was Matthew *Hope*, and besides, it was ridiculous to believe they would come back after me, since they'd done such a wonderful job the first time around.

And yet I was still afraid.

And I told myself, *Jesus, you're not going to hide in a closet*

*the rest of your life, are you? Just because a pair of hoodlums beat
you to within an inch of your life?* And I thought, *But suppose it's
a burglar out there, I'd better call the police.* But there hadn't
been any car in my driveway, and the only car parked anywhere
nearby was the red Porsche in front of the widow lady's house.
Were burglars driving Porsches these days? And why would a
housebreaker be *swimming* in my pool? And wouldn't he have
run when I turned on the house lights? I decided to turn on the
pool lights, but I didn't do that for a moment because I was still
wary, even though the television lady had stopped screaming and
the man was only telling her he was going to slit her throat. Then
I thought, *Come on, Hope,* and I walked swiftly to the wall switch
and took a deep breath and snapped on the pool lights.

It wasn't a raccoon out there, and it wasn't a burglar, either.
It was Sunny McKinney, and she was naked.

My first reaction was one of unreasoning anger. At her for
having scared me, at myself for having been scared. The sudden
explosion of the pool lights caught her standing in water to her
waist. She couldn't have been surprised, because I'd turned on
the house lights the moment I'd come in, but she affected a startled look nonetheless, and immediately dove beneath the surface,
the shimmering suntanned length of her wavering in underwater
illumination as she swam toward the deep end. I unlocked the
sliding glass doors, yanked one of them open, and stepped out
onto the baked clay tiles. Sunny was still underwater. In a moment her head broke the surface, long blonde hair plastered to
the sides of her face, mouth opening wide around a gasp for
breath.

"Hi," she said. She was treading water now, only her shoulders, neck, and head visible. "Could you turn out the pool lights,
please? I didn't bring a suit."

"I see that."

She smiled and dove beneath the surface again. Strands of
underwater light ensnared her submerged body as she swam

toward the shallow end again, her long blonde hair floating about her head in a tangle of liquid golden snakes. The surface broke like shattering glass as she came up for breath again, her arms emerging first, stretched above her head as though she were diving in reverse into the air itself, and then the blonde hair and the exquisite face, her body arcing upward out of the water and then sinking again as if in slow motion, ripples of light spreading out from it in widening circles. Standing in water to her waist now, she began wading toward the steps. I went into the house and snapped out the lights.

She was coming up the steps when I went outside again. Like an actress discovering a key light, or a maiden worshipping the moon, she raised her arms over her head and slowly turned her extended hands in the wash of moonlight, palms upward, as though she were allowing silver coins to cascade through her fingers.

My partner Frank maintains, though it is not on his list of ten rules, that a partially clad woman is infinitely more exciting than an entirely nude one. Perhaps he is right. I know only that Sunny McKinney naked was more spectacularly beautiful than any living creature had a right to be. I glanced quickly to the right and to the left. There were people living on either side of me, but the owner from whom I was renting was known in the neighborhood as "Sheena, Queen of the Jungle," a sobriquet applied after she had planted more trees, bushes, shrubs, and vines on her property than could be found on the entire six acres of Calusa's Agnes Lorrimer Memorial Gardens. Even the far side of the pool was shielded from the bayou beyond by low-growing mangroves and taller Australian pines. There was no one but me to witness Sunny's silent paean to the moon, and she herself seemed totally unconcerned by my presence. Her clothes, I noticed, were piled haphazardly on one of the lounge chairs. A pair of blue clogs rested on the tiles near the chair, alongside a purple leather shoulder bag.

"You wouldn't have a towel, would you?" she asked, sweeping

her wet hair back from her face. "Sorry about using your pool. It got so hot waiting for you."

"I'll get one," I said, and went back into the house.

When I came outside again, she was lying full length on her back on the other lounge chair, her eyes closed, her hands clasped behind her head, her legs slightly parted. She looked very blonde.

She opened her eyes.

"I'm almost dry already," she said.

I handed her the towel.

She patted herself here and there with it, and then dropped it onto the tiles. It was very difficult to keep my gaze fastened on her face. She seemed to be enjoying my discomfort. A small, wicked smile played about her lips.

"Is that your Porsche outside?" I asked.

"The red one, yeah. Well, the M.K.'s, actually—red and black, those are our colors. I didn't want to block your driveway."

"You parked it outside the wrong house."

"I was looking for the address. You don't have one on your mailbox."

"I keep meaning to put one on."

"You can buy those stick-on numbers at a hardware store," she said. "You just peel off the backs."

"I'll have to do that."

"They glow in the dark, some of them."

It occurred to me that I was having this conversation with a woman who was totally naked.

"Maybe I ought to get you a robe," I said.

"What for?" she said.

I didn't answer. I went back into the house and into my bedroom. In the closet there, I found a robe that belonged to Dale, decided against taking it out to Sunny, and brought her instead a Japanese-style kimono that was mine, white and sashed and scrawled front and back with black Japanese calligraphy. She was standing naked in front of the television set when I came back

74

into the living room, her eyes glued to the screen, her body flickering with blue electronic light.

"Oh, Japanese, good," she said, and took the kimono, but made no move to put it on. Instead, she kept watching the television screen. "Have you got anything to drink?" she asked.

She was twenty-three years old and very much a woman, legally and physically, but I couldn't shake the thought that I'd be impairing the morals of a minor if I mixed her a drink. On the television screen, a cop was explaining in detail how he'd been able to reach the screaming lady before she'd had her throat slit.

"What would you like?" I asked.

"Gin, if you have any. With a twist."

"Ice?"

"Please."

On the television screen, they were showing previews of next week's exciting show. "Do we need this?" I asked. Sunny shrugged. I snapped off the set, and went to the bar. When I turned to her again, the drink in my hand, she was still naked, walking around the living room, examining the place like a county appraiser.

"I wish you'd put on that kimono," I said, and handed her the drink.

"Oh, relax," she said, "I won't bite you. This is nice. You do it yourself?"

"It came furnished."

"Nice," she said, and nodded. "Aren't you having one?"

"In a minute."

I went back to the bar and mixed myself what my partner Frank calls a mother-in-law martini: straight up, very dry, and very cold.

"Cheers," Sunny said.

"Cheers," I said.

"Mm, good," she said. "Tanqueray?"

"Beefeater," I said.

"Good," she said.

75

"Why don't you put on that kimono, okay?"

"I hate clothes," she said, but she put her drink down on an end table near the imitation Barcelona chair, and then picked up the kimono and shrugged into it. "Nice fit," she said. "Your girlfriend's?"

"Mine."

"Nice," she said, and tied the sash.

The kimono seemed slashed in a wider V than I remembered. It also seemed far too short on her. She picked up her drink, sat carelessly—recklessly, in fact—in the Barcelona chair, and said, "I guess you're wondering why I'm here."

"It crossed my mind. How'd you find me?"

"Your number's in the phone book. Your address too. I tried to call first, but there was no answer." She shrugged. "I figured I'd take a chance. It's not a very long drive."

I nodded. She smiled.

"Aren't you glad I'm here?" she said, and took a long swallow of her drink.

"*Why* are you here?" I asked.

"I want to talk to you," she said. "About Jack."

"Your brother or your boyfriend?"

"My boyfriend is *Jackie*," she said. "My brother is *Jack*." She shook her head. "Or *was*, I suppose would be right. No *more* Jack, is there?" She shook her head again. "How'd *you* know about him? *Jackie*, I mean."

"I met him this afternoon. Out at the ranch. I understand you were with him the night your brother was killed."

"Yeah. Boy, was *that* ever embarrassing! Having to tell that to the cops."

The way she was sitting, I wouldn't have thought she'd be embarrassed by anything. I suddenly thought of my partner Frank's dictum on partially clothed women. I looked away. Sunny smiled, as though she had caught me doing something she never would have imagined of a doddering, dithering old man.

"Men sure are funny," she said. "I really *did* come here to talk, you know."

"So talk," I said.

"Sure," she said. "Haven't you been wondering where Jack got that forty thousand dollars?"

"Do *you* know where he got it?"

"I've got a few ideas. Mm, this is good," she said, and gestured with the glass. "Mother disapproves of my drinking, you know. Mother *also* disapproves of my boyfriend. *And* my language. *Fuck* mother," she said. "Or have you already thought of that?"

"Where do *you* think your brother got that money?" I asked. "Assuming he had it at all."

"Oh, I think he had it, all right," she said. "Where do *you* think he got it?"

"I thought inheritance at first, but that doesn't seem to be . . ."

"No, my father didn't leave him a dime. Me, neither. Everything went to Mother." She drained her glass and said, "I wouldn't mind some more of this."

I took the glass from her hand. She smiled again, for no reason that I could detect. I refilled it and carried it back to her.

"Thanks," she said. Sipping at the gin, she said, "What do the police think? About where he got the money?"

"You understand, don't you, that they haven't yet *found* any money. For all we know, the forty thousand never even existed."

"Well, he gave that farmer four thousand down, didn't he?" she asked. "That's what Mother said, anyway."

"Yes, but that doesn't necessarily . . ."

"*What* kind of gin did you say this was? It tastes expensive."

"It is," I said.

"I love expensive things," she said. "So what do the police think?"

"I don't know what they think now," I said. "Earlier on, they mentioned narcotics, but . . ."

"Narcotics?" she said, and laughed. "My brother once caught me smoking a joint, and he spanked me so hard I couldn't sit for a week." She seemed reflective for a moment, recalling the incident. "No," she said, "dope is definitely out of the question. You wouldn't have any, by the way, would you? Grass, I mean?"

"I'm sorry, no."

"I should have brought some with me. I'm always afraid to carry it in the car, though. I'm afraid I'll pass a red light, and next thing you know I'll be in jail for intent to sell, or whatever they call it. No, Jack didn't get that money through—what did they think? That he was trafficking?"

"We didn't go into it very deeply."

"Good thing, it's a dead end. Typical brilliant thought for a Mickey Mouse police department. I can just see Bloom putting it all together, can't you? This is Florida, so how *else* would a kid like Jack come into forty thousand dollars? Dope, naturally." She shook her head. "You can tell your friend Bloom my brother wasn't involved in dope. No way."

"Why don't you tell him yourself?" I said. "In fact, if you have any *real* notion of where your brother got that money . . ."

"I don't like talking to cops, and I *especially* don't like talking to Detective Bloom," she said. "The way he went after me and Jackie, you'd have thought we were both ax murderers or something. All we did was *sleep* together, is that a crime? But Bloom . . ."

"A crime *was* committed," I said. "Your brother was murdered. Detective Bloom was . . ."

"Detective Bloom was getting some weird kind of kick out of it."

"I doubt that very much."

"Yeah? Then why'd he want to know *where* we were doing it, and at what *time* exactly, and everything but what I was wearing? Your friend's some kind of closet sex freak," she said, and smiled again.

"My friend is a cop," I said flatly, "who was doing his job."

"If he's doing his job so great," she said, "then why hasn't he

78

found out where my brother got that money? You think it just *might* occur to him that if forty thousand dollars is involved . . ."

"It *has* occurred to him. And if you *know* where your brother . . ."

"I *don't* know. I didn't *say* I knew. I said I had a few ideas, is all."

"Then tell them to the police."

"No. You were my brother's lawyer, right? And from what Mother tells me, you're representing *her* now, right?"

"Yes."

"So who better to talk to?" she said, and shrugged.

"Whatever you tell me, I'll repeat it to Bloom," I said. "If it has any bearing at all on the crime . . ."

"Are you really as square as you seem?" she asked, smiling again. "Anybody else I know would've been very happy to see me marching around here starkers."

I made no comment.

"I *was* starkers, you do remember that, don't you?"

"I remember."

"'Cause memory is the first thing to go, I'm told. Would you mind filling this glass again?"

"Why?" I said.

"I told you. It's nice gin."

"That doesn't mean you have to finish the bottle."

"I can drink you under the table any night of the week," she said. "I was raised on a *ranch*, mister. I've spent more time with cowboys . . ." She let the sentence trail. She extended the glass to me. "Please?" she said, pouting. "Pretty please?"

I took the glass and poured a little gin into it. She watched me.

"Don't be so generous," she said.

I poured a bit more, and then carried the glass back to her.

"Thanks." She held the glass up to the light. "Are you sure you can spare this?" she said, and shook her head, and drank. "So here's what *I* think," she said. "I think my brother was a thief."

"Uh-huh."

"What does that mean, 'uh-huh'? Does that mean you find the idea inconceivable?"

Judging from the way she stumbled on the word "inconceivable," it occurred to me that her speech, although not yet quite slurred, was getting a bit sloppy, and I suddenly wondered how often and how heavily Miss Sylvia McKinney hit the sauce. Her glass was almost empty again. I did not want a drunken twenty-three-year-old on my hands. Or did I?

Once, back in Chicago while I was still a teenager, I'd tried to get a sixteen-year-old girl drunk so that I could pry her out of her virgin fortress panties. She'd passed out cold on me, and I felt like a burglar as I fumbled around under her skirt. I quit when the shame and the guilt got too heavy for my seventeen-year-old conscience. I never knew whether she was really drunk or not. I did not know whether Sunny was drunk now, but she certainly seemed on the way toward Blotsville.

"Why are you staring at me?" she asked.

"No reason."

"There's a reason. I'm a beautiful girl in a loose kimono—do you know who wrote *The Open Kimono?*"

"Who?" I said.

"Seymour Hare," she said, and smiled. "You're wondering where all this is going to lead, aren't you?"

"No, I'm wondering if you're getting drunk."

"You don't have to worry about that. Let me reconstruct it for you, okay?" she said, having a little trouble with the word "reconstruct" this time. "My brother Jack needed forty thousand dollars so he could realize his lifelong dream of becoming a goddamn *snapbean* farmer . . ."

"*Was* that a dream of his?"

"I'm being facetious. Who knows *what* was in his head? *Ever?* So, fine, he wanted to own a snapbean farm. I suppose that's better than a string of empty stores to rent to gypsies. Listen, do I *really* have to beg for a little gin around here? Sunny's very thirsty, Mr. Hope."

"Sunny's getting sloshed," I said.

She said nothing. She shoved herself out of the chair, exposing a great deal of smooth suntanned thigh when the kimono parted, and went directly to the bar. "Help yourself, Sunny," she said. "Thanks, I will," she said, and poured freely into her glass. "Are you looking at my ass?" she said.

"Yes," I said.

"I thought you might be," she said, and turned and smiled and said, "Cheers. Where was I?"

"Your brother needed forty thousand dollars . . ."

"Correct. So he decided that the way to get it was illegally. To great men come great thoughts. All he needed was something to rob."

"Which bank did he hold up?"

"No, not a bank, Mr. Hope. Would *you* rob a bank if your mother owned a cattle ranch?"

"I'm not following you," I said.

"Cows," she said.

"Cows," I repeated.

"Yes, sir. My brother was stealing cows."

"Your mother's cows?"

"Yes, sir, my mother's cows."

"How do you know that?"

"I *didn't* know it. Until I started piecing it all together. I'm a lot smarter than Mother gives me credit for, you know." She sipped at her drink, looked at what remained in her glass, and then said, "I guess you know October is a busy time for us—well, from the beginning of October to the middle of November. Busy time on any ranch. We normally put the bulls on the cows come early spring . . ."

"Put them on the cows?"

"Well, yes, put them out for breeding, take them off in the summer sometime. Figure February to June for them to do their work, the bulls. It takes nine months from conception to delivery, same as a human. We'll have heifers dropping calves all through the late fall and early winter—depending on how well the bulls covered them. That means the calves are ready to be taken off the cows . . ."

"Taken off the cows?"

"Weaned. Usually when they're ten months old. We separate the cows and the calves in different pastures, put the calves on feed for a week or ten days, till they're ready to get out there and eat grass on their own. This is usually in October, November sometime. That's when we run our pregnancy tests, too—did my mother show you our squeeze chute?"

"Yes."

"Front end holds the cow's head up while we drench her— that's giving her the medicine she needs. We use a big syringe, the hands do the actual work, no need for a vet there. A vet works the *back* end, though, wears a long plastic sleeve while he shoves his arm up the cow's cooze—are you familiar with the word 'cooze,' Mr. Hope?"

"I'm familiar with it."

"Feels around up there to see whether there's the beginning of a calf or not. We hope for an eighty-five-percent pregnancy rate—which varies, of course. But that's what we hope for. We turn the pregnant cows out to pasture again, put the open cows in another pasture for . . ."

"You're losing me again."

"Open cows? The ones that aren't pregnant. We sell them, Mr. Hope. Simply because we can't afford to keep them unless they deliver a calf every year. October's our biggest selling time. Not only for open cows, of course, but for whatever's ready to move on."

"Move on to *where?*" I asked.

"Mother's what's known as a cow-calf lady, Mr. Hope. Bottom end of the food chain. Next step up is the stocker, he's a buyer who comes to the ranch to look over the herd, we'll sell him five, six hundred head at a time, by what we call private treaty. He'll put the calves out to richer pasture—wheat, oats, rye, what have you. We'll sell some of the calves at four hundred fifty to five hundred pounds, right off the cow. Some of what we sell are calves we've already wintered, they'll weigh maybe six-fifty, seven hundred pounds. We sell them *all* at live weight, put them on the scale right in the pens, before they're loaded. The price will fluctuate, depending on the supply of cattle at the time we're selling. It'll vary, oh, from a high of a dollar a pound to a low of fifty-five cents. The current price on steer calves is sixty-eight cents a pound. Anyway, your stocker'll fatten them up by a couple of hundred pounds, and then sell them to the *next* man up the line—what we call a feeder, or a feed-lot operator."

"What does *he* do?"

"Pens them, feeds them from troughs—corn, soybeans, very rich stuff, we're talking U.S. Choice here, Mr. Hope. He'll add another few hundred pounds to each of them, and then sell them to the packer. Your average steer going to slaughter will weigh somewhere between a thousand and twelve hundred pounds. Your packer will dress the steer and send it on to your butcher, and he'll end up as a steak on your dinner table—the *steer*, not the butcher. End of the food chain."

"Okay," I said. "What makes you think your brother . . . ?"

"Hold on just a second," she said. "I told you we sell any open cows we find, usually for the going hamburger price of about forty cents a pound. At the same time we sell any cows who aren't good for breeding anymore. Usually they're seven or eight years old, in there someplace. You've got to remember it takes almost four years for a cow to be worth anything to a breeder. Figure a year for her as a calf, another year as a yearling, a third year as a bred heifer, and then seven or eight months for suckling her calf—almost four years. That's a sizable investment to carry. This is a *business*, Mr. Hope. Those cows out there *aren't* pets."

"I realize that."

"So we'll sell off any open cows, or used-up cows, or crippled cows, or bad-eyed cows . . ."

"Bad-eyed?"

"Cancer of the eye. The crippled ones and the bad-eyed ones usually go to the cat-meat man. He sells them to the pet-food people, or if there's a circus in town—well, lions and tigers eat a lot of raw meat, and they don't care if it's stamped U.S. Choice. Are you following all this?"

"I think so."

"Okay. We take one herd at a time to the crevice the night before we weigh them and sell them. Makes it easier than doing it at the crack of dawn. Each herd is about two hundred head, give or take. Out of that two hundred, we'll find maybe fifty open cows—twenty percent of them—and maybe another ten *bad* cows, your crippled ones, your sick ones. Those all go for hamburger or cat meat. We leave the culls in the crevice, move the good cows into the pens." She paused, looked into her glass, found it was empty, and went to the bar to fill it again. She turned from the bar, lifted the glass, drank without toasting this time, and then said, "I think my brother was winnowing off some of those cows. The open ones, the sick ones . . ."

"What makes you think so?"

"The phone rang one night at the beginning of last October—this was long before Jack moved into his condo. I know it was a Wednesday night because the stocker was coming the next day, a Thursday, to look over the herd we'd already penned. I picked up the extension phone downstairs. Jack was on one end of the line. A man with a Spanish accent was on the other."

She drank again. By my count, she had already consumed four glasses of gin, and was working on a fifth. I wondered how she was able to keep all of this straight with so much alcohol inside her.

"The man with the Spanish accent said, 'Are we still on for tonight?' Jack said, 'We are.' The man said, 'How many?' Jack said, 'Fifteen at thirty.' The man said, 'Same time?' Jack said, 'Yes,' and hung up."

"What'd you make of that conversation?"

"Nothing—at the time. I only began thinking of it since he was killed."

"And what does it mean to you now?"

"I think they were talking about cattle. I think Jack was going to raid the crevice, cull out fifteen of the sick or open cows, and sell them at thirty cents a pound live weight."

"To this man with the Spanish accent?"

"Yes."

"Does your cat-meat man have a Spanish accent?"

"No, Ralph's a cracker through and through."

"So this was someone else."

"Someone willing to buy cattle in the dark with no questions asked."

"Are your cattle branded?"

"Yes, but that doesn't matter. No one's going to question anybody about where he got the cows he's selling farther on up the line. Branding isn't even *required* in the state of Florida."

"How'd you hit on thirty cents a pound?"

"Ten cents less than the price of hamburger or cat meat. These cows were being *stolen*, Mr. Hope—they had to be sold under the market price."

"And these cows would weigh what?"

"Eight, nine hundred pounds each."

"That would come to something like two-fifty a cow."

"Two-fifty, three hundred, somewhere in there."

"Times fifteen cows . . ."

"I figure he'd have netted something like three, four thousand dollars. On one herd *alone*, remember."

"And you say there are five herds?"

"Five herds. I think Jack milked all of them—excuse the pun."

"So you're figuring he culled from all five herds . . ."

"Right. Made himself something like twenty thousand dollars."

"How'd he get the cows off the ranch?"

"He was stealing only fifteen at a clip. All he had to do was wait till everybody was asleep, and then unlock the southwest gate near the crevice. His Spanish buyer rolls in, and it's off to market in a gooseneck trailer."

"With no one seeing them?"

"At two, three in the morning? Anyway, Jack probably gave Sam a cut to keep him looking the other way."

"Sam?"

"Watson. Our former manager. Who suddenly got it in his head to pick up and head west. About the same time Jack moved into his condo."

"Wouldn't your mother have realized what was going on? So *many* cows missing? Fifteen from each *herd*? Doesn't anyone *count* them?"

"Every spring and every fall. But who does the counting, Mr. Hope?"

"Who?"

"The manager. And if Jack paid him off . . ."

"To falsify the count?"

"Sure. You think anyone would know? My mother sees a bunch of cows out in the pasture, you think she knows exactly how many are out there?"

"Well, it sounds . . ."

"It sounds right, admit it."

"Except for one thing," I said. "*Twenty* thousand dollars ain't *forty* thousand dollars."

"Twenty for *October* alone," she said. "How about if he'd been doing this for a long time? How about if he started right after my father died? My mother didn't know her ass from her elbow about cows, he could've stolen the whole *ranch* from under her, for all she knew about the business."

"You're saying . . ."

"I'm saying Dad died two years ago, on the glorious Fourth, a week after Jack's birthday. Okay. Let's say Jack started culling the minute Dad was gone. That would have given him the fall calf crop *that* year, and the spring and fall calf crop *last* year. Three crops, Mr. Hope. At twenty thousand a crop. Well, maybe a little less. Maybe he started small, a few cows at a time. Even so, it's easy to see how he could've put aside forty thousand, isn't it?"

"You've got a whole lot of maybes in there," I said.

"Have the police got anything better?"

86

"Even if he *was* stealing, how does that explain his murder? Who do you think killed him?"

"*That* I *don't* know. His Spanish partner? A burglar who found out he had a big pile of money under his mattress? Who knows? The point is, if he was involved in cattle rustling—that's a felony, Mr. Hope, you can get five years in prison for it—Jack had to be running with some pretty hard types. He could have got himself into *any* kind of mess, is what I'm saying. And ended up dead for it."

"*Maybe* again."

"Maybe, sure. But no maybes about stealing those cows. I *know* what I heard on the phone, and I *know* he was talking discount hamburger prices with a guy who had a Spanish accent. And I *know* he ended up with forty thousand bucks to spend on a snapbean farm. The numbers don't add up to coincidence, Mr. Hope, I'm sure of that."

There was a long silence.

She looked at me.

She smiled over the rim of her glass.

"Are there any bedrooms in this house?" she asked.

"Two," I said.

"Why don't we go use one of them?"

I looked at her.

"You'd like to, wouldn't you?" she said.

I kept looking at her.

"Am I wrong?" she said.

"You've had too much to drink," I said.

"*In vino veritas,*" she said.

I looked at the clock. A mistake.

"The night is young," she said.

"Sunny," I said, "if I thought for a minute you were sober . . ."

"I am dead cold sober," she said, and stood up and loosened the sash of the kimono, and opened the kimono, and then shrugged out of it and let it fall to the floor at her feet in a tangle of black-and-white Japanese squiggles. She put her hands on her hips. "Don't you think I look dead cold sober?" she asked.

I thought a *lot* of things in those next several moments while she stood with her legs apart and her hands on her hips, her head tilted somewhat defiantly, her eyes challenging and wide as they moved from my face downward over my chest and my waist, and then lower, and held lingeringly to ascertain what she already knew, a thin certain smile widening her mouth, the languid eyes coming up to meet my own again. I thought, oh, so *many* things. I thought first that she was old enough to know what she was doing, and I thought that if she said she was sober, then who was I to doubt her word? And I thought back to Chicago and the back seat of my father's steamy Oldsmobile where a sixteen-year-old girl named Joy Patterson lay back with her eyes closed and her breath heavy, and her legs spread, either really drunk or feigning drunkenness while I explored the ribbed tops of her nylon stockings and the soft white thighs above them, and drew back my trembling hand when at last it touched the silken secret patch of those undefended panties. Pulled it back with the certain knowledge that if Joy was drunk, this was rape, and if she wasn't drunk, this was not the way to go about making love on a starry summer night with a partner pretending to be lox spread upon a sacrificial bagel.

And then, oddly and suddenly, I thought of Dale O'Brien, and I remembered that I'd spoken to her not five hours ago (my eyes glancing at the clock again, Sunny's eyes following them, "Oh, we have time," she murmured) and I remembered what Dale had said about feeling like some kind of whore, and I thought this wasn't the way to forget her, *however* much she loved someone else, the way to forget Dale was not through substitution but by choice, and Sunny McKinney was offering no choice; Sunny McKinney was about to throw me and brand me the way she might have a steer. And I realized that allowing her to claim me would only be the equivalent of that unconsummated Chicago rape all those years ago, Joy either drunk or joylessly submissive, a seven-dollar rape for sure because that was what I'd paid for the bottle of booze we'd consumed in the back seat of my father's car while somewhere out on the lake somebody played a mandolin.

So I stood there looking at Sunny, both of us motionless, our eyes locked, brown against pale blue, both of us aware of my visible masculine response, her eyes flicking downward again to ascertain and to verify, and I thought suddenly of Charlie and Jeff, and I thought of all the offers ever made by American gangsters who were certain they would not be refused. And I thought of the extravagant gift Sunny was offering, and it seemed to me that it was as much a *genuine* present as a chunk of meat in an iron-clawed trap would be to a bear searching for honey in the woods.

I did not think I wanted my head banged yet another time against a varnished hatch-cover tabletop. So I looked at Sunny one last time, and then I turned away and sighed heavily and said, "Please put on your clothes," and I felt like what my daughter would call a nerd, but I also felt somehow better than I had since the night Charlie and Jeff had beaten me senseless, and I didn't know why, and I didn't *care* why, and I didn't even watch while Sunny went out onto the terrace and dressed silently in the moonlight.

She searched in her purple leather shoulder bag for the car keys—she was wearing a denim wraparound skirt now, and a purple halter top to match the bag, and the pair of blue clogs—impatiently rummaging among Kleenex tissues and a crumpled package of cigarettes and several sticks of chewing gum and a purple leather wallet, and finally found the keys, and went to the door, and turned to me before going out and said, in all seriousness, "You're not a fag or anything, are you?" And without waiting for my answer, she went up the walk to where she'd parked the red Porsche. The car started with what sounded like an angry roar, and then scratched away from the curb.

I didn't know whether to laugh or cry.

4

I did not talk to Bloom until Monday morning.

I had learned early on in my relationship with him that it was best to tell him everything I knew as soon as I knew it, because things left unsaid had a way of coming up later either to haunt or to embarrass me. But a call to his office on Saturday informed me that he had the weekend off, and I was reluctant to disturb him at home. I frankly didn't know whether Sunny's theory about a series of cattle thefts committed by her brother in cahoots with a Spanish-speaking stranger would hold up under police scrutiny, but it seemed to me that Bloom should know about it; whatever he did with the information later was *his* business. At the same time, I didn't want to break in on his weekend; Monday morning would be time enough. Telling him, of course, would also mean telling him about Sunny's moonlight visit, but I did not plan to mention her naked dip in my pool or her later modest proposal. There were some things even Bloom did not have to know.

The first question he asked was, "What was she doing there?"

"Well . . . she was swimming," I said.

"In your pool?" he asked.

"Yes, in my pool, of *course* in my pool."

"You mean she came there for a swim?"

"No, but she was swimming when I got there."

"Did you know she was coming?"

"No, it was a surprise."

"You mean she just came over with her bathing suit, and popped into your pool . . ."

"Well, no, she wasn't wearing a bathing suit."

"Oh, she was *nude*," Bloom said.

So much for keeping secrets from Detective Morris Bloom. I told him everything she'd told me.

"She was nude during all this?" Bloom asked.

"No, she was wearing a kimono," I said.

"She's a very beautiful girl," Bloom said thoughtfully.

The telephone line went silent. Bloom did not ask, and I did not offer. Gentlemen both, I thought.

"And she thinks he stole *how* many cows?" Bloom said at last.

"Fifteen at a clip."

"From five herds?"

"Right."

"How much is five times fifteen?"

"Seventy-five."

"So he could've stolen seventy-five cows each spring and fall, is that what she told you?"

"Something like that."

"That's a lot of cows, Matthew."

"I wouldn't want them in my bedroom, that's for sure."

"Did she have any idea who this Spanish guy might be?"

"None."

"Well," Bloom said, "if he really *was* stealing cows, that would let out dope, wouldn't it? As a source of the money, I mean."

"Sunny doesn't think he was involved in dope," I said, and then told him about Jack's having spanked her when he'd caught her smoking a joint.

"Spanked his older sister, huh?" Bloom said.

"According to her, yes."

"Kinky," Bloom said. "Don't you think?"

"Well," I said.

"You spank a six-year-old, that's discipline," he said. "You spank a twenty-three-year-old who's your sister, that's kinky. Didn't the girl think it was kinky?"

"She didn't seem to."

"Was this a regular thing between him and her? Spanking her, I mean?"

"I have no idea."

It suddenly occurred to me that Bloom and I lived in two different worlds. On Bloom's block, a murder had been committed, and he wanted to know why, and a twenty-year-old boy spanking his twenty-three-year-old sister was an unnatural act that warranted thought and discussion. The spanking had been mentioned only casually by Sunny, and I myself hadn't given it a moment's further thought. But now that Bloom had focused attention on it, it *did* seem somewhat peculiar, and I wondered— as he had a moment earlier—whether it had been a regular occurrence in the McKinney household. And then I wondered what *other* unnatural actions or deeds or possibly even thoughts confronted Bloom on a daily basis. Given the undisputed fact that he dealt day and night with the aftermath of violence, how far *beyond* that did his professional horizons extend? What undreamt-of horrors was he forced to contend with as a routine part of his working day? And what sort of man could hope to deal continuously with murder, rape, sodomy, child abuse, burglary, robbery, assault—the list seemed endless—without having his entire perspective distorted by a world he accepted as "natural"? What did Bloom talk about when he was with his wife? I felt suddenly as if I did not know him at all.

"Take down her panties, or what?" he asked.

A matter-of-fact question.

Bloom's world.

"She didn't say."

He was silent for a moment. Then he said, "Kinky. Twenty-three-year-old beauty shacking up with a pimply-faced kid who stacks oranges, and meanwhile getting her ass spanked by her younger brother. Very kinky. I think I'll give the mother a ring, find out if her son was in the habit of taking down his sister's pants. Thanks a lot, Matthew, this is all very helpful. Have you given any thought to when you want to go a few rounds with me? How about this afternoon, does that sound okay?"

"Sounds fine," I said.

"Drop by here around five, five-thirty, okay?" Bloom said. "We'll walk over together, the gym's right next door. Wear an iron jock," he said, and hung up.

At two o'clock that afternoon, I received a phone call from Harry Loomis. He told me he'd discussed the entire matter with his client, and they had a counter-offer for me, and he wanted me to come to his office to hear it. When I asked why he couldn't simply give it to me on the phone, he said, "You want to hear it, you come on out here," and hung up. I called Bloom to tell him we'd have to postpone the lesson, and we set a tentative date for the next day at five. It was two-fifteen when I left the office, and I did not get to Ananburg till three-thirty. I was in an extremely foul mood after the long trip, and the Iron Maiden in Loomis's outer office did nothing to raise my spirits. Neither did Loomis himself. His counter-offer, as it turned out, was something he *could* have given me on the phone, and I was mad as hell that he'd dragged me all the way out here to listen to it.

"As I understand this," I said, "Mr. Burrill . . ."

"If you been listenin', you got it," he said.

"Mr. Burrill is willing to settle the matter if Mrs. McKinney pays him an *additional* five thousand dollars—out of her own pocket—for any damages he may have suffered."

"Never mind '*may* have suffered,'" Loomis said. "Burrill lost all his potential buyers 'cause of that boy's promises."

"You know, of course, that Mrs. McKinney herself is not personally responsible for any debts her son may have incurred . . ."

"Yes, I know all that," he said. "A'*course*, I know it. But I'm figuring somebody with Mrs. McKinney's kind of money'd be willing to part with a mere five thousand of it just to get us out of her hair. You know how much she's worth?"

"I have no idea."

"She's sittin' on four thousand acres of land worth at *least* fourteen hundred an acre. That comes to five million six, where I come from. She's got—what?—a thousand head of cattle on that ranch? Say a good brood cow's worth seven hundred dollars, and a good bull somewhere between twelve and fifteen hundred. Well, that comes to *another* six, seven hundred thousand dollars in stock, Mr. Hope. Add the machinery and whatnot, the horses, I'd say she's worth six, seven million dollars. Don't know how much of that's only on paper, but I don't rightly care. Five thousand ain't gonna hurt her. You tell her that's what we want. Five thousand in damages, forfeit of the four in escrow, and all the kid's personal belongings. The farm stays with us, of course. How does that sound to you?"

"Rotten," I said.

Loomis chuckled.

"Thought you might say that," he said. "But maybe your client'll think different."

"Not if *I'm* advising her," I said. "Good day, Mr. Loomis."

It began raining again the moment I started the long drive back to Calusa—a big surprise here during the summer months, our daily reminder that there was indeed a God. I drove slowly, hunched over the wheel, trying to see through whatever patches of clear windshield the faulty wipers provided. The rain came down as though it were spilling from a huge bloated sack that had ripped open from end to end, unleashing torrents of water that pelted the car and the land outside.

Great plops of water exploded on the asphalt ribbon, silvery plunks erupting everywhere ahead in the gloom. There was a sudden flash of lightning and then a boom of thunder. I winced, and then remembered that an automobile was supposed to be the safest place you could find in a thunderstorm. It had something to do with the rubber tires serving as conductors—or something. If a bolt of lightning hit your car, it was supposed to travel all around it and down to the tires, which would absorb it—or something. Physics had never been my strongest subject. The road ahead was steaming now, the baked-in heat of the day evaporating rapidly, rising, shifting, dissipating in the fiercely falling rain. I started thinking about that shyster Harry Loomis, and I got angry at him all over again, and then I got angry at the rain, and then at the windshield wipers, and then at God, and then I passed Burrill's brown mailbox on the right and knew I had crossed over into Calusa County and began to feel a little better until another flash of lightning, very close by, caused my hair to stand on end and I pulled my head into my shoulders like a turtle when the boom of thunder immediately exploded overhead.

The wind whipped through the palmettos flanking the road, setting up a fearsome rattling in counterpoint to the steady drumming of the rain. I kept pushing the small car through the tunnel of wind and water, flinching each time there was more lightning and thunder, having no real faith in the theory of protective rubber tires. Anyway, my tires were synthetics, weren't they? Would a combination of rubber, nylon, and steel save me from instant electrocution? I was perhaps three-tenths of a mile past Burrill's mailbox when I spotted the huge puddle ahead, and tried to brake, and changed my mind for fear of skidding, and ploughed through it like a drunken sailor—and the engine quit.

I thought, *Shit*.

I knew that what you were supposed to do when your battery got wet was wait five or ten minutes before you tried starting the car again. So I sat there in the middle of nowhere for the next ten minutes, listening to the rain. It showed no sign of abating. I looked at my watch, and tried the key again. There was more lightning when I turned it, one of those coincidental happenings that always scare the hell out of me, as if my own hand had unleashed the lightning flash and the following boom of thunder. The car did not start. I tried the key again. And again. And again. I knew I was doing exactly the wrong thing, but I was getting impatient. The starter whined and complained each time, the engine almost catching, encouraging me. I kept trying. And finally, of course, I drained the damn battery of whatever juice it had left in it, and there I was. Some twenty miles from downtown Calusa, with a storm roaring all around me, and a dead battery, and no other pilgrims abroad on the road, and an umbrella with two broken ribs on the back seat—or what passed for a back seat in a Karmann Ghia. I reached over the seat to grab the umbrella, and opened the door on my left, rain lashing in at me immediately, and then took the keys from the ignition and tried to open the broken umbrella before I stepped fully into the storm.

The wind turned it inside out at once. I said the hell with it and tossed it over the roof of the car into the palmettos lining the road. I stood in the rain, then, and got soaked clear to the skin in the next forty seconds while I locked a car that wouldn't start.

Avery Burrill's farm was just up the road, a short distance back, if three-tenths of a mile could be considered minimal in a raging storm. There was a telephone at the farm, and even if I had to wait forever for the talkative lady on his party line to get off, I could nonetheless eventually contact a service station that might send someone to help me get started, or even tow me if worse came to worst. When you are thoroughly drenched, there is no longer any need to worry about getting wet. I walked through the downpour feeling somewhat lighthearted, in fact, a latter-day Gene Kelly who—while not actually *singin'* in the rain—jogged along at a brisk pace broken only once, when I tried to flag down a truck carrying a load of chicken crates. The driver went by me without even slowing, sending up a spray of water that fazed me less than did his disregard. I reached Burrill's mailbox, and turned left onto his driveway.

The driveway was a dirt road, potholed and rutted and running with water so that it resembled more a muddy brown stream than it did any manmade thoroughfare. I had no idea how long the driveway might be when I started up it, but after I'd been trudging along for what must have been five minutes and saw no sign of a house anywhere ahead, I began thinking that perhaps this was only a service road that led to where the snapbeans grew, and not to any proper residence. I fought the mud for another five minutes, already convinced that the better part of valor would have been to stay in the car till the storm ended, which— small consolation—it showed no sign of doing in the immediate future.

The land on either side of the driveway did not seem suitable for growing anything but cabbage palm and palmetto. I wondered where the hell Mr. Burrill planted his snapbeans, and I wondered where the hell his house was, and I wondered what the hell I was doing out here in the middle of a godforsaken landscape lashed with wind and water, and then I saw a rusting yellow tractor some little way ahead, and I figured if there was a tractor there had to be a farm, and if there was a farm there had to be a farmhouse, and there it was at last, a ramshackle structure as gray as the rain, sitting on top of a low rise behind which was a gully rushing with water. Beyond that I saw what appeared to be cultivated land, and still beyond that, a row of slash pines that filled the horizon and screened from view whatever acreage might have been behind it.

I climbed a pair of rickety steps and was grateful at once for the overhanging roof of the porch, which, however leaky it was, provided welcome shelter from the rain. I looked for a doorbell and found none. I opened the tattered screen door and knocked on the wooden entrance door. No answer. I knocked again. "Mr. Burrill!" I shouted, and a flash of lightning scared the hell out of me, and the following boom of thunder drowned out my second shouted "Mr. Burrill!" I pounded on the door. "Mr. Burrill, it's me," I shouted. "Attorney Hope!" My formal title seemed not to impress either Mr. Burrill or whichever storm-god decided to unleash another bolt of lightning and another boom of thunder.

I tried the doorknob.

The door was unlocked.

I opened it and stepped into the house.

"Mr. Burrill?" I said.

The house was dark. Not a light showing anywhere; odd, when one considered the storm. Or had the power failed? And if the power had failed, would the telephone be working?

"Mr. Burrill?" I said again, and a flash of lightning illuminated something lying just inside the door to the other room, and the immediate boom of thunder drowned out my scream when I realized it was a dead body.

I actually screamed, that's right.

I had never in my adult life screamed until that moment, but that's what I did when I saw the blood-soaked body. The thunder rolled away and faded. I was in the dark again. I backed away toward the door, tripped on something, caught my balance, and fumbled for a light switch on the wall inside the door. I flicked it up, and a pair of lamps came on across the room. One of the lamps was lying on the floor, overturned. There were overturned chairs, their cushions slashed. There were open books and magazines scattered all over the floor. The body lay just this side of a door leading into a kitchen. There were utensils and pots and pans strewn everywhere on the kitchen floor. The dead man was lying on his back. His face and chest were covered with blood. There was a hole in his face, still dripping blood, and there were several more bloody holes in his white shirt.

I decided to get the hell out of there.

I was backing away toward the door again when I saw the phone sitting on a wooden table between two shabby upholstered chairs, their backs and arms slashed, their stuffing pulled out. I went to the phone. I lifted the receiver and got a dial tone. I called Calusa Public Safety then, and asked for Detective Morris Bloom.

So now there was the ritual and routine of murder.

The whole grisly entourage arrived in dribs and drabs during the next hour or so: first a pair of uniformed cops coming up the muddy drive in separate City of Calusa police cars, and then Bloom in an unmarked car, with another detective whose name I didn't catch, and then the captain in command of Calusa's detective bureau, and then an assistant medical examiner, and then a man from the State's Attorney's office whom I happened to know because I'd spoken to him on the phone during the George Harper tragedy, and then the technicians from the Criminalistics Unit, arriving in their Ford Econoline van, and then an intern and two ambulance attendants from Southern Medical.

The rain had stopped.

My clothes were drying.

I stood in the living room and watched the professionals go about their work, and then I explained to the captain in command what I had already explained to Bloom, how *I* had happened to be the one who'd discovered Avery Burrill's body on a rainy afternoon in the middle of August. The assistant ME had already pronounced him dead, and the hospital team was carrying him out in a rubber body bag. There was blood all over the floor, inside and around the chalked outline of his body. There were people taking photographs and people dusting for fingerprints. The two patrolmen in their black rain slickers were standing near the entrance door, talking about getting laid. One of the patrolmen laughed. The captain in command seemed satisfied with my story, but he frowned when I told him I'd been handling a real-estate transaction between Burrill and Jack McKinney, who, he remembered at once, had been killed two weeks ago. His face told me that he didn't like the smell of that. Bloom didn't like it much, either. He had told me that on the phone, but not in so many words. He had said, "Oh, *no*," and then told me to stay right where I was till he got there. He was there now. *Everybody* was there now, except Burrill himself, who was being loaded into the ambulance outside.

"Who else was involved in this transaction?" the captain asked me. His name was Harley. I think it was Harley. He hadn't introduced himself, but I had heard one of the technicians calling to him, and I thought it sounded like Captain Harley. Maybe it was Captain Holly. Either way, he was looking at me very intently now, his sharp blue eyes seeming to linger on the faint discoloration that still showed under my own eyes. He was taking me for the kind of guy who got into fistfights, I thought. He was taking me for a street brawler.

"No one," I said. "Just the principals and their attorneys. I'm an attorney," I said, thinking I'd better make that very clear from the start.

"McKinney's attorney, huh?"

"Yes, sir," I said. I don't know why I called him *sir*. I think I was thinking he felt I was somehow involved in this. I think I was kissing his ass a little.

"And the victim's attorney?" he said, and turned to Bloom. "What's his name again, the victim?"

"Burrill," Bloom said. "Avery Burrill."

Harley, or Holly, turned back to me again. "Who was *his* attorney?" he asked. "The victim's?"

"Man named Harry Loomis in Ananburg."

"And that's all the parties to the transaction, is that right?" he asked.

"Well," I said, "not entirely."

"What do you mean, 'not entirely'? Were there just the four of you, or were there some other parties involved?"

I explained to him in detail that McKinney had died without leaving a will, and that under Florida's intestate-succession statutes, whatever estate he'd left would go to his mother. I further explained that McKinney had intended to pay for the farm in cash, but that so far—and Detective Bloom would corroborate this—no cash had been found, and therefore the estate could be said to have no assets but the boy's personal belongings. I went on to tell him that I had been discussing a possible settlement with Harry Loomis today.

"So there's a lot more people involved in this than you said at first, is that right?"

"Not really," I said.

"You just told me there's a mother and a sister."

"Yes, but there's no way they can be held responsible for any of McKinney's obligations. The *estate* is responsible, and as I just told you, in essence there are no assets in the estate."

"Except this cash McKinney was supposed to have had," Harley said. Holly. *Whoever* the hell.

"We haven't been able to locate that yet, sir," Bloom said. "I think I ought to tell you, too, that both the mother *and* the sister had ironclad alibis for the night McKinney was killed."

"Did I see a report on that?" the captain said.

"I sent it up, sir, I don't know whether you saw it or not."

"Fill me in," the captain said. "I see a lot of reports." Which meant he hadn't even looked at it.

"The mother was home watching television with a vet who'd come to dinner that night . . ."

"Which war?" the captain said.

"Sir?"

"This veteran."

"A veterin*arian*, sir," Bloom said. "She breeds cattle. He was out there looking at a sick cow, and she asked him to stay to dinner, and they sat around later watching television."

"Did you check with the vet?"

"Yes, sir."

"And he confirmed?"

"Yes, sir."

"What about the sister? Where was she?"

"In the sack with her boyfriend."

"Confirmed?"

"Yes, sir."

"What's the boyfriend's name?"

"Jackie Crowell. He's an eighteen-year-old kid, works in the produce department at a supermarket in Calusa."

"And he said he was fucking her that night?"

"In his apartment, yes, sir."

"At the time of the murder?"

"We set the time of death at about nine, sir. She went out to dinner with him . . ."

"Where?"

"McDonald's."

"That's *dinner*?" the captain said.

Bloom shrugged. "Had dinner with him at seven, went back to his place, spent the entire night there."

"All confirmed, huh?"

"Yes, sir."

"You think he might be covering for her?"

"That's possible. But there's a kid at McDonald's who knows them both, and he said he served them hamburgers at a little after seven."

"Still, there's nobody but the two of them to confirm she was with Crowell all night, is that right?"

"That's right."

"Stay on that, Bloom, I want to know more about it."

"Yes, sir, we *are* on it. We're canvassing Crowell's neighborhood, trying to find anybody who might have seen him and the girl going in or coming out."

"What the hell's taking you so long?"

"Big neighborhood, captain. He lives in a housing project in New Town."

"He's a *nigger*?" the captain said. "She was fucking a *nigger*?"

"He's white," Bloom said. "There are whites in the project, too. It's a low-income project."

"I thought it was only niggers in New Town," the captain said, and shook his head.

"No, sir."

"And you say McKinney was killed at nine o'clock?"

"That's the coroner's estimate, sir."

"Well, stay with it."

"Yes, sir."

"Captain Hopper?" someone said.

So much for total recall.

The captain walked over to where someone was standing near the telephone I'd used earlier. He handed something to the captain. Hopper looked at it.

"Some dump here," Bloom said, looking around. "McKinney was paying forty K for it, huh?"

"There's fifteen acres of land," I said.

"Must be *some* land," Bloom said. "Must be *oil* on it."

"Take a look at this," Hopper said, handing me a slip of paper. My name and phone number were handwritten on it. "This you?"

"Yes, sir."

"You talk to Burrill recently?"

"He called me the day after McKinney was murdered," I said.

"What'd he want?"

"He'd heard about the murder, and he wanted to know what would happen next."

"How'd he seem to you?"

"Eager to close the deal."

"You talk to him since?"

"Just his attorney."

"How'd you get here?" Hopper asked suddenly.

"I walked," I said.

"All the way from Calusa?"

"My car's up the road. The battery went dead."

"Convenient," Hopper said, and walked over to look at the chalked outline on the floor.

"Shmuck," Bloom whispered under his breath. Aloud, he said, "Okay if Mr. Hope goes now?"

"Who's Mr. Hope?" Hopper asked, without turning to look at us.

"I am," I said.

"Sure, go ahead," he said.

Bloom shook his head, and then walked me outside.

"You want a lift back to town?" he asked. "I'll be here awhile yet, but as soon as His Royal Shmuck is gone, I'll get one of the blues to drive you back."

"I'd appreciate it," I said.

I did not get back to the office until a quarter past six. I called the service station I usually dealt with, told them what had happened and where the car was, and asked if someone could stop by to pick up the keys. They promised that someone would be there within the next half hour. There were several pink message slips on my desk, but it was too late to return any calls.

There was also a handwritten note from Frank. It read:

Dear Partner,

Have you given up lawyering in favor of ranching? It would be nice to see you here at the office occasionally. Please, remember that you have a closing at Calusa First tomorrow morning at eleven.

Kindest regards,
Frank

P.S. What did you think of my ten rules?

The tow truck arrived some ten minutes later. I gave the mechanic the keys and asked him when he thought I could have the car back. He shrugged. Mechanics, I've discovered, shrug almost as often as doctors do. It must have been about seven-fifteen when I left the office. I was just locking the door when the telephone rang. I debated going in again to answer it, and decided against it. I had dinner alone at an Italian restaurant within walking distance of the office—there is not a single good Italian restaurant in all Calusa; most of them are owned and operated by Greeks from Tarpon Springs—and then took a taxi home. It was almost nine o'clock when I got to the house.

A red Porsche was parked in my driveway.

I paid and tipped the cabbie, walked around to the kitchen

door, unlocked it, stepped into the house, and immediately heard the sound of someone splashing around in my pool. This time I did not turn on any lights. I went directly to the sliding glass doors, unlocked them, pulled them open, and stepped out onto the terrace.

I had a distinct feeling of déjà vu.

Sunny McKinney was in my pool again.

Sunny McKinney was swimming underwater.

Sunny McKinney was naked.

Her body, tanned and long and supple, moved effortlessly and gracefully beneath the moonstruck surface, a triangle of white flesh showing where the sun had not touched her, arms pushing water in a strong breast stroke, legs frog-kicking behind her, blonde hair reflecting glints of whatever pale light there was. Underwater, she touched the tiles at the far end of the pool, executed a swift turn, still submerged, and started back for the shallow end. Midway between the far end of the pool and where I was standing, she came up for air. I caught only a glimpse of her blonde hair before she went under again, but it was enough to tell me that the lady in my pool wasn't who I'd thought she was.

Still unaware of my presence, she surfaced near the pool steps, touched the bottom step for support, stood up, and began climbing the steps. She was not, as I had earlier surmised, entirely naked. What I'd taken for an untanned triangle of flesh was in reality a pair of white bikini panties, soaked through now and showing a darker triangular patch above the joining of her legs. Her hair was cut in a short wedge, but her body could have been Sunny's exactly, long and tan and supple and firm. Veronica McKinney still didn't know I was standing there. The moment, for her at least, was a private one. She shook out her short hair. She put a finger in her left ear, jumped up and down on her left foot, did the same to her right ear and on her right foot, ran her hands over her breasts to stroke water from them, and did the same with her belly and thighs. She went to the lounge chair where her clothes were neatly folded, reached into her bag for a tissue, and blew her nose.

"Hi," I said.

She turned, startled.

"Hi," she said. "You're home, huh?"

"I'm home."

We looked at each other. She smiled.

"Caught me trespassing, huh?" she said. "Will you prosecute?"

"I don't think so."

We kept looking at each other.

"You want a towel, right?" I said.

"Wrong," she said.

She rummaged around in her handbag again, found a package of cigarettes, shook one free, and lit it. "Mm, good," she said, exhaling, and sat on the edge of the lounge next to the one with her clothes folded on it. There was a faint chill on the air; her nipples were puckering.

"I tried you at the office," she said, "but I got no answer."

"When was this?"

"Seven, seven-thirty? I was at a very dull cocktail party in that new condo on the Gulf—what's it called?"

"Bayview?"

"Bayview, yes. Stuffy and boring. I also called you here. No answer. I figured you had to come home sooner or later, so I drove on over. Your address is in the phone book, you know."

"Yes, I know."

"Well," she said, "aren't you going to offer me a drink?"

The feeling of déjà vu persisted.

"Sure," I said. "What would you like?"

"Sour mash on the rocks, if you've got any."

"I think so," I said, and paused before going back into the house. "Would you like a robe or something?" I asked.

"No, thanks, I'm fine," she said.

I went to the bar and poured a generous splash of bourbon into a short glass. I mixed myself a Dewar's and soda. I picked up an ashtray and carried that out to the terrace as well, a drink in each hand, the ashtray pressed against my ribs with my right elbow.

"Oh, good," she said, "I was *wondering* what to do with this."

She stubbed out the cigarette and accepted the drink. "Thanks," she said. "Your pool was delightful, I hope you don't mind my using it. It got so hot."

I was wondering why she was here. Had she heard about Burrill's murder on the six o'clock news? It didn't seem likely that someone had turned on a television set at a cocktail party.

"Cheers," she said.

"Cheers," I said.

We drank.

"Why don't *you* take a swim?" she said.

"Maybe later," I said.

"At least take off your jacket and tie," she said. "Aren't you suffocating?"

I took off my jacket and draped it over the back of the lounge chair behind her clothes. She'd been wearing white tonight. A silky-looking white dress neatly folded on the seat of the chair, a pair of high-heeled white patent slippers side by side on the tiles. No bra, I noticed. And she was *wearing* the panties that completed the outfit. I yanked down the knot of my tie, and unfastened the top button of my shirt.

"There," she said, "isn't that better?"

"Much," I said.

"Always listen to Mama," she said. "Does it embarrass you, my sitting here like this?"

"No," I said.

"You keep averting your eyes," she said. "You needn't."

I felt as if I'd been reincarnated by mistake into the same life I'd already lived last Friday night. Remembering Sunny, I suddenly wondered how far from the tree the acorn ever really fell, and I wondered again why Veronica had come here. Perhaps I was avoiding the obvious. I was certainly old enough and experienced enough to accept without question a partially clad woman sipping a poolside bourbon and telling me I didn't have to worry about where my eyes wandered. But I had never flattered myself into believing I was irresistible to women; I had, in fact, spent the better part of my life convincing myself that I could be even slightly attractive to any member of the opposite sex, despite the knowledge that many of the women I'd known in my adult life were, at the very least, pretty. Perhaps unfulfilled teenage yearnings died hard. I know only that I felt as if I were back in Chicago again, scrawny and acne-ridden and steaming with adolescent passion. Here and now was Calusa, Florida, on a sweltering night in August. Here and now was Veronica McKinney sitting casually, albeit half naked, in the moonlight while I sat fully clothed, looking at all the beautiful foliage, *and* the sky, *and* the moon, *and* the pool, and anything but her. Maybe it had something to do with her age. Maybe, by comparison, I *was* a teenager.

"Cat got your tongue?" she asked.

"Just thinking," I said.

"About what?"

"About why you came here."

"I was bored. Also, I remembered you had a pool."

"Okay," I said.

"I don't know why I'm making you so nervous," she said. "But I'll dress if you like."

She looked at me questioningly. I said nothing. She rose suddenly.

"Turn your back," she said.

I did not turn my back.

"Naughty boy," she said, and rolled the wet panties down over her thighs and ankles and stepped out of them. She picked up the white dress, pulled it over her head, and smoothed it over her hips and thighs. "There," she said, "is that better? Don't look so stern and disapproving, Matthew."

"Is that how I look?"

"Indeed."

"Actually, I'm glad you're here."

"You seem positively overjoyed."

"I planned to call you in the morning, anyway."

"Ah? What about?"

"I went to see Loomis again this afternoon."

She raised her eyebrows expectantly. I did not know how much I should actually tell her. She seemed not to know that Burrill had been murdered, and I didn't think I should be the one to inform her. At the same time, Loomis had made his counter-offer on behalf of a client who was now *dead*. Would Burrill's heirs, if there were any, insist on the same terms for settlement? I decided to tread very cautiously.

"He made a counter-offer," I said. "He wants you to pay five thousand dollars in damages."

"*What* damages?"

"He claims his client lost potential buyers."

"Yes, I'm sure the woods are just *full* of aspiring snapbean farmers. I hope you told him to go to hell."

"In effect. I wanted to check with you first."

"Then why didn't you call me?"

"Something came up."

"Like what?"

"Busy afternoon at the office," I said.

"Would you mind if I freshened this?" she asked, and without waiting for an answer, she started for the house. Here we go again, I thought. Like mother, like daughter. Same magnificent bodies, same blonde hair, same blue eyes, same thirst. She stopped just outside the sliding glass doors.

"Where's the light switch?" she asked.

"I'll get it," I said, and went into the house ahead of her. I turned on the living room lights and then the pool lights. She followed me into the house and looked around, appraising it. "Nice," she said. "Did you do it yourself?"

"Must be an echo in here," I said.

"What?" she said.

"It came furnished."

"Very nice," she said, padding over to the bar. "How big is it?"

"Two bedrooms," I said. "My daughter comes to visit every other weekend."

"You're divorced?" she asked, and found the bourbon bottle.

"Yes."

"Would I know your ex?" She put two ice cubes into her glass, and poured liberally over them.

"Her name's Susan."

"Does she still keep the Hope?"

"Yes."

"Don't know her," Veronica said, and turned from the bar. "Cheers," she said, and drank. The white dress clung to her. I was unashamedly aware that she was wearing nothing at all under it. "Are you otherwise attached?" she asked, and looked at me.

"Not at the moment."

She nodded.

She was silent for what seemed a very long time then, sipping at her drink, looking out over the bayou whenever a mullet jumped, apparently gathering her thoughts before she spoke again.

At last she said, "I've been doing a lot of thinking about Jack these past few days."

I said nothing.

"About how it could have happened," she said. "How someone could have got in there and stabbed him."

I still said nothing.

"My son had a gun. A .38 Smith & Wesson that Drew gave him on his eighteenth birthday. The twenty-seventh of June. Two years ago," she said. "Just before Drew died. I find that ironic, don't you? Macho Drew giving un-macho Jack a great big symbol of masculinity when he reaches manhood, maybe because he himself—ravaged by cancer—was feeling intimations of mortality. He was right, as it turned out. He died a week after Jack's birthday. On the Fourth of July, went out in a blaze of fireworks. Here's *to* you, Drew," she said, and drank. "I hope there are lots of fat cows wherever you are, all of them *barbecued*, you son of a bitch." She drank again. "Jack actually learned to use it," she said. "Amazing. He never *was* worth a damn when it came to practical matters."

I remembered what she'd told me about her son's never having learned to brand a calf or ride a horse, and I assumed that on a ranch, learning to use a gun was just another one of those "practical matters."

"He took it with him when he moved out to Stone Crab," she said. "Have the police mentioned a gun to you?"

"No," I said.

"Me neither. They gave me a list of everything in the apartment, right down to a pair of sweaty tennis socks. I guess they do that to protect themselves, wouldn't you say? Against later charges of theft?"

"I suppose so."

"Because it's not unheard of, you know. The police taking whatever isn't nailed down. The firemen too."

"In New York, they call them the Forty Thieves."

"The police?"

"The firemen. My partner Frank told me that. He's a New Yorker."

"And you?"

"Chicago."

"I love that city," she said. "Hog butcher to the world. Sandburg, you know."

"Yes, I know."

"Yes, of course you would. But if the gun wasn't in his apartment, where *was* it?"

"You're sure it wasn't . . ."

"Not according to the list they gave me. They *would* have listed a gun, wouldn't they?"

"I'd guess so."

"A *weapon*? Well, certainly. And another question. Wouldn't Jack have tried to *use* the gun? On a man intending serious damage with a knife?"

"Assuming the gun was there."

"Yes, but that's exactly my point, don't you see?"

"I'm afraid I don't."

"*Was* the gun there?"

"You seem to think it should have been."

"Well, he took it with him when he moved, didn't he?"

"Which was back in June."

"Yes. So where was the gun on the night of the murder? And where is it now?"

"Maybe the police confiscated it."

"Without listing it?"

"Maybe they didn't want the killer to know about it."

"Do they think *I'm* the killer?"

"I'm sure they don't."

"The list was prepared for *me*, Matthew. As next of kin. If they found Jack's gun, it would've been on that list."

"Maybe the killer took it with him."

"Maybe," she said. She sipped at her drink thoughtfully. "Which brings up yet another question. How'd the killer get in? Jack normally kept his door locked. There's a peephole in the door. He would have seen whoever was out there in the hall before he unlocked the door. Yet he unlocked it. And let his own murderer in. And didn't even try to use the gun to protect himself."

"What does that indicate to you?" I said.

"First, that he knew whoever killed him. Knew him well enough to let him into the apartment. And second, that the gun wasn't in Jack's possession on the night of the murder. He'd have gone for it otherwise. To protect himself."

"Well," I said, "no one *really* knows what happened in that apartment. Except the killer, of course . . ."

"And Jack. Who's dead."

"Yes, of course."

There was another silence.

"Could I have a smidgin more of this?" she asked.

I took her glass and carried it to the bar.

"Bloom asked me a lot of questions that night," she said.

"What night?"

"The night Jack was killed. I think he considered me a suspect."

"They *have* to ask a lot of questions," I said, and carried the drink back to her. "Especially of the family."

"Is that why he wanted to know whether Dr. Jeffries and I had a thing going? Thanks," she said, and took the glass.

"Dr. Jeffries?"

"My veterinarian. And Bloom's word exactly. A *thing*. I guess he meant an affair. Wouldn't you think he meant an affair?"

"I would suppose so."

"With a man who's seventy-five years old?"

"Well . . ."

"I realize I look mummified, but really . . ."

"You look nothing of the sort," I said.

"Thank you," she said, "you're very kind. But Dr. Jeffries *is* considerably older than I am, and the idea of Bloom suggesting a *thing* with him . . ." She shook her head.

"He was undoubtedly checking your alibi," I said.

"Because we were together, do you mean? On the night of the murder?"

"Yes."

"And if we *were* lovers, of course, we would most certainly lie for each other."

"I guess that's what Bloom was thinking."

"Or *with* each other," she said.

"Sorry?"

"Lovers. Lying *with* each other. Or *on* each other, as the case might be."

"Uh-huh."

"We were watching television," she said.

"So Bloom mentioned."

"Did the thought occur to you as well?"

"Which thought is that?"

"That Ham and I might be lovers?"

"Ham?"

"Hamilton Jeffries. My vet."

"Never occurred to me," I said.

"Why? Because he's seventy-five years old?"

"I didn't know *how* old he was until you mentioned it."

"But it never occurred to you, when Bloom was filling you in on where everyone was that night, that Ham and I *might* have been covering for each other? That Ham and I *might* indeed be lovers?"

"No, that never occurred to me."

"What if I told you we were?"

"Lovers? Or covering for each other?"

"Take your choice."

"I would say you were suggesting complicity in murder, and you ought to be telling this to the police, not to me."

"We were," she said. "Lovers. *Past* tense. He was fifty-one, I was thirty-three. Nice age spread, wouldn't you agree? My husband was more interested in cows than he was in me. Spent a lot of time running around for the Cattleman's Association, Drew did, while I languished back at the ranch, swatting flies and wondering what the hell I was doing there in the middle of the wilderness."

"This was . . . ?"

"Twenty-four years ago. Twenty-four plus thirty-three equals fifty-seven. Elementary, my dear Watson. Fifty-seven is what I am, remember? No, I guess you don't. You once told me you'd already forgotten how old I was."

"I remember how old you are," I said softly.

She crossed her legs as though to emphasize the absurdity of discussing chronological age with a woman so emphatically beautiful. The white dress rode up over her knees, and there was a sudden flash of suntanned thigh. Her eyes met mine.

"Does it embarrass you to hear me talk about my youthful escapades?" she asked.

"Not particularly."

"In that case," she said, "*there* I was. Thirty-three years old, married for six years, and sitting on a cattle ranch while my dashing husband raced off to Denver and Tallahassee and God knows where else to talk about *cows*. I *hated* cows, still do, for that matter. I don't think I'd even *seen* a cow till I met Drew. Well, that's an exaggeration. But it *was* an alien world to me. My father used to be an investment banker in Dayton, came down here to open his own bank. Calusa was still a fishing village then; you have no idea how beautiful it was, Matthew. Drew borrowed a sizable amount of money from my father. That's how we met. I was a late bloomer, twenty-seven when I got married, didn't have any children till I was thirty-four. If I'd been a heifer, they'd have sold me off in a minute. Anyway, there I was, alone on the M.K. one steamy night at the end of September, with a sick calf and Ham there to fix her. And to fix *me* as well. Am I shocking you, Matthew?"

"No."

"He fixed me, all right. Delivered me straight out of boredom and loneliness into a rapture I hadn't thought possible." She sighed deeply. "'But that was in another country,'" she said. "'And besides, the wench is dead.'" She paused. "Marlowe," she said. "*The Jew of Malta*, circa 1587. I used to read a lot while Drew was off talking cattle."

"How long did it last? This . . . *thing* with Ham?"

"Are *you* checking my alibi, too? Or have I captured your interest?"

"I find you interesting, yes," I said.

"I thought you did," she said, and smiled over the rim of her glass and uncrossed her legs. There was the briefest flash of thigh. She sat with her legs slightly apart, fully aware of the intimate knowledge we shared: she was wearing nothing under that pristine white dress.

"Not too very long, I'm sorry to say, Ham and I. We fell in love in September, and it was already over by February. Short season, easy come, easy go. I settled down—isn't that the expression one uses?—and became a faithful wife and loving mother, not necessarily in that order. Sunny was an August baby, full of rain, cried day and night, I sometimes wanted to strangle her, sometimes wish I *had*. A lost cause, that girl. Jack came three years later, Drew's son exactly, same dark hair and dark eyes, spitting image except for the swagger and bravado, in which departments he was sadly lacking. Which is maybe why he got rid of a gun he should have kept—and ended up dead for it. While *I* was watching television with a former lover." She smiled wanly. "Why is it that people *watch* television," she said, "whereas they go to *see* movies? Have you ever heard anyone say, 'Let's go *watch* a movie tonight'? Have you ever heard anyone say, 'Let's go *see* television tonight'? It's peculiar the way language evolves, isn't it? Or is the choice of words a qualitative one? Do people *watch* television only because there's really nothing to *see* on it?"

She looked into her glass.

I had the feeling that the last little verbal exercise had served to transport her safely and easily from her past memories of Hamilton Jeffries and her present concern about a gun her son should have had in his apartment on the night he was killed. She kept staring into her glass.

"What makes you think he threw that gun away?" I asked.

"Well, it wasn't *there*, was it?"

"Why would he have got rid of it?"

"Who knows? Maybe he robbed a bank to get that forty thousand dollars. Maybe he felt the gun would incriminate him. My son was a *dip*, Matthew—Sunny's word for him. By the way, Bloom called me today, wanted to know whether Jack was in the habit of *spanking* Sunny. I couldn't believe my ears. *Spanking*? He does come up with some good ones, your Bloom."

I didn't mention that Sunny was the one who'd come up with it.

"First he gives the third-degree to a pair of former lovers . . ."

"Former lovers, Veronica . . ."

"Yes, don't say it. Can lie for each other through force of habit. No, Matthew. We really *were* watching television when my son let someone he knew into his apartment."

"Who do you think the someone was?"

"I have no idea."

"Sam Watson didn't have a Spanish accent, did he?"

"My former manager?" She shook her head. "No. A Texas drawl, if anything."

"How about any of the people you do business with? Your cat-meat man . . ."

"No. How do *you* know about cat-meat men?"

"Your stocker?"

"No. Have you been visiting the library?"

"Do you know anyone at *all* with a Spanish accent?"

"What's all this about a Spanish accent?"

"*Do* you?"

"Well, no. Well, *yes.*"

"Who?"

"We used to have a Mexican cook . . . oh, ten, twelve years ago, I guess."

"Where is he now?"

"He went back to California."

"Anybody else?"

"Not that I can think of. This isn't Miami, you know."

She drained what was left in her glass. I thought she might go to the bar for another refill. Instead, she put the glass down and said, "I'm getting tired, aren't you?"

I looked at her.

"Why don't we go to bed?" she said.

A smile touched her mouth. She arched one eyebrow.

"Why don't we?" I said.

5

We were both dressed and out of the house by a quarter to nine the next morning, a scant fifteen minutes before Lottie and Dottie were certain to arrive. Lottie and Dottie were the two women who came to clean my house and do my laundry every Tuesday and Thursday. I called them the Speed Queens because, rather than hourly payment, we had settled on a flat weekly rate, which gave them license to go through the house like a pair of cyclones. They usually arrived at nine, by which time I was normally at the office. That was why I'd given them a key.

The widow lady next door was out picking oranges when Veronica and I came out and walked to the Porsche. The widow lady, whose name was Mrs. Martindale, was forty-seven years old, ten years younger than Veronica. Her husband had died of a heart attack at the age of fifty. She told me that this was because he'd refused to drink the orange juice she squeezed fresh each morning from the oranges she picked in her own modest citrus grove of two trees. She was constantly inviting me in for fresh-squeezed orange juice. I was constantly finding excuses. She looked at us now, doubtlessly reflecting on the early morning hour, reflecting as well on the white nylon cocktail sheath and high-heeled slippers Veronica was wearing. I could just imagine what thoughts would be racing through her mind as she squeezed her oranges this morning.

I opened the door on the driver's side of the car. Veronica climbed in. I had held her naked in my arms the night before, but I could not resist looking at her legs now as she slid in behind the wheel. She grinned in appreciation. I called a cheery good morning to Mrs. Martindale, went around to the other side of the Porsche, and got in.

"Where to?" Veronica asked, and turned the ignition key.

"My office, please," I said. "Corner of Heron and Vaughan."

She backed the car out of the driveway. Mrs. Martindale was still watching us. I waved as we went by her house. I was hoping she'd realize Veronica was ten years older than she was. I was full of praise for older women this morning.

"When am I going to see you again?" Veronica asked.

"Tonight?"

"Greedy man," she said, and smiled. "What time?"

She had smiled a lot last night, too. I had kissed the smile off her mouth more times than I could remember. She had told me that people of her generation were very good kissers. This was because when she was growing up (and here she smiled wickedly), young girls weren't even allowed to attend the weekly chariot races. "Going all the way" was unthought of back then, when everyone was a vestal virgin, and so there'd been a lot of kissing. Kissing at parties, kissing in the back seats of automobiles, kissing at the movies, kissing on the beach or in the park, kissing whenever and wherever the opportunity presented itself, which seemed to be quite often. The people of her generation had had a lot of practice kissing. They were experts at kissing. The trouble was that when they grew out of their teens, they *still* thought kissing was all there was to it. It had taken her a long while to learn that kissing, even *good* kissing—even *soul* kissing, which she'd learned when she was seventeen—wasn't the be-all and the end-all of sex.

"I was a virgin when I married Drew," she said, "can you imagine? Twenty-seven years old and a *virgin*! A very good kisser, yes—do you like the way I kiss, Matthew?—but *oh*, such a late bloomer."

It was a well-known fact, I told her teasingly, that women reached the peak of their sexual prowess at the age of thirty-two, and that after that it was all downhill. "Late bloomer," she said, and pounced on me again. We had pounced on each other a lot last night. When the alarm woke me at eight, I was exhausted. Veronica was still asleep, lying on her back, the sheet pulled to just below her breasts, one arm bent, her hand lying palm upward on the pillow above her head. She looked serene and radiantly beautiful and completely irresistible—but the Speed Queens were due at nine.

I touched her cheek gently.

"Mm," she said.

"Veronica?"

"Mm?"

"My cleaning women are on the way."

"That's right," she said, and rolled over, turning her back to me.

"We have to get up," I said.

"Okay."

"Veronica?"

"Uh-huh."

"We really do have to get up."

She rolled over again, opened her eyes, and looked at me in surprise. "Matthew?" she said, and grinned, and snuggled into my arms. "Oh, good *morning*," she said, and kissed me, and despite the imminent arrival of the wondrous whirlwinds, we lost ourselves completely for the next twenty minutes.

I kept watching her as she maneuvered the Porsche through the early-morning traffic.

"You're staring," she said.

"I'm dying to kiss you."

"The next light."

I kissed her at the next light. I kissed her at the light after that.

"We'll get arrested," she said.

I put my hand on her knee.

"*Matth*-yew," she warned.

I began sliding my hand up under her dress.

"Matthew!" she said sharply, and closed her thighs on my hand, and looked swiftly at the traffic on her right and left. She was blushing. "Where do I turn off?" she asked, flustered.

"Where are you going after you drop me?"

"To my chiropractor," she said, and turned to smile at me. "You weren't very good for my back, Matthew."

"I'll go with you."

"Why?" she said, surprised.

"I don't want to leave you yet."

"Don't be silly, you'll be seeing me tonight."

"What time did we say?"

"We didn't. How's eight o'clock?"

"Why so late?"

"Seven?"

"Make it six. No, wait, I have to see Bloom at five."

"I'll be there at seven-thirty."

"Too long to be apart," I said. "I'm coming with you to your chiropractor."

His office was on Main Street, a white cinder-block structure wedged between a store selling jeans and a store selling inexpensive kitchenware. A large plastic chiropractic symbol hung on the wall beside a mustard-yellow entrance door; it looked very much like a hybrid between a medical caduceus and a representation of Christ hanging on the cross. The naked man depicted, however, had no beard and no crown of thorns and his arms were spread wide against a pair of oversized wings. In place of the glow of light that normally shimmered above Jesus' head, the word HEALTH was lettered on a trailing banner that curved serpentinely behind the man's body and then emerged below his hips to cover his groin with the word CHIROPRACTIC. Hanging horizontally and slightly to the right of the figure was a white plastic sign lettered in blue with the words CHIROPRACTIC CLINIC. Whenever anyone talked about reviving Calusa's downtown area, they had in mind these one-story cinder-block buildings that lined Main Street like dwarfed Apache pueblos, most of them painted a mildewing white, some of them painted a mildewing pink, which was infinitely worse.

"I hope you like back-issue magazines," Veronica said, and pushed open the yellow door. I followed her into a small reception area furnished with a green metal desk and several padded green metal chairs. The cinder-block walls were painted the same white as the exterior walls. A young girl in a white blouse and a black skirt sat behind the desk. She looked up as we came in. The door on this side, I noticed, was painted green, to match the beautiful furniture. There was a calendar advertising feed and grain hanging on one of the walls. Its illustration showed a farm girl in ragged cutoff jeans, a red blouse knotted under her full breasts, a straw hat angled back on her head, a wide grin around a piece of hay tilted rakishly in her mouth. The slogan read FATTEN 'EM WITH SIMMONS FEED AND GRAIN, but the only reference to cattle was a minuscule cow standing against a wooden fence in the far background. This was August, but the calendar had not yet been turned from the month of July. Aside from the calendar, nothing else hung on the spartan white walls.

"I'm Mrs. McKinney," Veronica said. "I was just passing by. Do you think he can take me?"

"Oh," the girl said. "You don't have an appointment?"

"No," she said.

"Oh, then this is going to be *complicated*," she said, fluttering her hands aimlessly in the air and conveying the distinct impression that anything more complicated than "run, Spot, run" would naturally be overwhelming to a mere country girl. She studied the buttons on the base of her phone as though they were numbered in Sanskrit, and then—with a bewildered look on her face—pushed down boldly on one of them. "Doctor?" she said into the phone, seemingly surprised that her haphazard stab had produced *any* result at all. "There's somebody here doesn't have an appointment. Her name . . ." She looked at Veronica, her eyes widening in panic. "What was your name again, ma'am?" she asked. "McDonald, did you say?"

"McKinney," Veronica said.

"I thought you said McDonald."

"No, McKinney. I'm a regular patient here, the doctor knows . . ."

"Well, let's not get into *that*," the girl said, and rolled her eyes. "Her name's McDonald," she said into the phone, "I mean *McKinney*." She looked at Veronica again. "Phew, what a name," she said. Into the phone she said, "Shall I send her in or what?"

She listened for a moment, cautiously replaced the receiver on its cradle, and then said, "You can go right in, Mrs. McKinley. Through the door there, and then . . ."

"I know the way," Veronica said. "And it's McKinney. Veronica McKinney."

"Yeah," the girl said. "Right."

Veronica winked at me and disappeared through another green door, on the opposite wall. The girl looked in surprise at her electric typewriter, as if discovering that a Martian spaceship had landed on her desk. Placing both hands carefully on the keyboard, she began moving her fingers. Nothing happened. Either to herself or to me, she said, "You have to turn it on first." She looked for the on-off switch. She looked on the right of the typewriter and then on the left. She lifted the typewriter and looked under it. She found the switch, at last, on the left-hand side of the machine, near the back. She was reaching to turn it on when her eyes opened wide and she said, "Oh!" and looked at me and said, "What's *your* name?"

"Hope," I said.

"Come on, that's a *girl's* name," she said.

"It's my last name."

"Then what's your *first* name?"

"Matthew."

"Do you have an appointment, Mr. Matthews?"

"No, I'm waiting for . . ."

"Did you want to see the doctor?"

"No," I said.

"Then why are you here?"

"I'm with Mrs. McKinney," I said.

"Oh, right," she said. "Well, have a seat, okay?" She looked at the typewriter. She looked up at me again, bewildered. "Where'd that switch go?" she said, and began searching for it all over again.

The door to the inner office opened not ten minutes later. Veronica, in white and in mid-conversation, came through into the white reception area, followed by a man who was also dressed in white. For a moment it looked like a sudden snowstorm.

". . . ever you did, it feels much better already," Veronica said.

The man nodded, pleased. He was tall and burly, with an olive complexion that seemed deeper against the white of his tunic. His eyes were brown. There was a shaggy black mustache under his nose.

"Matthew," she said, "I'd like you to meet Calusa's miracle worker. If ever you've got a muscle that refuses to behave, you just call him. Dr. Alvarez . . . Matthew Hope."

"Nice to mee' you," Alvarez said, with an accent I could have spread on a tostada.

I called Bloom the moment I was in my office.

I told him that Veronica McKinney's chiropractor had a Spanish accent.

He said, "Yeah?"

I reminded him that Sunny McKinney had overheard her brother in conversation with a man who had a Spanish accent and that—

124

"Yes, I know," he said.

—according to her they'd been discussing the theft of cows.

"I've been giving a lot of thought to that telephone conversation," Bloom said. "I'm not so sure they were talking about cows. Remember my first impression when I heard this kid had forty thousand in cash? I thought *dope* is what I thought, the kid was involved some way with dope. Okay, last October he gets a call from a guy with a Spanish accent—all your cocaine comes up from Colombia, Matthew, the dope heavies in Florida are mostly all Spanish. And the guy says how many and the kid says fifteen at thirty. Okay, Matthew, I know this is far out, I know it's pretty much off the wall. But the going rate for *good* cocaine in Miami is fifty grand a kilo. Okay. Suppose you could get *shitty* cocaine for *thirty* grand a kilo?"

"You think Jack McKinney was selling *cocaine* to this man? Instead of *cows*?"

"No, sir."

"You just said . . ."

"I think it could've been the other way around, Matthew. The guy with the Spanish accent was selling the girl . . ."

"What girl?"

"The dope. Girl, coke, snow, nose candy, they're all names for cocaine. 'The brighter the blue, the better the girl'—you never heard that expression?"

"Never."

"Your hotshot dope dealers'll test the coke with cobalt thiocyanate to make sure it isn't Johnson's Baby Powder or something. If it turns blue, it's the McCoy. The *really* pure stuff turns a *bright* blue. Live and learn," he said.

"And that's what you honestly think? That McKinney was buying cocaine from this guy with the Spanish accent?"

"It's possible. Fifteen kilos of not very good dope. At thirty thousand bucks a throw."

"That comes to four hundred and fifty thousand dollars."

"It does."

"You think McKinney had that kind of money, huh?"

"If he was trafficking in dope, that's peanuts."

"Well," I said.

"What does 'well' mean?"

"It means this all sounds like sheer speculation."

"It is. That's the business I'm in, Matthew. Speculation. Until all the pieces fall together, that's all it is—speculation. What'd Mrs. McKinney have to say about her Spanish chiropractor?"

"She told me he's Cuban."

"You asked her?"

"Right after I met him. She was driving me over to my . . ."

"Oh," Bloom said, "you *met* him?"

"Yes. His name is Ramon Alvarez."

"How'd you happen to meet him?"

"I went to his office with her."

"This morning?"

"Yes."

"And in the car afterwards, you happened to ask her whether he was Cuban, is that right?"

"Well, I'd asked her last night if she knew . . ."

"Oh, you were with her last *night*, too?"

"Yes."

There was a silence on the phone. I knew just what Bloom was thinking. Veronica had been with me last night, and she'd been with me again early this morning. Bloom was thinking just what Mrs. Martindale had thought.

"Did *she* come over for a swim, too?" he asked.

"She came over to talk."

"About her chiropractor?"

"No. But during the course of the conversation, I asked if she knew anyone with a Spanish accent . . ."

"And she told you her chiropractor was Spanish."

"No, she could only remember a Mexican cook who used to work for them."

"She couldn't remember her *chiropractor*?"

"Well, what she said, actually . . ."

"When was this? Last night, or in the car today?"

"In the car. She said she thought I'd meant anyone connected with the ranch. The chiropractor never occurred to her."

"I don't believe in chiropractors, do you?" Bloom said.

"Well, they seem to help people."

"So let me get this straight. Last night, out of the blue, you happened to ask Mrs. McKinney if she knew anyone with a Spanish accent. And she told you . . ."

"Not out of the blue," I said. "We were talking about her son's murder, and I remembered Sunny telling me . . ."

"Is that what she came there to talk about? Her son's murder?"

"Yes."

"What'd she have to say about *that*?"

"She thought Jack knew the person he let into his apartment. Because there's a peephole on the door. He would have seen who was outside. He wouldn't have opened the door for a stranger."

"That's occurred to us," Bloom said dryly. "Did it occur to Mrs. McKinney that the killer may have had a key?"

"Well . . . no. She didn't say anything about a key."

"The resident manager's office has passkeys to every apartment in that condo," Bloom said.

"Oh."

"So it didn't *have* to be a pal the kid let in. He didn't have to *let* anyone in at all, in fact. The killer could have used a key."

"She also mentioned a gun. Did you find a gun in that apartment, Morrie?"

"No. A gun? No."

"Veronica says her son kept a gun."

"Oh, it's 'Veronica' now, is it?"

"Well . . . yes."

"You've been busy, Matthew."

I suddenly remembered something Bloom had said to me a long time ago. "Counselor," he'd said, "it would be nice to have your word from this minute on that you won't be running all over the city of Calusa questioning anybody you think might have some connection with this case." He still referred to that case as "the German dwarf mess." I referred to it as "the Vicky Miller tragedy." His warning back then had been prefaced by the word *counselor*, which in my profession was often used sarcastically by opposing courthouse attorneys. Cops used it the same way in *their* profession, I discovered that day, inflecting the word so that it seemed synonymous with *shyster*. I didn't know now whether his comment about my having been busy referred to Veronica or simply to the fact that I'd been asking questions he felt I had no right to ask. Either way, it sounded like a reprimand. I said nothing. The silence on the line lengthened. I didn't know now whether Bloom was thinking or sulking.

"Where'd he get this gun?" Bloom asked at last.

"A birthday present from his father."

"His father's been dead for two years now."

"He gave it to him just before he died."

"*Veronica* told you this?"

It seemed to me he put the same inflection on her name that he'd put on the word *counselor* all those years ago. I decided he *was* sulking, after all.

"Yes," I said. "Veronica."

"Where was this gun supposed to be?" Bloom asked.

"In his apartment. He took it with him when he moved off the ranch in June."

"What *kind* of a gun, did she say?"

"A .38 Smith & Wesson."

Bloom was silent for what seemed like a very long time.

"That's very interesting," he said at last.

"How so?"

"Because I've got here on my desk in front of me a report from Ballistics saying the gun that killed Burrill was a .38 Smith & Wesson. Now that is what I call an even *bigger* coincidence than the going rate for a kilo of coke. I think I better have another talk with Mrs. *Veronica* McKinney, find out a little more about this gun her son owned. A birthday present, huh? They give nice birthday presents down here in sunny Florida. You don't even

128

ave to register them, you can pick a gun off the shelf like it was a ripe banana." He paused. "What else did she have to say?"

I debated telling him about her long-ago affair with Hamilton Jeffries, the veterinarian. I decided, perhaps wrongly, that revealing this would be unfair to her. Even though she'd told me about it *before* we'd gone to bed together, I nonetheless considered it pillow talk. And pillow talk, on *my* scale of values, rates almost as high as the privileged communication between an attorney and his client—which, in fact, we *also* were.

"Matthew? Did she say anything else?"

"Nothing," I said.

"Did she know about Burrill? His getting killed?"

"She didn't seem to."

"What do you suppose he was looking for?"

"Who?"

"Whoever shot Burrill."

"*Was* he looking for something?"

"Well, you *saw* the place, didn't you? Looked like a tornado went through there. Same as McKinney's apartment, everything thrown upside down, mattresses tossed and slashed, drawers spilled all over the floor. Guy living like a Bowery bum, what the hell could he have been *hiding* in that pigsty? She said he couldn't have been involved in dope, huh?"

It was sometimes difficult to follow Morris Bloom's stream-of-consciousness meanderings. I gathered he was referring to Sunny McKinney and her brother, Jack.

"She didn't think so," I said.

"Because doesn't it sound to *you* like dope?" Bloom said. "I mean, what *was* all that shit about 'fifteen at thirty'? It sure sounds like the going price for a kilo of beat snow, doesn't it? Thirty grand, something like that? Your really *good* stuff goes for fifty. You think Burrill and McKinney were running dope together? You think maybe *that's* what the killer was looking for? Dope?"

"I don't know."

"Assuming it was the same guy who killed them both," Bloom said. "The gun makes it look like there's a real connection, doesn't it?"

I realized that Bloom was thinking out loud. He no more needed me on the other end of the line than he needed a mirror. I suddenly knew what he and his wife talked about when they were alone together.

"Well, I'll give her a ring," he said, "the cow lady. Meanwhile, don't forget we're going to the gym today."

"I have it on my calendar," I said.

"See you at five," Bloom said, and hung up.

I did not get back from the eleven o'clock closing at Calusa First until almost one o'clock. I asked Cynthia to phone out for a hot pastrami on rye and a bottle of Heineken beer, and I was just unwrapping the sandwich when Frank came into my office.

"Howdy, Tex," he said.

I uncapped the beer.

"How are the deer and the antelope playing these days?" he asked.

I bit into the sandwich.

"I'm *sure* the *enormous* fee we'll be earning on this McKinney shit will justify all the time you're putting in on it," he said. "Loomis called while you were out, wants you to get back to him."

I nodded.

"Have you been stricken mute?" Frank said. "How'd the closing go?"

"Fine."

"How'd you like my ten rules?"

"Fine."

"They're not supposed to be *trick* rules, you know."

"Oh, I thought they were trick rules."

"Lots of people think so."

"Do you hand them out to lots of people?"

"Only those who need help desperately. The reason lots of people think they're *trick* rules is because of the first two."

"Which ones are those?"

"Always treat a lady like a hooker. Always treat a hooker like a lady."

"Ah, yes," I said.

"People automatically assume," Frank said, "that in all the rules *following* those two, you're supposed to substitute lady for hooker and hooker for lady. But that isn't the case. In other words, where Rule Number Five says, 'Never try to buy a lady into bed,' it doesn't mean 'Never try to buy a *hooker* into bed.' It means just what it says. Lady."

I looked at him.

"You're not supposed to think that because you're supposed to treat a hooker like a lady that where it says, 'Never try to buy a *lady* into bed,' it really means 'Never try to buy a *hooker* into bed,' which is how you're supposed to treat a *lady* if you're observing the first rule. Like a *hooker*. In which case, if you're treating her like a *hooker*, you should never try to *talk* her into bed, the *lady*, and that's wrong."

"I see."

"It can get complicated," Frank said, "but it's not meant to be tricky."

"I'm glad you told me that."

"Have you tried any of them yet?"

"I don't know any hookers."

"I don't know any hookers, either," he said, looking offended.

The buzzer on my desk sounded. It was Cynthia, telling me that Attorney Loomis was on five.

"Loomis," I said to Frank, and took a swallow of beer.

"You *really* think I know hookers, don't you?" he said, and shook his head and walked out of the office. I pressed the five button in the base of the phone.

"Hello, Mr. Loomis," I said.

"Mr. Hope?"

"Yes, sir."

"Looks like we've got ourselves a pair of dead clients, don't it?"

"Looks that way."

"Which don't change the situation none, the way I look at it."

"I didn't think it would."

"Burrill wrote a will leaving everything he had to his only daughter, woman named Hester Burrill in New Orleans, named her personal representative too. I've been trying to reach her all day. She's either busy talkin' on the phone, or else it's off the hook or out of order. Anyway, I wanted you to know I'm going to recommend the same thing to her I recommended to Burrill. She keeps the property, a'course, and you forfeit the four thousand, plus you fork over the Mustang and five thousand in damages. You had a chance to talk this over with Mrs. McKinney yet?"

"I mentioned it to her."

"What'd she say?"

"She said I should tell you to go to hell."

"Sounds like a right nice lady," Loomis said.

"She is," I said.

"Well, you know our position, and we ain't budgin' an inch from it. Save us all a lot of trouble if your client agreed to it now. 'Cause otherwise, what I'll recommend to Burrill's daughter is to file an action against the estate, see if we can't turn up that cash."

"I'm not going back to Mrs. McKinney on this," I said. "She's already refused your offer."

"Suit yourself," Loomis said. "You'll be hearin' from me soon's I talk to the daughter."

The buzzer sounded again almost the moment he'd hung up.

"Your wife," Cynthia said. "On six."

"I don't *have* a wife," I said.

"Shall I tell her you're out?"

"I'll take it," I said, and sighed, and pressed the button. "Hello?" I said.

"Matthew?" she said. "How *are* you?"

132

The Waif.

"Fine," I said. "And you?"

"My eyes are watering a lot," she said. "My allergies."

The Waif, for sure.

"I'm sorry to hear that," I said.

"One of these days I may just leave Florida," she said.

She knew she couldn't take up residence outside the state until Joanna reached the age of twenty-one. I'd made damn certain of that in the settlement agreement. I refused to rise to the bait.

"So what's on your mind?" I asked.

"Matthew, I feel embarrassed asking you this, you'll think I'm taking advantage of you."

I thought, perhaps unkindly, that she had taken everything *else* in the divorce settlement, so what would it matter if she took mere *advantage* now? And then I wondered what catastrophe Susan the Witch had conjured for Susan the Waif to lay on me in order to spoil whatever little time I'd be spending with our daughter this weekend. In the next three seconds, I felt I was getting omniscient when it came to Susan.

"Matthew," she said, "I don't want Joanna to be sulking around your house all weekend. You know how she can get when she's been deprived."

I did not know how she could get when she'd been deprived. To my knowledge, I had never deprived her of anything but my presence in her mother's house.

"Matthew," she said, "do you remember Rhett Robinson?"

"I remember her," I said.

"She got divorced just about the time we did, do you remember?"

"I remember."

"She's getting married again this weekend. To a lovely man from Bradenton."

"That's nice," I said.

"Do you remember her daughter? Daisy?"

"I remember her."

The Robinsons all had rather fanciful names. Rhett had been named after Mr. Butler in *Gone with the Wind*; I assumed her mother had been hoping for a boy. Her former husband, Bruce, had been named after Bruce Cabot, the actor who'd played Magua in the film based on *The Last of the Mohicans*. Their daughter, Daisy, had been named after Daisy Buchanan in *The Great Gatsby*. An entirely literary family, the Robinsons. I seemed to recall, however, that Bruce had remarried just before Christmas, and his new wife's name was Mary—plain as any name can be. The last time I'd seen *Daisy* Robinson was when she was ten years old and sleeping over at the house Susan and I then shared. I remembered her as a runny-nosed little girl who kept calling Joanna a cheat, because Joanna consistently beat her at the game of jacks.

"What about her?" I said.

"She and Joanna are *such* good friends," Susan said.

This was news to me. I had not heard Joanna so much as *mention* Daisy in the past several months. I suddenly remembered what we used to call *The Great Gatsby* back when I was an undergraduate at Northwestern. *The Light on Daisy's Dock*. This was supposed to have sexual connotations. When I was an undergraduate, *everything* had sexual connotations. "Daisy's dock" referred to Daisy's vagina. The possibility that it had a *light* on it was enough to send all of us pink-cheeked sophomores into gales of hysterical laughter. We also used to enjoy singing a song called "I Wonder Who's Kissing Her Now," the "now" being synonymous with the "dock" Daisy had a light on. Oh my, we were such great wits back then.

"It would be a shame," Susan said morosely, "if Joanna couldn't be there."

"Be where?" I said.

"The wedding," Susan said. "She virtually grew *up* with Daisy, you know, and her mother *is* getting remarried, after all, and I know she . . ."

"No," I said, "I'm sorry."

"What?" Susan said.

134

"I won't forfeit another weekend."

"I haven't even *asked* yet," Susan said.

"You've asked. And the answer is no."

"The wedding's on Saturday. I thought I might bring Joanna over to your place on Sunday morning . . ."

"No."

"This means a *lot* to her, Matthew!"

"I doubt it. But if she *really* wants to go see Rhett Robinson marry—who's she marrying, anyway? Some guy named Heathcliff? Ahab? Beowulf?"

"His *name* happens to be Joshua Rosen," Susan said coldly. "He *happens* to be Jewish."

"That's very nice," I said, "but I don't care if the *Pope* is marrying Bo Derek. The last time I saw Joanna was on . . ."

"Do you know what you are?" Susan asked, and suddenly the Witch rode into view on a broomstick trailing brimstone and fire and eyes of newt. "You are an unmitigated son of a bitch. Your daughter's best girl friend in the *entire* world . . ."

"Daisy Robinson is not Joanna's best friend. Susan, I really don't want to get into an argument, okay? If Joanna *really* wants to go to the wedding . . ."

"She *does* want to go!"

"Then have her call me. If she honestly wants to go, I'll . . ."

"You'll pressure her, right?"

"No, I won't pressure her. All she has to do is say, 'Dad . . .'"

"*Dad!*" Susan sneered, as if the word, coming from my lips, were sheer blasphemy.

"I *am* her father," I said with some dignity.

"*Some* father," Susan said. "Denying her the opportunity to . . ."

"Not if she wants to go," I said. "All she has to do is tell me so herself."

"I sometimes wonder why God made you so fucking mean," Susan said.

"Just ask her to call me, okay?" I said, and hung up. My hands were trembling. I truly hated these bouts with Susan. I was still shaking when Cynthia knocked on the door and came into my office.

If a person didn't know that Cynthia Heullen had a mind like a switchblade knife, he would automatically assume she was a beach bum. This was because she spent every weekend outdoors—swimming, boating, shelling, gardening, walking, whatever—and as a result had become the tannest, blondest young woman in all Calusa. I think she even spent *rainy* weekends outdoors. Cynthia was twenty-five years old and blessed with a grasp of the law that sometimes caused envy in our modest offices. Frank or I would often be fumbling around for a pertinent section in the Florida Statutes, fitfully leafing through pages, and Cynthia would pop up out of the blue with "Child Abuse, Section 827.03," even though she had never studied law in her life, and had come to us as a receptionist directly after she'd earned her Bachelor of Arts degree at USF. Frank and I kept begging her to go to law school, promising to take her into the firm the moment she passed the Florida bar exams. But Cynthia was happy with being exactly what she was. I knew very little about her private life; Karl Jennings, the youngest lawyer in our firm, told me in confidence that she was living with an itinerant folksinger out on Sabal Key. I told him I didn't want to hear anything more about it. Whatever Cynthia did on her own time, in the sun or out of it, was her own business. In the office, she was resourceful, hardworking, even-tempered, quick-witted, and good-humored. And that was more than enough.

She looked at my face.

"I'm never going to put her through again," she said. "*Never.*"

"We occasionally have to talk," I said.

"I don't even *know* her, and I hate her," Cynthia said, shaking her head. "Your car's here. The mechanic's outside, wants to know if you'll pay for it now, or should they bill you?"

"Ask them to bill me. What'd he do to it?"

"Put in a new battery and a new fan belt."

"Why a new fan belt?"

"He said the old one was shot."

"Did he fix the windshield wipers?"

"He didn't say anything about windshield wipers."

"I guess I forgot to tell him about them."

"Do you want him to take the car back? To fix the . . . ?"

"No, no. Don't forget to get the keys from him."

"I won't. Also, there's a lady outside to see you. A Miss McKinney."

"*Mrs.* McKinney, do you mean?"

"*Miss* McKinney," Cynthia said. "About my age, I'd guess, long and lovely and almost as blonde as I am. She says it's personal."

"Ask her to come in," I said.

"She's dressed for the beach," Cynthia said, and surprised me with a wink.

Sunny McKinney wasn't quite dressed for the beach, but neither was she dressed appropriately for a visit to a law office. You get to know a person's colors; her mother's were white, hers were purple. She was wearing very short purple shorts and purple sandals, and a braless purple T-shirt. She was carrying the same purple leather shoulder bag she'd had with her last Friday night at my house. Her tanned legs looked very long indeed, and her long blonde hair was swept to the back of her head and clasped there with a silver barrette. She seemed very nervous. I did not think it was because she felt underdressed.

"Hi," she said. "I hope you don't mind my breaking in on you this way."

"Not at all," I said.

"I was doing a little shopping, thought I'd drop in."

"Sit down, won't you?"

"Sure," she said, and took the chair opposite my desk and crossed her long legs.

"So," I said, "what's on your mind?"

"Well, first off, I wanted to apologize for Friday night. For using your pool, you know. And for trying to turn you on and all. I realize it was a mean trick. You're old enough to be my father."

Her apology made me feel ancient, which I was sure hadn't

been her intention. I told myself I couldn't *possibly* be old enough to be her father, not unless she'd been born when I was fifteen. But I made no comment.

"So that's the first thing," she said. "I really *am* sorry for the way I behaved that night."

"Okay," I said.

"You mind if I smoke?" she asked.

"Go right ahead."

She reached into her bag, found her cigarettes, shook one free from the pack, and held a purple disposable lighter to it. Everything color-coordinated. The hand holding the lighter was shaking as badly as my own hands had after my little chat with Susan. She blew out a cloud of smoke. I pushed an ashtray across the desk to her.

"I *do* hope I'm forgiven," she said, and smiled suddenly— and a trifle wickedly, I thought—as if absolution were the furthest thing from her mind. The smile dropped from her face almost instantly. It had been a smile generated by habit; Sunny McKinney was a natural flirt. She could not help being seductive even while she was *apologizing* for having been seductive. I waited. I remembered Cynthia's wink just before she'd left the office. Sunny uncrossed her legs, and then recrossed them in the opposite direction. I kept waiting.

"I suppose you told Bloom everything I said that night, huh?" she asked at last.

"I did."

"What'd *he* think?"

"He thought it was interesting."

"About Jack stealing my mother's cows, I mean."

"Yes, I know."

"That's all he found it, huh? Interesting?"

"He's still toying with the idea that your brother may have been trafficking in dope."

"No, no," Sunny said. "You tell him he's wrong."

She was silent for several seconds, puffing on her cigarette, reaching over to flick the ash into the ashtray. She was jiggling one foot now. I wondered why she was so nervous.

"Are you all right?" I asked.

"Huh? Oh yeah, sure."

"You seem worried about something."

"No, no," she said, and shook her head, and stubbed out the cigarette. "Well, yes," she said, "I guess I am. Worried, I mean."

"About what?"

"You remember I told you I was listening in on this conversation? With Jack and the Spanish guy? Last October, remember?"

"Yes?"

"The guy he was selling the cows to, remember?"

"*If* that's what he was doing."

"Oh sure," she said, "that was it, all right. So . . . I've been thinking . . . suppose it was this Spanish guy who stabbed Jack? I mean, suppose he was afraid Jack would *tell* on him or something? And he went there to . . . well . . . to make sure he *wouldn't* tell. 'Cause this is *rustling*, you know, this is serious. I mean, it didn't even have to be the Spanish guy *himself*. He could've sent somebody else to kill Jack, you know what I mean?"

"Your mother thinks Jack knew whoever killed him," I said.

"She does?" Sunny looked suddenly nervous again. She reached into her bag for another cigarette. "How does she . . . I mean, how does she figure *that*?" She held the purple lighter to the cigarette. Her hand was shaking again.

"The door has a peephole in it," I said. "He wouldn't have let in anyone he didn't know."

"Maybe the guy had a key," Sunny said.

"The police are considering that possibility."

"They are?" she said, and puffed on the cigarette. "Well, sure, it's a good possibility. Jack used to all the time tell the resident manager it was okay to let me in. Whenever I was supposed to meet him there, he told the lady in the office to let me in. With her passkey, you know? Maybe whoever killed him knew somebody in the office. Who gave him a key to get in."

"Maybe," I said.

"Sure, that's a possibility," she said, and nodded.

"Did you go there often?" I asked. "To visit your brother?"

"Oh, every now and then." Her eyes widened. "You don't think *I'm* the one who was there that night, do you?"

"No, I simply . . ."

"I mean, is that what *Bloom* thinks? That *I'm* the one Jack let into his apartment?"

"I'm sure he doesn't think that. And neither do I."

"Then why'd you ask me if I went there a lot?"

"I was only wondering how close you and your brother were."

"Close as most brothers and sisters," she said. "If *that's* what Bloom thinks, that I killed him, he ought to be put away, I mean it. In a hospital for the mentally deranged, I mean it. Jesus, would I even *be* here if I had anything to do with . . ."

"I still don't know why you're here," I said.

"I *told* you why. I'm worried. I'm *scared*, all right?"

"Why?"

"Because whoever killed my brother might decide to kill me next."

"What makes you think so?"

"I heard them talking on the *phone*, didn't I?"

"Yes, but they didn't know you were listening, did they?"

"How do *you* know that?"

"Well, I *don't* actually know it for a . . ."

"Neither do I. Suppose they heard a click or something? Suppose they heard me breathing?"

"They still wouldn't have known who it was."

"Who else *could* it have been? There're only two people living in that house, my mother and me. It had to've been either one of us, am I right?"

"Assuming they *did* know someone was listening in . . ."

"It's a possibility," Sunny said.

"Then your mother would be in danger as well."

"Yeah, well, I'm not worried about my mother, she's old enough to take care of herself. I'm worried about *me*, Mr. Hope.

About somebody coming at me with a knife or a gun, the same way . . ."

"What makes you mention a gun?"

"What?" she said.

"Your brother was stabbed."

"I'm just saying. *Any* weapon. A club, a hatchet, *whatever.*"

"But you specifically mentioned a gun."

"It was the first thing that popped into my mind. What *is* this?" she said sharply, her pale eyes flaring.

"I'm only trying to . . ."

"Trap me," she said. "I shouldn't have come here. I thought if I told you . . ." She stopped abruptly. She shook her head.

"Told me what?"

"How worried I am, how *scared* I am . . ."

"Your brother was killed on the eighth of August," I said. "Today's the twenty-third, that was more than two weeks ago. When did you start getting scared?"

"I was scared when I came to your house Friday night."

"You didn't seem scared."

"I told you what Jack was *into*, didn't I? I told you he was stealing my mother's cows."

"But you didn't seem scared."

"I was *scared*, believe it. I wouldn't have come on with you the way I did if I wasn't scared."

"But you're even more scared now. Why?"

She stubbed out her cigarette. "Forget it," she said. "This was a mistake."

"Does your fear have anything to do with Avery Burrill's murder?"

"I don't know anybody named Avery Burrill," she said.

"He's the man who was selling your brother a bean farm."

"I don't know him. I never heard his name before this minute."

"He was shot to death," I said.

"I didn't know that."

"Yesterday," I said.

"This is the first I'm hearing of it."

"It's in the newspaper this morning."

"I never look at the Mickey Mouse papers down here."

"It was on the radio too. And on television."

"I don't *know* the goddamn man!"

"He was shot with a .38 Smith & Wesson."

"All right, I believe you."

"Your brother owned a .38 Smith & Wesson, didn't he?"

"I don't know what kind of gun it was."

"But you know he owned a gun?"

"Yes. He used to keep it in his dresser drawer."

"You *saw* the gun?"

"I saw it."

"Where?"

"In his dresser drawer, I just *told* you. Out at the ranch. Before he moved."

"What were you doing in his dresser drawer?"

"I was looking for something."

"Looking for what?"

"Nail clippers."

"And you found your brother's gun."

"Yeah. He was mad as hell. He really smacked me around good that day. For fiddling with the gun. I think he was afraid I could've hurt myself with it."

"Sounds like that was a regular thing with him," I said. "Smacking you around."

"He had big hands, my brother."

"When was the last time you saw that gun?"

"That day when I was looking in his dresser. Four, five months ago."

"Do you know if he took it with him when he moved into the condo?"

"No, I don't."

"Did you ever *see* it in his apartment? At the condo?"

"I just told you the last time I saw it was four, five months ago. In his dresser drawer."

"And not after that?"

"No."

"Then you don't know whether it was in his apartment on the night he was killed."

"No, I don't. You're really terrific, Mr. Hope, you know that? I come here because I'm scared out of my wits, and you turn it all around . . ."

"I haven't turned anything around, Sunny."

"Yes, you have," she said. "You think just what Bloom thinks, don't you? You think *I* had something to do with . . ."

"I didn't say . . ."

" . . . my brother's death. Well, I *didn't!* So long, Mr. Hope," she said and rose suddenly. "Thanks a lot for nothing." She went immediately to the door, opened it, said, "See you around," and then walked out, slamming the door behind her.

I had the distinct impression that I'd blown it.

She had come there to tell me something, but I'd bludgeoned her with questions before she could get it out. A frightened young girl had run from my office because I'd been too damn impatient to listen. A good lawyer, like a good actor, is supposed to listen. I had behaved like a bad lawyer and an inexperienced cop, sticking my nose into business that was rightfully Bloom's, and causing Sunny McKinney to panic and run. My partner Frank kept telling me that I was entirely too guilty for a WASP. He said only Jews and Italians were supposed to feel as much guilt as I did. Maybe I had Jewish or Italian ancestors. All I know is that I was *still* feeling guilty when I left the office at a quarter to five for my scheduled meeting with Bloom. In fact, I was wishing he'd beat my brains out and leave me bleeding and unconscious on the gymnasium floor.

Considering the size of the Calusa P.D., the police gym was spacious and well equipped. Cops—I assumed they were cops—swarmed all over the place, lifting weights, working out on the ropes and the parallel bars, shadowboxing, generally getting themselves in shape for their day-to-day combat with the bad guys. Bloom and I came out onto the polished wood floor, hauled a pair of mats to a relatively clear area, and squared off facing each other.

"You ready?" he asked. He was wearing a gray sweatsuit that looked a bit baggy on him, the result of his recent bout with hepatitis and his subsequent weight loss.

"Ready," I said, and Bloom jackknifed a flat-footed kick at my groin, aborting the attack an instant before what would have been an excruciatingly painful collision.

In the next hour or so, I learned a great deal from Detective Morris Bloom.

My phone was ringing when I let myself into the kitchen. The clock on the wall read ten minutes to seven. I hadn't heard from Joanna before I'd left the office, and I was hoping it might be her now. It was Veronica.

"Hi," she said, "I've got a problem."

"What's the matter?"

"Sunny took the car this morning, and she isn't back yet. I've been trying you at the office . . ."

"I was with Bloom."

"Oh?" she said. "Anyway, the Jeep's gone too, Rafe took it to Ananburg with him. And the hand is out somewhere in the pickup truck. I just don't have any transportation."

"I'll come there," I said.

"Are you sure you want to? It's a long way, Matthew."

"I'm sure I want to."

"I'll get some steaks ready," she said. "Hurry."

I showered and changed my clothes and was on the road by a quarter to eight. The Ghia ran like a Rolls-Royce, through flat pasture land flecked with grazing cows. Behind the car, the sun was beginning to drop slowly below the rim of the horizon, tinting the sky a fiery orange-red that spilled over into the countryside as a lush purple. In the palmettos and cabbage plants, the birds chirped their incessant sunset songs. As I drove eastward through the lingering dusk, I thought of Veronica waiting for me, and I remembered her brief excursionary flight on the verbs *to see* and *to watch*. I wanted to *see* her. I also wanted to *watch* her. I thought with pleasure of my new battery and my new fan belt, and of how reassuring it was to be driving along on such a glorious night, secure in the knowledge that my battery wasn't dead and my fan belt wasn't shot. My mind soared imaginatively, the way Veronica's had last night.

To a mechanic, a "shot" fanbelt was a worn one. To a bartender, a "shot" was a one-ounce glass of whiskey. To a decathlon champion, a "shot" was an iron ball to be thrown as far as he could throw it. To a tennis player, a "shot" was what he stroked over a net. To a junkie or a physician, a "shot" was an injection by hypodermic syringe. To a motion-picture director, a "shot" was any given camera setup. And to Morris Bloom, who discussed sibling spanking with all the aplomb of Krafft-Ebbing, a "shot" was something fired from a gun you could buy off a shelf like a ripe banana. I was very happy I wasn't learning English as a foreign language; I was far too old to be taking a shot at such a formidable task.

Grinning, I drove through the open gate of the M.K. Ranch and onto the dirt road that led to the big white house. The sky had gradually shaded from purple to deep blue and then to the blackest of blacks, with only a few faint stars timidly glowing. Out on the pasture, I heard the lowing of a solitary cow, and then there was silence except for the chatter of the insects in the grass on either side of the road. The compound was empty and still, not a vehicle in sight anywhere. The mobile trailer home and the manager's house were both dark, but the main house was aglow with light. I parked the car near the rusting gas tanks and went up the steps to the front entrance. I opened the screen door and knocked on the closed inner door.

"I'm out back!" Veronica called.

Following her voice, I went around the side of the house to a small patio that began where the greenhouse ended. Veronica was standing over a barbecue grill, looking at the glowing red coals under the grate. Amber light from inside the house spilled onto the patio. She was wearing white again—white shorts and sandals, a white T-shirt. A white plastic apron covered her to her thighs. The red lettering on it read, DON'T KISS ME, I'M COOKING.

I kissed her.

I kissed her hungrily.

She said, "Wow."

I kissed her again.

"I missed you," she said.

"Me too."

"I'll put the steaks on," she said. "We'll eat here, if that's all right, and then we can go to your place later. Will that be all right?"

"Sure," I said.

She was still in my arms. She looked up into my face.

"It's just . . . Sunny may be home later, I don't like to . . ."

"I understand."

"Are you sure? I hate to sound so damn Puritan."

"You don't sound Puritan."

"Especially when the wandering child in question . . . well, never mind. I'd just feel more comfortable at your place."

"So would I."

I kissed her again.

"You have to stop doing that," she said. "Until later. Otherwise, I'll lose all my maternal resolve."

"Okay," I said, and kissed her again.

"Oh, wowwwww," she said, and fell limply against me. "Is this how Jesus felt in the wilderness?" She kissed me on the chin. "Let me get the steaks," she said. "What would you like to drink? I made a pitcherful of martinis, but I can mix anything you . . ."

"A martini would be lovely."

"I'll bring the pitcher out," she said.

As she started around the house, a phone began ringing inside. She looked up, listened, nodded, and then said, "That's Sunny's, upstairs. I never answer it." She blew me a kiss and disappeared into the night. I sat near the grill and looked up at the sky. There were more stars now. I could even make out some of the constellations. It would be a beautiful day tomorrow—in the morning, anyhow. The telephone upstairs stopped ringing. I thought suddenly of Sunny's visit to my office. I did not relish the thought of telling Veronica about it, but I knew I would have to. I sat there thinking it was sad when a man of thirty-eight could remember most clearly only the mistakes he'd made in his life. I wondered if Veronica was a mistake. Fifty-seven years old, I thought. And then she came into view around the corner of the house again, juggling a martini pitcher and a platter of meat and three ears of corn wrapped in foil and a pair of short glasses, and she looked so utterly, adolescently helpless in that moment that all I wanted to do was hold her close again and reassure her that fifty-seven didn't mean a damn and this definitely wasn't a mistake. I rushed to unburden her.

"Just in the nick," she said, and the telephone upstairs began ringing again. "Never rings when she's here," she said, rolling her eyes. "Only when she's out. The most maddening thing in the world. Pour us some martinis, okay? How do you like your steaks? Did I tell you how handsome you look? Satan, get thee behind me."

The martinis were cold and crisp and very, very dry. As Veronica put the steaks on, she mentioned idly that beef sometimes made a big circle out of Florida to the feeding pens out West and then back again to Florida, where it ended up on the dinner table. "For all I know," she said, "these steaks may once have been calves on the M.K."

I thought about her eating her own cows. "Do you ever get attached to any of them?" I asked. "The cows?"

"Never. It's a business, Matthew."

I thought of Sunny telling me those weren't pets out there. I sighed.

"What is it?" she asked at once.

"Sunny came to see me this afternoon," I said.

"Oh? what about?"

I told her she'd been there to tell me about something that was obviously troubling her. I told her I'd blown it by bearing down too hard on her, asking a lot of questions, generally behaving like a benevolent bully. I told her I felt guilty as hell about scaring off a girl who was *already* scared.

"But of *what*?" Veronica asked, and I realized all at once that I'd never told her about Sunny's speculation that her brother had been rustling cows right here on the M.K.

I hesitated.

"Matthew," she said, "never keep anything from me, okay? I was married to a man who was as secretive as a rock. What happened with Ham might never have happened if Drew had ever dared to *reveal* himself to me. Whatever it is, you can tell me."

I told her.

She listened intently. The steaks sizzled and popped on the grill. Occasionally she nodded. Once she said, "I didn't think Sunny knew that much about cows." I kept talking. When I got to the end of it, she was silent for several moments. Then she said, "I feel like running out there right this minute to count all my damn cows." She shook her head. "It's hard to believe . . . but it's equally hard to disbelieve. He could have done it, Matthew. I wouldn't put it past him." She was silent again. "That's why you were asking me about people with Spanish accents, right?" she said, and nodded. "Is that who Sunny's afraid of? The man she heard on the phone?"

"Well, that's what seemed so farfetched to me. That's when I began asking all my questions. She seemed genuinely convinced that the man might have known she was on the line, but . . . I just don't know. I had the feeling there was something else she wanted to tell me. She seemed so damn *scared*, Veronica . . ."

"Well, *I'd* be scared too. If I thought a murderer . . ."

"Yes, but why all of a *sudden*? Last Friday night, she didn't seem at *all* . . ."

I cut myself off.

"Oops," Veronica said.

I looked at her.

"What *about* last Friday night?" she asked. "You saw her? My daughter? Last Friday night?"

"Yes."

"Where?"

"She came to my house."

"Oh?"

"That's when she told me about Jack."

"At your house?"

"Yes."

"How long was she there?"

"An hour or so."

"Did you go to bed with *her*, too, Matthew?"

"No."

"Are you sure?"

"I'd remember," I said, and smiled.

Veronica smiled back.

"I'd better check those steaks," she said.

I wasn't sure I trusted that smile. She stood at the grill silently, her back to me, cutting into the steaks to test them, forking them onto separate plates, clasping the corn with tongs, and finally carrying the plates over to a picnic table and bench already set with utensils, glasses, and napkins. She took two bottles of beer from a cooler, and plunked them down beside each plate.

"Eat," she said. "Before it gets cold."

We began eating in silence.

The steak was very good, but the silence was foreboding.

"If I thought for a *minute*," she said at last, "that you went to bed with Sunny . . ."

"I didn't."

"I'm glad," she said. "Because I'd stick this steak knife right in your heart."

I believed her.

She smiled radiantly. Lowering her voice confidentially, she said, "Of course, Sunny *can* be very flirtatious, I know that, outrageously so." She looked across the table at me. The smile was still on her face. "Provocative, too," she said, "a maddening child, really." Her eyes met mine. "Did she flirt with you, Matthew?"

"Yes."

"Was she . . . provocative?"

"Yes."

"But you didn't touch her."

She was watching me expectantly. The smile on her mouth encouraged complete honesty. The smile was telling me she was my friend as well as my lover. The smile was assuring me that if indeed I *had* been intimate with her daughter, she would be understanding and sympathetic because she knew full well how outrageously flirtatious and maddeningly provocative Sunny could be. But the smile never quite reached her pale eyes, and a moment ago she had told me she would stick a steak knife in my heart. I was very glad I was able to tell her the truth.

"I didn't touch her," I said.

She nodded.

"Why not?" she asked.

I told her why not. I told her about my attempted seven-dollar rape in Chicago. I told her about breaking up with Dale. I told her about Charlie and Jeff using me for a beanbag. I told her there were some things a person just didn't do if he expected to live with himself ever again. She listened the way she'd been listening when I'd told her about her son stealing cows. When I finished, she said, "I think I love you, do you know that?"

We both turned at the sudden sound of an automobile out front.

"There's Sunny," she said. "If you so much as *look* at her, Matthew . . ."

"Do you realize what you just said?"

"Can't remember a word of it," she said airily, and got up and called, "We're out back!" She came around to my side of the table. She cupped my chin in her hand. She kissed me so fiercely that I almost fell off the bench. She squeezed my chin hard, said, "Mm, *you!*" and then released it and went to sit on the other side of the table again, the prim and proper mother awaiting the arrival of her prodigal daughter.

Jackie Crowell came into view around the corner of the house. He was wearing blue jeans, boots, and a striped T-shirt. He stood awkwardly at the far end of the patio, looking very much like a shit-kicking bumpkin. "Hello, Mrs. McKinney," he said. "Mr. Hope." His dark eyes looked very somber and concerned. He was not smiling.

"Where's Sunny?" Veronica said, glancing into the shadows beyond the house.

"She's not here, huh?" Crowell said.

"No, she isn't."

"I was hoping she might be. I been calling, but I got no answer. I figured she might be downstairs, didn't want to run up to answer the phone. When I drove her here this morning . . ."

He hesitated. He looked at me. He looked at Veronica.

"She . . . uh . . . was at my place last night," he said apologetically, and shrugged his massive shoulders. "Anyway . . . uh . . . before I went to work this morning, I drove her back here. She said she wanted to pick up the Porsche, go do some shopping. She said she'd be back at the apartment sometime this afternoon. But when I got back from work . . ."

"What time was that?" I asked. Sunny McKinney had come to my office at about one-thirty. She'd left about twenty minutes later. Assuming she'd already done her shopping . . .

"When I got back from work, you mean? Around five-thirty," he said. "She wasn't home yet."

I could see that Veronica took mild offense at his use of the word *home* to define Sunny's residence, much the same as I did whenever Susan referred to *her* house as Joanna's home. But she said nothing.

"I'm a little worried about her," Crowell said. "She's usually either home or here, so . . . I mean, where can she be?"

Veronica looked at her watch. I looked at mine. It was close to nine-thirty. In Calusa, the department stores in the malls were open till nine. There was no conceivable way that Sunny could still be out there shopping. The knowledge was on Veronica's face. It was on Crowell's as well.

"Her clothes are gone, too," he said. He looked at Veronica, apologetically again. "The clothes she kept at my place. Only thing she left was a bathing suit."

"What was she wearing the last time you saw her?" I asked.

"Purple shorts. A purple T-shirt."

"What time was that?"

"When I dropped her off here? Must've been about eight-thirty this morning."

"And she said she planned to do some shopping?"

"Yeah. Downtown."

"Did she say anything about wanting to see me?"

"What do you mean?"

"Coming to my office?"

"No. *Did* she come there?"

"At about one-thirty."

"No, she didn't mention that," Crowell said. "Just that she was going shopping."

The silence was almost palpable. The intrusive chatter of the insects in the grass sounded like a sudden musical sting in a horror movie, presaging dire events to come.

"Well," I said, "It's only nine-thirty . . ."

My voice trailed off. The insects kept up their ominous chatter, intensifying the silence on the patio.

"Maybe I ought to check around town," Crowell said. "Places we hang out in."

"That might be a good idea," I said. "But really, I don't think there's any cause for alarm."

I looked at him. His eyes told me he thought there *was* cause for alarm.

"Well, sorry to've bothered you," he said. "I'll look around, let you know if I find her."

"Matthew, give him your number," Veronica said. Apparently her own concern was not great enough to keep her glued here to the ranch all night. I fished in my wallet for a card, and wrote my home phone number on the back of it. "You can call us there when you find her," Veronica said. "Meanwhile, I'll keep trying here. I'll let you know when she gets home." She stressed the word *home*. Whatever else Crowell may have thought, home to Veronica was not a dinky little apartment in New Town. She had also used the word *when*. Veronica was obviously less concerned about her daughter's meandering than I'd thought; "*when* she gets home" was a far cry from "*if* she gets home."

"Do you have *my* number?" Crowell asked.

"You'd better give it to me," I said.

I wrote it down on the back of another card, and stuck the card in my wallet.

"Well," he said, and stood shuffling his feet for another moment. "Sorry to've interrupted your supper." He turned awkwardly and walked off the patio into the darkness. Moments later, we heard his car starting. We listened to the sound of its engine fading on the road to the main gate. The insects took over again.

"Good," Veronica said.

"Good?"

"She's packed up and left the little jerk. Maybe there's hope for her yet." She smiled and came around the table to where I was sitting. "The hell with the dishes," she said. "Let the raccoons have a field day." She kissed me fiercely. "You ready to go?" she asked.

Pillow talk.

Privileged communication.

She told me she was seriously concerned about the difference in our ages. I told her she had the body of a goddess, the intelligence of a computer, the wisdom of a guru, and the passion of a

154

fanatic. She told me that if all that was meant to be flattering, I had a lot to learn about sweet-talking. I told her that in the past two nights she'd taught me more about women than I'd learned in all my thirty-eight years. She said, "That's exactly what I *mean*, Matthew. There's a nineteen-year difference. When will you be thirty-nine?"

"In February."

"God," she said, "that makes it even *worse*! I'll be fifty-eight next *month*!"

"The better to eat you," I said.

"What on earth does *that* mean?" she asked, grinning.

"Pretending to be Grandma," I said. "Shame on you."

"It was the *wolf* who pretended to be Grandma."

"It's the wolf right here in bed with you," I said, and bared my teeth.

"I hate fairy tales; I think they're designed to frighten children," she said. "I'd better try Little Red Riding Hood again. It's almost eleven." She had tried the number at ten-thirty, and there'd been no answer. She reached over me for the bedside phone. I ran my hand along the smooth curve of her back. "Not while I'm talking," she said, and dialed the number again. My hand wandered, seeking her out. "*Matth*-yew!" she warned. She held the receiver to her ear, listening. She let the number ring for a long time. She put the receiver back on the cradle then, and rolled over to her side of the bed again. People had their favorite sides in bed, I'd noticed. Veronica's side was the right.

"That's what the *real* problem is," I said. "Never mind our ages."

"Am I supposed to be reading your scattergun mind?" she asked.

"We both prefer the right-hand side of the bed."

"Where do you suppose she is? If she *really* moved out of his apartment . . ."

"Well, we don't know that."

"She packed all her clothes, didn't she?"

"Maybe she was taking them to the cleaners."

"All of them?" She shook her head. "That's my good profile," she said.

"Talk about scattergun minds."

"The left one. That's why I always position myself on the right. In bed."

"Is that an intractable position?" I asked. "Or can it be negotiated?"

"Maybe," she said. "Posit me an alternate position."

"How about the missionary position?"

"You know any good preachers?" she asked, and threw her arms and her legs wide.

"I prefer practicing to preaching," I said.

"Come practice," she said.

We were still practicing at midnight.

"Think we'll ever get it right?" she asked.

"We have all eternity," I said.

"Until Grandma drops dead on you one night."

"Grandma still seems reasonably healthy," I said.

"Except for her heart," Veronica said. "Grandma has lost her heart. *And* her daughter, it looks like. I'd better try her again."

She reached for the phone.

"Keep your hands where they belong," she said, and began dialing.

"Just trying to keep them warm," I said.

"You make me jump when you do that."

She was holding the receiver to her ear now, listening intently.

"Anything?" I asked.

"It's ringing."

She let it ring.

"Where the hell *is* she?" she said, and slammed down the receiver. "Maybe you ought to call Jackie, find out if she's there. I hate talking to that little moron."

I got out of bed and went to where I'd left my wallet on the dresser.

"You have a beautiful behind," Veronica said.

"U.S. Prime," I said. "Plenty of fat."

"We call it marbelization. And you're *not* fat."

"A hundred and ninety pounds, live weight. What'd I do with that card?"

"*I'm* the one who's fat," she said. "Fat and *old*."

"Young and slender," I said.

"'And tall and lovely,'" Veronica sang, "'the girl from Ipanema comes walking . . .'"

"Here it is," I said.

"You don't like the way I sing, huh?"

"I *love* the way you sing. Do you know 'I Wonder Who's Kissing Her Now'? It's from a musical called *The Light on Daisy's Dock*."

"I never know what the hell you're talking about, do you realize that?"

"Sex talk," I said.

"Big talker," she said. "Come here and kiss me."

"I thought you wanted me to call Jackie."

"Jackie can wait. Grandma feels an urgent need."

"Grandma's insatiable."

"Grandma's in Matthew Hope's bed, *that's* what she's in. Come over here."

"Oh my, you have *such* big eyes, Grandma."

"The better to see you," she said, opening them wide. "God, look at that thing!" she said, and reached for me.

I didn't get to call Crowell till almost one o'clock. He sounded fuzzy with sleep when he answered the phone. "Hullo?" he said.

"Jackie," I said, "this is Matthew Hope. Have you had any luck?"

"Huh?" he said.

"Finding Sunny?"

"Oh," he said. "No. I looked everyplace I could think of."

In the background I heard someone ask, "Who is it, Jackie?"

"She's not there with you now, is she?" I said.

"No . . . uh . . . that's the television. I was watching television."

I thought it remarkable that the girl on television knew his name, but I made no comment.

"You let us know if she comes back there, will you? You have my number."

"Yeah, okay," Crowell said.

"Whatever time it is, you call, okay?"

"Sure," he said.

"You want me to give you the number again?"

"No, I have it."

"Sorry I woke you up," I said.

A trick shyster-lawyer ploy. He did not fall for it.

"I was watching television," he said, and hung up.

I put the receiver back on the cradle.

"There's a girl with him," I said.

"Sunny?"

"I don't know."

"Let's go there," she said. "I *hate* it when she makes me worry this way. If she's there with him . . ."

"We can't just break in on him in the middle of the night," I said. "If the girl *isn't* Sunny . . ."

"Then let's call the police. Call your friend Bloom."

"At one in the morning?"

"My daughter's missing," she said flatly. "If she's not with that little twerp and she's not home, then she's missing. I want a cop to go over there, Matthew. I don't think Bloom will find that an unreasonable request."

"How reasonable will his *wife* find it?" I asked. "Calling at one o'cl—"

"Five *past* one," Veronica said. "Nobody asked her to marry a civil servant. Call him, Matthew. Will you please call him?"

I tried the Public Safety Building first, on the off-chance that Bloom was working the night tour. The detective who answered the phone told me he was expected at eight tomorrow morning.

He amended this to say they usually came in at seven-forty-five to relieve what he called the graveyard shift. That meant that Bloom would have to be up and around by seven at the very latest—and it was now one-ten by the bedside clock. Reluctantly, I dialed his home number. He sounded wide awake when he answered the phone.

"I was sitting here watching a beer commercial on television," he said. "I can't even have a *beer* till October fifteenth. I'm sitting here counting the minutes. You recovered from all that kicking and scratching this afternoon?"

"I'm sorry to be calling you at home," I said, "but . . ."

"Don't be ridiculous. What is it?"

I told him about Sunny McKinney's visit to my office that afternoon. I told him how frightened she'd seemed at the time. I told him that she'd left Crowell's apartment and had taken all her clothes with her. I told him she hadn't gone back to the ranch and Crowell claimed she wasn't with him now, although I'd heard a girl's voice in the background when I'd talked to him a few minutes ago. He listened to all of this very patiently.

"You don't know if it was her or not, huh?" he asked at last.

"I couldn't tell."

"If it *was* her, he would've said so, wouldn't he?"

"I can't see any reason for him to have lied."

"So then it *wasn't* her," Bloom said. "Which means we got a missing person on our hands."

"It looks that way."

"And you say she was worried about whoever killed her brother maybe coming after her?"

"That's what she said."

"So she ran," Bloom said. "Better to run than to end up on a slab. First thing I want to do is go over to Crowell's place, find out if that *was* her you heard. If she's there, we got no problem, right? If she isn't there . . ." His voice trailed off. "Well, let's cross that bridge when we come to it. Where are you now, Matthew?"

"Home," I said.

"I'll call you in a little while. Stay put, okay?"

"I'm not going anywhere."

"Talk to you later," Bloom said, and hung up.

He did not call back until two-thirty. Veronica and I were both sitting in the living room, waiting for his call, sipping cognac. Only the pool lights were on. I was wearing my Japanese kimono. Veronica was wearing one of my shirts. When the phone rang, I went into the kitchen and snatched the receiver from the wall hook.

"Hello?" I said.

"Matthew? Sorry to have taken so long," he said. "I just got back from New Town. Here's how it . . ."

"Mr. Bloom?" Veronica's voice said. "This is Mrs. McKinney, I'm on the extension. I'd like to hear this, if you don't mind."

I turned and looked into the living room. It was empty.

There was a long silence while Bloom digested the fact that Veronica was at my house at two-thirty in the morning.

"Sure," he said at last. "This is the way it looks." And he proceeded to tell us how it looked.

He had gone to Crowell's apartment in the New Town housing development, and had banged on the door and announced himself through the door, and at last Crowell had come to answer it in his undershorts. Bloom had asked if he might come in; a lot of people had gathered in the hallway by then, because a police officer in New Town at 1:30 A.M. could only mean that somebody had either been the victim of a crime or the perpetrator of one. Crowell had let him into the apartment, a tiny little place that looked even more cluttered than it had the last time Bloom was there, with dirty laundry and magazines and newspapers all over the floor, but Bloom supposed that was the way teenagers liked to live, like pigs. He went into a side excursion on teenagers, then, to the effect that they were all really uncivilized barbarians until they reached the age of twenty-four or so (I did not bother to mention that adolescence officially ended at the age of twenty), by which time they began to realize that there was more to life than hot-rodding around the city streets and smoking pot and chasing after ladies old enough to be their mothers. I assumed he was referring to Crowell's relationship with Sunny McKinney— or perhaps he was referring to mine with Veronica. I was suddenly very aware of her on the bedroom extension.

Crowell asked to what he owed the pleasure of Bloom's visit (those were the exact words Bloom used, but I doubted Crowell had ever uttered them), and Bloom told him he had hoped to find Sunny there, and asked if she was in the bathroom or something, and Crowell said she was not, but Bloom checked out the bathroom anyway, and found in there a black woman in her early thirties who was wearing nothing but a bath towel, and who told him she didn't know nothing about nothing and she was only there to take a shower 'cause the shower in her apartment wasn't working.

Bloom had then looked around the apartment, and had seen no female clothing in it, except for the black woman's clothes draped over one of the chairs, and a purple bikini bathing suit on the floor. He had asked the black woman how long she'd been there, and she'd told him she'd seen Jackie driving up around eleven and decided to ask him could she use his shower 'cause hers wasn't working and all. Crowell confirmed that he'd concluded his tour of the local hangouts by then, looking for Sunny in vain, and was parking his car outside when Lettie—the black woman's name was Letitia Holmes—had come over to him and asked if she could use his shower. Lettie had indeed smelled of soap. So had Jackie Crowell. ("He always smells of *soap*, did you notice that?" Bloom asked. "He must wash a lot.")

Anyway, Bloom had thanked them both, and had apologized for interrupting their showers or whatever it was he'd interrupted, and then had gone down to the street to find a lot of black people sitting out there on the front stoop. In New Town, he explained, where there wasn't any air conditioning in the apartments, you sometimes found the tenants sitting outside till all hours of the night, hoping to catch a breath of fresh air. The blacks in New Town weren't overly fond of cooperating with the police, not since a cruising Calusa patrolman had senselessly killed a black businessman two years ago and then got off with nothing but a slap on the wrist. But Bloom took great pride in his color-blindness, and he knew that "attitude" was something black people could sense about a white man. He was not surprised when one of the old guys sitting on the stoop told him he'd seen a young blonde girl coming out of the building around four that afternoon, carrying a suitcase and looking like she was in a big hurry. He'd watched her put the suitcase in a red automobile, and he'd seen her driving off toward U.S. 41. A woman confirmed that she had seen the same thing from her window upstairs; a favorite pastime in New Town was spreading a pillow on the windowsill, and then leaning over it to watch the passing parade downstairs. Bloom had thanked everybody, and then found a phone booth in an all-night billiards parlor down the street. He first called the ranch on the off-chance that Sunny had found her way back there, got no answer, and then called his office to have the detective on duty put her name on the missing-persons sheet and send out a BOLO.

"What number did you call?" Veronica asked on the extension. "At the ranch, I mean."

"Well, the number I have for . . ."

"But not my daughter's number? She has her own phone."

"I don't have that number," Bloom said. "If you'll give it to me, I'll try it now."

"I don't want to trouble you," Veronica said. "I can make the . . ."

"I'd rather make it myself, if you don't mind," Bloom said. "Tie up all the loose ends."

Veronica gave him the number and then asked, "What's a Bolo?"

"A be-on-the-lookout-for," he said. "It isn't what it sounds like, it's not only for wanted desperadoes. We usually tack it on to any missing-persons report. It goes out on the computer, covers Florida and six other states."

"Then you must consider this serious," she said.

"Two people have been killed, and your daughter's on the

run," Bloom said. "Yes, Mrs. McKinney, I consider this *very* serious." He sighed and then said, "I'll try your daughter's number now. If I don't get back to you, it means she isn't there. Matthew?" he said.

"Yes, Morrie?"

"What was she wearing when you saw her this afternoon?"

"Purple shorts, purple sandals, and a purple T-shirt."

"Then she changed her clothes before leaving the apartment. The witnesses who saw her go say she was wearing a purple dress and high-heeled shoes. Oh yeah, the red car. Was that *her* car, Mrs. McKinney?"

"The ranch's. It's registered to the M.K."

"What kind of car is it?"

"A Porsche."

"Can you give me the year and registration number, please? I'd like to add those to the BOLO."

She gave him the information he wanted. There was a long silence on the line. Then she said, "Tell me, Mr. Bloom. Are you looking for a frightened young girl on the run . . . or a murderess?"

"I don't know yet, Mrs. McKinney," he said, and sighed again. "All I know is that she's taken off. I guess she'll have to tell us why when we find her."

"Thank you," Veronica said.

"Let's hope that's soon," Bloom said.

The phone rang early the next morning. Veronica was still in the shower. I was in the bedroom knotting my tie. The air-conditioned temperature in the house was seventy-two degrees. But the thermometer outside the bedroom window read eighty-four, and this was still only eight o'clock in the morning. I picked up the receiver.

"Hello?" I said.

"Dad? It's me."

"Joanna, hi," I said.

"Mom said you wanted me to call. The bus'll be here in a minute, so we'll have to make this fast."

"Honey, I wanted to ask you about this wedding . . ."

"Daisy's mother, you mean?"

"Yes. Mom says you want to go to it . . ."

"She shouldn't have told you that."

"That isn't the point. If you *want* to go . . ."

"I haven't seen Daisy in it must be six or seven months. Why would I want to go watch her mother get married? I don't even remember what her mother *looks* like."

"Well, it wouldn't just be *watching* someone get married, Joanna. I'm sure you're invited to the reception as well . . ."

"Sure, lots of grownups getting drunk," Joanna said.

"I'm sure there'll be some people your own age, too. People you and Daisy know."

"You trying to get rid of me or something?" Joanna asked, and I could visualize her grinning on the other end of the line.

"I'm trying to be fair, honey. If you really want to go . . ."

Veronica came out of the bathroom, naked and drying herself with a huge blue bath towel.

"Is it Bloom?" she asked.

I shook my head.

"Is Dale there with you?" Joanna asked.

I felt suddenly embarrassed, as though Joanna and I were hooked up on one of those science-fiction television-phones where we could see each other while we talked, and where she could also see Veronica standing just outside the bathroom door, drying herself.

"No, she isn't," I said.

"Then who was that?"

"One of the cleaning women."

"I thought they came on Tuesdays and Thursdays," Joanna said, puzzled. "Isn't this Wednesday? I keep losing track of what day it is, all those damn papers Mrs. Carpenter keeps assigning. Dad, don't sweat the wedding, okay? I'd rather be with *you*, really. Anyway, Daisy Robinson's a pain. She used to tell me I cheated at jacks, remember?"

"I remember. So what's your decision, honey? Do you *want* to go or not?"

"Of *course* not. What time will you pick me up Friday?"

"Five-thirty?"

"Terrif. I gotta go, Roadrunner's honking the horn. See you Friday, I love you, Dad."

"Love you too, honey," I said, but she was already gone.

I put the receiver back on the cradle. Veronica was watching me from the bathroom door.

"Your daughter?" she asked.

"Yes."

"Is this her weekend with you?"

"This one, and the next one too."

She nodded and went back into the bathroom to hang up the towel. She came out again a moment later, went to the chair where she'd thrown her clothes last night, picked up a pair of white nylon panties, and stepped into them.

"Will I be meeting her?" she asked.

I went back to the mirror and started knotting my tie all over again.

"Matthew?"

"I'm thinking," I said.

"Is there that much to think about?"

"I haven't yet told her about Dale."

"Your former lady friend," Veronica said, and picked up the white shorts. "Who left you for . . . what'd you say his name was? Jim?"

"Jim."

"Hardly ever brings me pretty flowers. Do you know that song? Or was it before your time?" She stepped into the shorts. She zipped them up the back. "That's right, you grew up with the Beatles, didn't you?" she said.

"I was already in law school when the Beatles came along."

"Who, then? Elvis?"

"*And* the Everly Brothers, *and* Danny and the Juniors, *and* . . ."

"Never heard of them," she said, and pulled her T-shirt over her head. "I keep giving away my age, don't I? Are you finished with that mirror? Never mind, I'll use the one in the bathroom." She picked up her handbag and carried it into the bathroom with her. I could see her at the mirror over the sink, brushing her lids with a blue that was a shade darker than her eyes.

"Why'd you tell her I was the cleaning lady?" she asked.

I had not enjoyed lying to Joanna. I liked to believe that our father-daughter relationship was built on mutual trust. But I hadn't seen any way of telling her, at eight o'clock in the morning, that the female voice she'd heard in the background belonged to a woman she didn't know, a woman she'd immediately realize I'd spent the night with. On Joanna's block, in Joanna's entire adolescent neighborhood, Dale was the woman I was supposed to be spending my nights with.

"She caught me by surprise," I said.

"So naturally you said I was the cleaning lady. It's a shame I don't do windows or floors."

"Well, I just didn't know *what* to tell her."

"Maybe you should have tried the truth."

"Not on the phone."

"Of course not."

"She's very fond of Dale."

"Of course she is. How old *is* Dale, anyway, did you tell me? At my age, it's so difficult to remember things."

"Thirty-two."

"Thirty-two, how nice," she said, an edge of saccharine bitchiness to her voice. "They must have been like sisters to each other."

I watched her as she applied lipstick to her mouth. She was the only woman I'd ever met who could look so radiantly beautiful in the morning. She didn't need eye shadow, she didn't need liner, she didn't need lipstick or blush. All she needed was that gloriously naked face with its spatter of freckles across the bridge of the nose. She saw me watching her in the mirror. She winked broadly, and then came out of the bathroom to look at herself in the mirror over the dresser, where the light was better. She tucked a stray wisp of blonde hair behind her ear. She dabbed with a tissue at a tiny smear of lipstick near the corner of her mouth.

"You could have told her I was *me*," she said softly, still studying herself in the mirror. "I *am* me, you know."

"Yes, I know that," I said, and smiled.

"I thought maybe you thought I was the cleaning lady," she said, and smiled back at me in the mirror. She turned and leaned against the dresser. "Will I be seeing you this weekend?" she asked.

"After I break the news to her."

"The news," she repeated.

"About Dale."

"Oh, the breakup."

"Yes."

"For a moment I thought you meant the news about *me*."

"I'll do that in person. When you meet her."

"*Will* I be meeting her, Matthew?"

"Of course you will."

"Of course I will. When?"

"I'll have to call you," I said. "Let me see how it goes with Joanna."

"After you tell her about Dale, you mean."

"Yes."

"Could be traumatic, I suppose."

"Well, she's very fond of her."

"I'm sure. When do you think that might be, Matthew?"

"I'm not following you."

"Sorry. You said you'd have to call me. You said you wanted to see how it went with . . ."

"Oh. Well, I don't *know*, actually. We'll play it by ear. I'll call you as soon . . ."

"I have a better idea," she said. "Call me a taxi instead. *Now*, okay?"

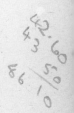

I looked at her.

"Blue Cab or Yellow," she said, "either one'll take me out to the ranch."

"I was planning to drive you out," I said.

"I wouldn't *dream* of troubling you," she said. "I'm sure you have a lot of work to do this morning. You'll probably want to prepare a brief on how best to break the news to your . . ."

"What *is* this, Veronica?"

"You tell me."

"What are you so *angry* about all of a sudden?"

"What makes you think I'm angry? And who says it's all of a sudden? You tell your daughter I'm your cleaning lady, you tell *me* you're not sure you can see me this weekend . . ."

"This is only Wednesday, why are you worrying about the weekend? We've got tonight, we've got . . ."

"That's what *you* think."

"Well, haven't we?"

She put her hands on her hips. She looked me dead in the eye. Her own eyes looked virtually colorless in the wash of light that streamed through the window. When she spoke, her voice was very low.

"The weekend depends on how Joanna reacts to this devastating news, doesn't it?"

"I suppose so."

"This awesome news. This shattering . . ."

"Veronica, you can't expect me to tell her it's over with Dale and then just spring . . ."

"Just spring Grandma on her, right?"

"I think we can drop the 'Grandma' routine, don't you? I don't find it funny anymore."

"Neither does Grandma. If this precious love affair of yours . . ."

"Veronica, you're totally misconstruing . . ."

". . . was so *memorable*, so goddamn *unique* that announcing its demise will cause earthquakes in Southern California . . ."

"For Christ's sake, we sound *married*! All I said . . ."

"All you *said*, Matthew, was that you want to put me on *hold*. Well, I'm afraid that isn't good enough. I spent too many years married to a man who kept me waiting on the other end of the line while he was off frolicking in Denver or Dallas or—look, the hell with it, let's just forget it, okay? *You* spend the weekend worrying about *your* daughter, and *I'll* spend the weekend worrying about *mine*. Roses are red, and violets are blue, so fuck it."

She picked up her sandals.

"Don't bother about a taxi," she said, "I'll *walk* home."

Barefooted, the sandals dangling from her hand by their straps, she walked nonetheless with great dignity out of my bedroom and out of my house.

Like a damn fool, I let her go.

Harry Loomis called me at two o'clock that afternoon. I did not feel like talking to Harry Loomis. I did not feel like talking to *anybody*. All morning long, listening to the various clients with whom I'd had appointments, I kept losing track of the conversations. One woman—who was there to see me about petitioning for a variance that would allow her to build an eight-foot-high wall around her property—actually said, "Mr. Hope, only my psychiatrist doesn't listen the way you don't listen," and stomped out of my office. Another client, who knew me somewhat better, said, "Matthew? Big night last night?" When I blinked at him, he said, "Maybe we ought to save this for another time, huh?" We'd been discussing an outlay of $1,600,000 for prime shorefront property; I could understand his ardent desire for me to get all the details straight. I tried to snap back. I tried to listen. I made notes. When he left the office, I realized that without the notes I wouldn't have been able to remember a word of our conversation. I took at least a dozen calls, doodling while I listened—women in profile, women with short pale hair, always the good profile, the left one. At lunch with a pair of attorneys to whom we'd farmed out a malpractice suit, I listened halfheartedly while one of them told a gynecologist joke. They were specialists in malpractice suits, these two. All their jokes had to do with the medical profession.

A woman goes to see a gynecologist.

The gynecologist says, "What seems to be the trouble?"

The woman says, "My husband keeps complaining I have a very large vagina."

"Well, let's take a look," the gynecologist says.

He puts her up on the table. He puts her feet in the stirrups. He takes a look.

"My *God*, what a huge vagina!" he says. "My *God*, what a huge vagina!"

"Well, you didn't have to say it *twice*," she says.

"I *didn't!*" he says.

The malpractice attorney telling the joke laughed out loud when he delivered the punchline. His partner, who had heard the joke before, laughed so hard I thought he would choke on his sea bass, the catch of the day. I smiled.

I did not feel like talking to Harry Loomis that afternoon. But Cynthia buzzed me at two o'clock to say he was waiting on six, and I sighed heavily and picked up the receiver, and then moved my doodling pad into place.

"Well," he said, "I finally got her on the telephone. Reason it's off the hook most of the day is she *sleeps* all day long."

I assumed he was talking about Burrill's daughter in New Orleans.

"Doesn't get to bed till the crack of dawn. What she is, Mr. Hope, she's a *workin'* girl is what she told me she is. What I mean is she doesn't get to *sleep* till dawn, she gets to *bed* a lot earlier'n that, and a lot more frequently. What she is, Mr. Hope, is a prostitute down there in N'Orleans, is what she is. Hester Burrill. Talked to her early this morning, I think she had a sailor in bed with her, way she kept callin' him 'Ensign,' though that mighta been the man's name, they got funny names in N'Orleans, comes from the French infl'ence, I suspeck. Point is, Mr. Hope, I'm a God-fearin' Baptist who don't want no more truck with prostitutes than's necessary. She's flyin' down here tonight, wants to look over the land tomorrow; you'd think she was inheritin' the Taj Mahal, way she sounded on the phone. The sailor kept tellin' her to stop jumpin' up and down on the bed, and she kept yellin', 'I'm an heiress, Ensign, I'm a fuckin' *heiress!*'—'scuse the language, but that's what she said. You listenin' to all this, Mr. Hope?"

"I'm listening," I said. I was also doodling another left profile.

"What I plan to do, I plan to draw a termination agreement ready for her signature on Friday. I don't want to spend any more time on this than I have to. What I'll recommend is she settle for the four thousand in escrow and the Ford Mustang, and be happy the farm's still hers, that's what I'll recommend. We'll forget all about his sneakers and dirty socks, how's that? Papers'll be all ready for her signature, if she knows how to write. I'd appreciate it if you came by Friday morning, picked them up, got your client to execute them, and that'll be that. I don't like dealin' with prostitutes, Mr. Hope. You can get yourself a terrible disease just shakin' hands with 'em. Can you stop by here Friday morning?"

"Why don't you just put them in the mail?" I said.

"Nossir, I want to expedite this entire matter. You come look them over, make sure they're okay for her signature, and then take 'em with you. I'll have her here in the office at eleven o'clock, that too early for you?"

"Eleven'll be fine," I said.

"Maybe you can drop them off at the ranch there on your way back to Calusa, get Mrs. McKinney to execute 'em, finish the whole thing off in one day."

"Well . . . maybe," I said.

"Anyway, I'll see you here on Friday," he said, and hung up.

7

It was raining when I started for Ananburg on Friday morning. It wasn't supposed to be raining in the morning. In August it was supposed to rain in the afternoon. Maybe the hurricane season was gathering full force. Maybe all of Calusa would get blown out to sea before September when we *normally* started worrying about getting blown out to sea. I kept kicking myself for not having told the mechanic to fix the windshield wipers. I kept telling myself that a fifty-seven-year-old woman should have known better than to place a thirty-eight-year-old man in conflict with his fourteen-year-old daughter. I kept thinking maybe Frank was right; I didn't know how to treat women. I kept thinking I should go over his rules more carefully, study them, learn them by heart. I kept thinking I was about to meet a bona fide hooker, and I wondered if I should treat her like a lady.

Hester Burrill did not look like what I supposed a hooker should look like. I expected her to be wearing a slinky red dress cut low over creamy white cleavage, and slit high on a shapely thigh. I expected her to be wearing bangles and bright shiny beads. I expected her to be swinging a red leather handbag. I expected her hair to be bleached blonde, maybe done in the frizzies, or else worn straight and long and hanging over one eye, the way Veronica Lake used to wear hers. I expected eyes made up to resemble Cleopatra's, heavy rouge on the cheeks, a scarlet lipstick slash on her mouth, and a scarlet letter on her breast.

Hester Burrill looked like a female accountant.

She was wearing a blue linen suit, with a simple white blouse under the jacket. She was wearing matching blue shoes with low heels. A blue leather shoulder bag sat on the floor near her chair. The only piece of jewelry she wore was a high school graduation ring on the middle finger of her right hand. Her hair was black and styled in a straight simple cut, cropped to just below her jawline. She had green eyes that did not seem to harbor all the obscene sexual secrets of the universe, and the only makeup she wore was a muted lipstick on her generous mouth. I guessed she was in her late twenties. The single clue to her occupation was her very pale complexion; I did not suppose Hester Burrill spent much time in the sun.

"Well, I'd like to get this over with soon's we can," Loomis said, searching on his cluttered desktop for the release he'd prepared. He was not chewing tobacco today, I noticed, and he was treating Hester with gentlemanly courtesy and respect; maybe he had read Frank's ten rules. "Miss Burrill took a look at the farm yesterday, and she tells me . . ."

"Some farm," Hester said, and rolled her eyes.

Loomis smiled. "Little run-down, from what she tells me," he said. "She plans on puttin' it on the market again, soon's she's in actual possession. Meanwhile, she's read these papers"—he had them in his hand now—"and she's willin' to sign 'em soon's you look 'em over and say they're all right."

He handed one set of papers to me, and another to Hester. She put her copy back on the desk again, without looking at it.

"What they are," Burrill said, "is a simple agreement by both sides to cancel the contract. The estate turns over the four thousand dollars in escrow and the car used t'belong to McKinney, and in return Miss Burrill here agrees not to press further for satisfaction of the contract between her late father and McKinney."

"This is all assuming, of course . . ."

"Assumin' she's the only heir at law, correct," Loomis said. "I've put that in the first paragraph, and cited Avery's will, as well, a copy of which is attached to the papers. I don't think there'll be any problem with probate, but if for some reason the estate *don't* go to her, you're covered."

"We would not, of course, turn over any property until . . ."

"Until we clear probate, that's in there too. We don't expeck the escrow check *or* the car till it's determined Miss Burrill is the sole heir. If you look at the will, though, you'll see there's no problem."

I looked at the will. I looked through the papers. Everything seemed in order. Hester Burrill smiled when I told this to Loomis.

"I'll get Harriet in here to witness the signature," he said, and pressed a buzzer on his desk. "You think you'll be able to stop by Mrs. McKinney's on your way back? Get the whole thing executed today?"

"I'll have to call her," I said.

"You can use the phone here," Burrill said.

I had not spoken to Veronica since she'd left my house on Wednesday morning. I was reluctant to call her now. "Maybe I'll just drop in," I said.

"Suit yourself," Loomis said. "Miss Burrill's headin' back home tonight, though, be nice if I could tell her before then that everythin's in order."

"I'm sure there won't be any problems."

"Where in hell *is* she?" Burrill said, and stabbed at his buzzer again.

The door opened a moment later. Harriet—the gray lady

from the outer office—came in, looked at me, sniffed the air the way she had the last time she'd seen me, and then said, "I was down the hall," before Loomis had a chance to ask her.

"I need you to witness Miss Burrill's signature," he said.

"Did you want it notarized too?"

"Mr. Hope? I don't think that's necessary, do you?"

"Not if you want this expedited. I'm sure Mrs. McKinney doesn't have a notary public on the ranch."

"Simple release, I don't think we need a notary. What do *you* think, Harriet?"

"Never hurts to have something notarized," Harriet said, and stared at me.

"That means Mrs. McKinney would have to come to the office to sign it," I said.

"Well, I guess it's best," Loomis said. "You want to sign here where I've put these little check marks, Miss Burrill? Both as sole heir and personal representative. Harriet, you go get your seal, will you?"

It took another ten minutes for Hester to sign all four copies of the release, and for Harriet to notarize them. Loomis put the papers into a manila envelope for me. I was standing up to leave when Hester said, "You had lunch yet, Mr. Hope?"

"Well . . . no," I said.

"Come on, I'll buy you lunch."

"That's very kind of you," I said, "but . . ."

"I'm an *heiress*," she said, and smiled. "Come on, let me splurge a little."

"Well . . . okay, sure. But I have an appointment at two . . ."

"We'll make it a quickie. Thanks a lot, Mr. Loomis," she said, rising and extending her hand. "You let me know when everything's settled, okay? How long you think that'll be, Mr. Hope?"

"I'll call Mrs. McKinney as soon as I get back to the office."

"You won't be stopping by the ranch, like you said?"

"Well, if we're going to have these notarized . . ."

"Right, you'd just be wasting time. Let's go eat, okay? I'm starved."

Harriet looked at us both disapprovingly.

The rain had slowed to a drizzle when we came outside. Cowboys stood in sheltered doorways, peering glumly out at the fine mist, their hats tilted low over their faces. We found a little restaurant some three doors up from Loomis's office. We were both mildly wet when we stepped inside; Hester reached for a tissue in her shoulder bag and dabbed at her face with it. A long counter covered the back wall of the place. There were a dozen or so formica-topped tables. The jukebox was playing a country-western song to a room that was vacant except for us and a wait-ress in a green uniform who stood near the juke, tapping her foot in time to the music. We found a table some ten feet from the entrance door. Hester took the chair facing the door. I sat with my back to it. She was putting her shoulder bag on the floor near her chair when the waitress came over.

"Letting up a bit out there?" she asked.

"Seems to be," Hester said, smiling.

"Prolly *snowin'* up north," the waitress said. "You like to see some menus, or you just here for cocktails?"

"I could use a drink," Hester said. "Mr. Hope? How about you? Drink to my good fortune, huh?"

"You win the lottery or something?" the waitress asked, smiling.

"Just about, honey," Hester said. "Let me have a Johnnie Walker Black on the rocks, please."

"And you, sir?"

"The same, with a splash of soda."

"Will you be wantin' menus too?"

"Please," I said.

The moment the waitress left the table, Hester said, "Loomis wants a thousand bucks for settling this for me. You think that's a lot?"

"I don't know how much time he's put in," I said.

"How*ever* much time he put in, it sounds high. How much are *you* charging?"

"I don't know yet. I'll have to figure out the hours. We work on an hourly basis."

"Really?" she said, and smiled. "So do I. How much do *you* get an hour?"

"A hundred dollars."

"Shake, pal," she said, and extended her hand across the table.

The waitress came back with our drinks and the menus.

"Take your time looking them over," she said, and left the table again.

Hester lifted her glass. "Here's to lazy days and easy nights," she said. "Johnnie Walker Black, how *about* that? Never thought I'd see the day." She clinked her glass against mine. "You know how many tricks I'd have to turn for four thousand dollars?"

"Forty," I said.

"Well, that would be the *gross*. I don't get to keep the *whole* hundred, you know. I figure it comes to maybe a seventy-thirty split, after all is said and done. Bobby pays for all my clothes, pays my rent too, gives me spending money. Seventy-thirty is what I figure."

"Who gets the seventy?"

"Oh, *Bobby*, natch. That's generous, though, really. *Some* pimps, they take every cent you earn, only clothes they'll buy you is what you need to work in. Tight across the ass, tits showing, like that. This Loomis character, he's behaving just like a pimp, wants a twenty-five-percent cut. That seems high to me. That paper he wrote up is mostly boilerplate, ain't it?"

"Mostly."

"How many hours you think he spent on it?"

"I have no idea."

"You think *he* gets a hundred an hour, too?"

"Probably seventy-five. Here in Ananburg, I mean. Maybe even less than that."

"Fifty, you think?"

"Maybe."

"So that'd mean he put in twenty hours. I don't see how he could've put in *that* much time, do you?"

"Well, that's something you'll have to discuss with him."

"I think I'll offer him five hundred. That sounds about right to me. You want another one of these?"

"I think we'd better order."

"Sure, but I'd like another one, anyway," she said, and held up her glass to the waitress. The waitress nodded. "I was out looking over Papa's farm yesterday," she said. "Have you seen it? Sheesh, that's some house. Water leaking in all over the place— it sure rains a lot down here, don't it?"

"In the summer months," I said.

"I've seen waterfront whorehouses in Houston that look better than Papa's house. Somebody shot him, huh?"

"Yes."

"I wonder who," she said idly, and turned to the waitress as she brought another round of drinks to the table. "We only wanted *one*, honey," she said, "but you just leave the other, it won't go to waste. We'll be ready to order in a minute." She lifted her fresh drink, said, "Here's to lazy days and easy nights," and then picked up her menu. "All I want's a hamburger and some fries," she said, "but you go on and order anything you like, it's my treat. You think anybody else'll want to buy that farm? I sure would like to sell it, I can tell you that. Maybe set up my own escort service, you know? That's how I got started in this business, I answered this ad said they needed attractive young girls for this escort service. I figured it was legit, who the hell knew? I mean, I was fresh out of high school, my mother was still alive then. She left Papa when I was six or seven, took me to New Orleans. She played jazz piano, Mama did. Not on Bourbon Street, she wasn't all that great. So I go to see this guy, he's interviewing girls for this escort service. He says I'm very elegant-looking and what he's looking for is brilliant conversationalists who can go to fancy restaurants with visiting executives. I'm eighteen years old, this is the first time anybody ever told me I looked *elegant*. As a matter of fact, I was a little dumpy back then, I've lost a lot of weight since—do I look fat to you?"

"No, you look fine."

"I'm still a little plump naked—well, *zaftig*, I guess you'd call it. Anyway, I take the job, and I go to this hotel where this executive is waiting to take me out to a fancy restaurant for some brilliant conversation, and the first thing he says when I get in his room is, 'Take off your clothes, baby.' I gotta tell *you*. I wasn't a virgin, sheesh, *nobody* gets to be eighteen in New Orleans and is still a virgin, but I mean, just like that? Take off your clothes? I told him I was there to go dining and conversing with him, and he lays a hundred-dollar bill on the dresser and he opens his fly and says how about dining on *this*, sweetheart? So I took off my clothes. What it was, you see, this escort service, it was an out-call whorehouse. There are no *real* whorehouses in New Orleans anymore, not since they closed down Storyville. What you've got, it's either the massage parlors or the escort services, or else you find yourself a pimp—he finds *you*, actually—and you drape yourself over a bar every night and wait for a trick to come along. So what'll it be?" she said. "Why don't you have a steak or something? How often do you get to have lunch with an heiress?"

"I'll have a hamburger and fries, too," I said.

"Cheap date," she said, and smiled again, and signaled to the waitress. Her smile was infectious. I found myself smiling, too. She gave the waitress our order, drained her glass, and said, "You sure you don't want this other one?"

"Positive," I said.

"You mind if I drink it?"

"Go right ahead."

She picked up the scotch with the splash of soda in it. "Anyway," she said, "it's safer to have a pimp up there. The escort service, you never knew what kind of creep you'd be meeting, and you didn't have anybody to protect you if like a guy's a weirdo who enjoys beating up girls, you know? I always carry a can of Mace in my bag, anyway, just in case I come up against rough trade, but it's nice to know Bobby'll go out there and beat the shit out of anybody who tries to mess with me. Listen, he's no bargain himself, I mean I wish I had a nickel for every time *he* beat up on me. Still, it's safer. Well, I guess the bartop route is safe, too, go-go dancing in some cheap dive on Bourbon, taking some guy to the back of the place and giving him a blow job in one of the booths—but that's coarse, who needs it?"

She drank.

"The thing is, if I could sell that farm, I could maybe open my *own* escort service, you know? Give it a fancy name like some of them have—Executive Delight or Sophisticated Ladies or whatever the hell—get myself a string of nineteen-year-olds, be better than turning over seventy percent of what I make to Bobby, am I right? I can just feature him sitting still for *that*, my taking off and starting a thing of my own, sheesh! But what this four thousand means is I got fuck-you money now. Bobby tries to lay a hand on me, I'll have both his legs broken in six places, cost me five hundred bucks to hire a goon—just what I plan to pay Loomis. You think anybody'll wanna buy that place?"

She drank again. The waitress came back to the table with our food. I noticed, for the first time, that there was a scar on Hester's chin. It looked like a knife scar.

" 'Cause I mean it, Mr. Hope, I never saw a dump like that in my life. *Never.* In Houston—I went to live in Houston for a while after my mother died—there are places you wouldn't be-lieve, the girls are all scaly-legged junkies, they march around in baby-doll nightgowns and frilly panties, take on any sailor who comes through the Ship Channel—the *pits*, believe me. But some of those places look like palaces compared to that dump Papa was living in. And the *land*! Sheesh! I walked all over it yesterday in the rain, it doesn't look to me like you could grow *diddly* on it. Why'd this client of yours want to buy it? He musta been real crazy about weeds, I gotta tell you. I hope there's some-body else crazy enough down here. If I could sell that farm, I'd be home free. Maybe even go to L.A., set myself up there. You get all these girls out in L.A., they go out to become actresses, next thing you know they're working in banks for peanuts, they sooner or later begin to figure they can earn more in one night at the Beverly Hills Hotel than in six months as a teller. Get myself a string of girls out there—black, white, Chicano, maybe even Chinese—treat them nice, I bet I could make a lot of money in L.A., don't you? But I got to sell that farm first. You know anybody crazy enough to buy it?"

The front door opened. There was a sudden gust of wind, and then the door closed again. Hester looked up. I turned in my chair to follow her glance—and my blood froze in my veins.

"Hi, fellas," the waitress called. "Long time no see."

Charlie had shaved off his black beard, but Jeff still sported the blond mustache. Charlie was wearing his identifying red kerchief. Jeff was wearing his blue one. They were both still wearing faded blue jeans and scuffed boots and fancy snap-button shirts. Their wide shoulders were damp from the drizzle outside. They both grinned the moment they saw me.

"Well, well, looka who's here," Jeff said.

"Got hisself a new girl," Charlie said.

"Wanna dance again?" Jeff said.

Grinning, they started for the table, boots clattering on the hardwood floor, fists clenching as they approached, eyes glittering in anticipation of another hoedown with the city slicker prom-boy from Calusa.

Never get caught sitting.

Bloom's words in the gym.

If you're in a car and somebody's coming at you, get clear of the door before he catches you with your ass on the seat and one foot on the pavement. If you're in a booth, the same thing, get out of it right away. If you're at a table, stand up and get ready for whatever's coming, 'cause it's gonna come fast.

I knew what was coming, and it was coming fast.

I was on my feet and clear of the table while they were still three feet away from it. But I was trembling.

"Oh look, he *does* wanna dance," Jeff said.

Don't wait. If you know you've got trouble, you *be the one to* *make the first move. And make it a good one. It's the best shot* *you'll ever have.*

"Come on, sweetheart, let's dance," Charlie said, and pulled me to him in what he planned as a bear hug that would crack every rib in my body. I melted into his manly arms, and went for his balls, pistoning my knee up into his groin, the way Bloom had taught me. His jaw fell open. He grunted in pain, his arms flying wide. I backed out of his open embrace as he doubled over to grab himself between the legs.

If you hurt him with your first shot, hit him again—fast! Put *him out of action before he has time to recover.*

His head was coming down, his face twisted in pain as he doubled over, clutching himself between the legs. I brought up my knee again, catching him just under the nose this time, my kneecap smashing against the ridge of his upper lip. His head jerked up. Blood spilled from his torn lip and smeared his teeth. I thought he was finished—

Never take it for granted. Make sure.

—but he came at me like an enraged bull, still doubled over, both hands clutched into his groin, his head lowered like a battering ram. I clenched my right fist, stepped slightly to the side— almost tripping over Hester's bag where it sat on the floor—and brought the bunched fist down sharply, wielding it like the head of a hammer with a handle, connecting hard with the base of his skull. He fell flat to the floor on his face, his arms spraddled.

Kick him when he's down. Put him away.

I kicked him in the head. He tried to get up, and I kicked him again, and this time he *was* finished. But there was still Jeff, standing there with his mouth open, as if he'd just witnessed Clark Kent taking off his clothes to reveal himself in his blue underwear and his red cape. I did not feel like leaping tall buildings or stopping locomotives with my bare hands. In fact, I felt a little sick to my stomach. I was aware of the waitress cowering against the back counter, aware of Hester watching me with what appeared to be a blend of amusement and amazement, aware of the ketchup bottle on the table, and the cutlery, aware of Jeff pulling himself together now, collecting his wits. He was a lot better at this sort of thing than I was. He knew everything Bloom had taught me, and then some. He grinned suddenly. The grin terrorized me. I wanted to turn and run, but there was no place to go; Jeff was standing between me and the only door in the place.

If there are two of them—

What the hell had Bloom said about there being two of them?

Take out the strongest one first—

Had Charlie been the strongest one?

And let the second one come to you.

I did not need this singular piece of advice. The second one *was* coming to me, and fast, his fists bunched, the grin still on his face. Oh, I am going to kill you, the grin said. Oh, I am going to leave you bleeding and broken on the floor. Oh, I am going to have such a good time murdering you.

Wait till he's close enough . . .

I waited.

Feint for his balls . . .

I jabbed a short sharp left-handed punch down toward his groin.

And then go for his eyes.

Jeff's hands dropped protectively.

Blind him if you have to.

Bloom's world.

I did not want to blind Jeff, but in three seconds flat he would recognize that my jab at his groin had been a fake, and the moment he brought his hands up again—

I clenched my right fist, extended the forefinger and middle finger stiff and straight, like a horizontal V-for-victory sign, and jabbed them directly at his eyes. He tried to cover his face, but it was too late. My fingers straddled the bridge of his nose and found the jelly of his eyes. I pulled back my hand in horror.

He roared in pain, both hands covering his face, and then he whirled away from me and banged into the table behind him, knocking glasses and utensils to the floor . . .

Don't just wound him—

I had pulled back my hand an instant too soon.

Take him out!

. . . flailing with both arms now, windmilling them as he staggered around the room. He collided with one of the walls and knocked a picture to the floor, and then let out a blood-curdling bellow . . .

Your most dangerous opponent is a wounded, angry man.

. . . and shook his head as if to clear it, and then turned and scanned the room, his eyes bloodshot and watering. He blinked to clear away the tears. He blinked again. And then he got me in focus at last, and he came at me, and everything Bloom had taught me went right out of my head.

He hit me in the face so hard that I thought he'd broken my neck. I staggered back and away from him, colliding with the chair Hester had been sitting in, knocking it over. Hester screamed. He hit me again, in the gut this time, and when I doubled over, he brought his knee up against my jaw and my head snapped up and I felt myself falling over backward, and then I hit the floor, and he was on me, straddling me, and his hands went for my throat. I tried to remember if Bloom had taught me anything about getting strangled. I tried to break his grip, sliding my hands up between his arms, trying to force open the vise, but pain was sapping all my strength and his hands were tightening and I realized all at once that I was choking. I flailed out with my arms, banging the backs of my hands on the floor, trying to twist away from him, hitting the leg of the table, and then something softer, something yielding, Heather's leather bag where she'd left it on the floor.

I always carry a can of Mace in my bag.

Hester's words, this time.

I groped for the bag. I found the opening. I fumbled inside it, Jeff's hands choking the breath out of me, squeezing the life out of me, my own left hand scrabbling behind my head, inside the bag, searching blindly inside the bag, my fingers tangling in all the debris a woman carries, my fingers closing on something hard and cylindrical—too late. White dots were swimming in front of my eyes, and then the dots turned gray, and the gray spread, and everything started to turn a thick ugly black, and I heard Jeff murmur, "Go, you bastard, *go,*" and I told myself I did not want to go, and I pulled the can free with my last ounce of strength, and shoved it into his face and pressed down on the pushbutton, pressed, pressed . . .

His hands came free.

I coughed, sucked in a deep breath of air, coughed again, and kept my finger pressed on that button. He was off me now, lurching blindly around the room again, choking and snarling and swearing, and I lay there gasping for breath, the air so fucking sweet, idiotically pressing the button on top of the can, spraying wildly until I realized I was in danger of breathing in the fallout. Take him *out,* Bloom had said, make *sure.* I lay there on my back for several moments more, breathing hard, counting the minutes, hearing Jeff raging around the room, and then I stumbled to my feet and grabbed the ketchup bottle from the tabletop and went after him again with the Mace can in one hand and the bottle in the other.

I hit him only once with the bottle because I remembered Bloom telling me that if I *killed* anyone, it would be too bad for both of us. I didn't honestly know whether that was blood spurting from Jeff's forehead or only ketchup. Either way, I did not feel too terrific. I stood looking down at him where he lay unconscious on the floor, and I thought, *Welcome to the jungle,* and then Hester said, with great admiration, "Sheesh, you'd make a terrific pimp."

I stopped at the house to shower and change my clothes before heading back to the office. There was blood on the knee of my pants where it had connected with Charlie's upper lip. There was blood on the cuff from when I'd kicked him in the head.

There was blood on the sleeve of my jacket. I took out the blood-stains with cold water. The punch that I thought had broken my neck had instead raised a huge welt under my left cheekbone. It was already beginning to discolor. There were bruise marks on my throat. My jaw was swollen where Jeff had brought his knee up against it, but it wasn't broken. I decided I did not want another fistfight until I was sixty-two years old. A fistfight every twenty-four years was a decent enough interval.

Cynthia made no mention of the way my face looked; maybe she was beginning to get used to the idea that one of her bosses was an inveterate brawler. She told me instead that I'd had eight calls while I was out, and that two of them were from Bloom and my daughter. I could not reach Joanna because it was three o'clock and she was still at school, so I called Bloom. First I told him what I had done to Charlie and Jeff. He sounded very proud of me. He asked me if the police had shown. When I told him they hadn't, he advised me to stay out of Ananburg for the next little while. I told him that we were on the way to settling the Burrill-McKinney mess. He said that was nice.

"No word on the girl yet," he said. "That's why I called. She hasn't tried contacting the mother, has she?"

"I haven't seen Veronica since Wednesday morning," I said. "Or talked to her."

"Oh?" he said.

"I'll be calling her this afternoon," I said. "I need her signature on this release."

"Ask her if she's heard from her daughter, will you?"

"I will."

"The girl taking off really bothers me, Matthew. I know she told you she was scared, but where is it written that she wasn't lying? There's a game—do you know it?—it's called Murder, and what you do, you hand out these playing cards to everybody, and the guy who gets the ace of spades is the murderer. You turn out all the lights—this is very popular with teenagers 'cause they get a chance to grope in the dark—and everybody circulates around the house, and the murderer hands the ace of spades to his victim, and the victim has to count to twenty before he yells 'Murder!' Then you turn on all the lights, and the guy who's supposed to be the detective starts asking questions, trying to find out who done it. One of the rules of the game is that everybody has to tell the truth about where he was and what he was doing *except* the murderer. The murderer's allowed to say anything he wants, make up any story he wants, lie like a used-car dealer. That's the *game*, Matthew.

"In real life, it doesn't always work that way; it's not only your *murderer* who makes up stories. You get people lying not because they committed a crime but because there're things they don't want anybody to know about them. I went to see this chiropractor, for example, because I wanted to nail down where he was the night McKinney got killed. I'm taking the girl's story for fact, you see, that she heard her brother talking to a guy with a Spanish accent, and that maybe they were discussing rustling. I don't know how many Spanish people we got here in Calusa, but the victim's mother is this guy's patient, and Christ knows there've been plenty cases cracked on connections even skimpier than that. So he doesn't want to tell me where he was on the night of August eighth, and I ask him why, and he says it's none of my business, and I tell him this is a *murder* we're investigating here, and he finally tells me he was with this lady who lives on Sabal Key, but he told his wife instead that he was with some buddies bowling, and if his wife finds out where he *really* was, he'll be the *next* one getting murdered, you see what I mean, Matthew?"

"I see what you mean."

"And also, I talked again with this vet who was supposed to have been watching television with Mrs. McKinney the night her son got killed, Hamilton Jeffries, he lives about three miles down the road from her, on the way to Ananburg. 'Cause, you see, if the girl's story is *true* about her having heard her brother talking about stealing cows, then maybe the mother *knew* he was robbing her blind, and maybe she decided to put a few dozen puncture wounds in him, do you see? Though, actually, it was only four-teen stab and slash wounds. The point is, if she wasn't *really* with Jeffries . . ."

"I feel confident she was," I said.

"Yeah, but on the other hand, *you* don't have Captain Hopper breathing down your neck, do you? Anyway, I went to talk to Jeffries again, and I ran through it all one more time, the television show they were watching, the time it went on, the whole shmeer. And then I asked him if they were doing anything *else* while watching the show, like maybe holding hands or necking or whatever, and out of the blue he tells me they used to be lovers, but they haven't been for a long time. Did you know they used to be lovers, Matthew?"

"Yes, I knew."

"But you didn't tell me."

"Only because I felt Veronica was telling the truth, and I saw no reason . . ."

"Yeah, but that's *my* job, isn't it, Matthew? To decide whether people are telling the truth or not?"

"I'm sorry."

"Like, for example, I went to see this twerp again yesterday, the orange-stacker, I find him in back of the store, he's watering down the produce, wearing an apron all covered with shmutz. I ask him what the McKinney girl was wearing the last time he saw her, and he tells me the purple shorts and shirt, and I ask him what they talked about before he left the apartment that morning, and he says she was going shopping and would see him later, the same thing he said the last time around. Only *this* time he tells me she seemed *scared* about something, which is just what *you* told me—did you happen to mention that to him?"

"No, I didn't. I don't think I did."

"So all of a sudden he comes up with her being scared, which makes it reasonable for her to run the way she did, but why didn't he tell me that *before*, the night the black girl was in his apartment taking a shower? All of a sudden, Sunny McKinney was scared that morning. So naturally I asked Jackie what she was scared of, and he said she was scared of getting killed like her brother got killed, which is also what *you* told me, and so it starts to sound even more reasonable that Sunny ran to protect herself. Unless she ran to get away *not* from the bad guy but from the good guy—*me*. In which case, she's maybe got something to hide. So I started questioning Jackie again about the night of the McKinney murder, and he tells me it couldn't have been Sunny who did it because he was there with her all night; neither one of them left the apartment from the minute they got back from McDonald's till early the next morning. The point is, I didn't once suggest to him that Sunny had maybe iced her brother, but he's coming up with the same alibi again, she couldn't have done it 'cause he was with her at the time.

"What I'm saying is, this isn't the *game* of murder, it's the real-life thing. Somebody killed McKinney and somebody killed Burrill too, and maybe it's one and the same person done it—it sure looks that way, with McKinney owning a thirty-eight and it was a thirty-eight used on the farmer—but it doesn't have to be just the murderer lying in his teeth, it can be *everybody*. Including you, Matthew, who when I asked you whether Mrs. McKinney said anything else, you told me no, when all the time you knew she used to have a thing going with Jeffries."

"I didn't feel I was lying," I said.

"Withholding evidence, then, okay?"

"It isn't evidence unless it has something to do with the murders. Otherwise, it's just gossip."

"If you hear any more *gossip*, let me know, okay?" Bloom said.

"Sure."

"You sound mad. You mad at me?"

"No."

"Sure, you are. Friends are supposed to say what's on their minds, Matthew. Otherwise, it ain't worth a shit," he said, and hung up.

My daughter called at a little past four.

"Daddy?" she said. "I tried to get you earlier, but you were out."

She rarely called me "Daddy" unless she wanted something. Usually it was "Dad." Sometimes it was "Pops."

"I've been thinking," she said.

I waited.

"About the wedding tomorrow," she said.

"Yes, honey?"

"Would you be very disappointed if I went? 'Cause what it is, Daisy called me last night, she was almost in tears, Dad. She said she doesn't even *like* this man her mother is marrying, and she wanted me to be there so badly, you know, for support and everything, her mother told her I wasn't coming, so she was calling to *beg* me to *please* come or she didn't know *what* she would do."

"Well, fine, honey. If that's what you want . . ."

"The thing is, I won't be able to see you tonight, either, 'cause Mom has to work on this gown we bought for me last year, and which is a little small on me, and I have to be there while she measures it and pins it up and, you know, makes it so it'll fit."

"I understand, honey. Don't worry about it."

"Nor Sunday, either," she said. "I know Mom told you she could bring me over on Sunday morning . . ."

"What's on Sunday?" I said.

"Daisy asked me to stay over. Her mother and this man she's marrying are leaving for their honeymoon right after the wedding, and there's gonna be this sitter with Daisy while they're gone, and Daisy *hates* the sitter, and she begged me to *please* stay with her after the wedding and all day Sunday. To see her through it, you know what I mean?"

"Well . . . sure. If you think Daisy needs you . . ."

"Oh, she *does*, Dad."

"I just didn't know you were such good friends."

"Well, we used to wet our pants together, you know."

"Uh-huh."

"I mean, we go back for *centuries*, Dad."

"Uh-huh."

"So will it be okay?"

"If it's what you want."

"Yeah, Dad, I really do." She hesitated. "You *are* disappointed, aren't you?"

"No, no."

"I can tell you are. I'm sorry, Dad, I really am. But you know . . . well . . . we have all the time in the world to see each other, haven't we?"

"Yes, honey, we certainly have."

"So will you forgive me this time?"

"There's nothing to forgive."

"Thanks, Dad," she said. "Do you remember the dress? It's the green one I wore to the Sugarcane Hop last year, the one with the big red flower in front." And she went on to explain how the flower had been necessary last year when she didn't have any bosom, but one of the *first* things they were going to do now was take off the flower and see what they could do about the bustline. As she went on to describe in detail the various other alterations she and her mother planned to make, I thought of what she'd said a few minutes.earlier, about us having all the time in the world to see each other.

And I thought of Sunny McKinney out there on her own, alone and running scared, and I wondered how much time Veronica had enjoyed with her as an infant, and then as a little girl, and then as a teenager, before she'd lost her to a world much wider than the ranch's four thousand acres. The irony, of course, was that we raised them only to lose them, we taught them to fly and they soared out of the nest. A successful parent was anyone whose child had learned to be self-sufficient. Well, fine, then, I was well on the way to becoming a successful parent. But I was also a human being with feelings of my own, most of them mixed, and I *was* disappointed that I wouldn't be seeing Joanna this weekend, and a trifle annoyed that she had felt it necessary to preface her decision with a con man's "Daddy." I was not, after all, a child.

But neither was she anymore.

She was, I realized, someone on the imminent edge of becoming an independent young woman. She had told me what *she*, in her own right, wanted and needed this weekend, and never mind the technicalities of the settlement agreement. And in her fourteen-year-old view of the eternal universe, she had gone on to assure me we had all the time in the world to see each other. I wondered now if perhaps I wasn't *seeing* her for the first time in my life. Maybe, until now, I'd only been *watching* her.

". . . up to the Circle this afternoon to get a new pair of shoes," she was saying, "'cause the green satin ones I wore last year are all scruffy looking."

I hesitated a moment, and then I said, "Joanna, there's something I have to tell you."

"Sure, Dad, what is it?"

I took a deep breath.

"Dale and I aren't seeing each other anymore."

There was a dead silence on the line.

"Gee," Joanna said.

The silence persisted.

"I'm sorry to hear that, Dad," she said. "I know she meant a lot to you."

Another silence. And then:

"Dad, I really have to go, we want to get to the Circle before all the shops close. I love you heaps, Dad, and thanks a lot, you don't know how much I appreciate this."

"I love you too, honey."

"You sure it's okay?"

"Positive."

"I'll talk to you Monday, then, okay?"

"Have a nice time, honey."

"'Bye, Dad," she said, and hung up.

I put the receiver back on the cradle, and sat staring at the phone. I had to call Veronica, of course, but not to tell her that my plans had changed for the weekend and I was now available. I was not a criminal lawyer, but I knew what compounding a felony was, and besides, I had too much respect for her to offer a last-minute prom invitation because the girl I'd originally asked had backed out.

I called only to inform her of the latest development on the land her son had contracted to buy. Her voice was cool and distant when she realized who was on the phone. She listened patiently while I told her about the release Burrill's daughter had signed. She consulted her calendar when I asked if she could come into the office on Monday morning to sign the papers and have her signature notarized. We settled on ten o'clock. She thanked me politely for having called, and then hung up.

I had dinner alone.

I drank two martinis before the meal, had a half-bottle of red wine with the meal, and then sat sipping cognac and reading the newspaper. It was still only eight o'clock, and I was all dressed up with no place to go. There used to be two daily newspapers in Calusa: the *Herald-Tribune* in the morning and the *Journal* in the afternoon. They were both owned by the same man, and the editorial viewpoint was identical. In fact, except for the comic strips, they seemed to be carbon copies of each other. Maybe that was why the owner stopped publishing the afternoon paper and sold the morning paper to *The New York Times*. The paper hadn't changed much since the purchase, except that it now carried book reviews originally published in the *Times*. This meant that a greater number of people (including my delighted partner Frank) could be treated to literary criticism, New York–style. I skipped over the book review, read the movie ads, and then turned to an item headlined LAW OFFICERS LIST ARRESTS.

"Calusa County law enforcement authorities announced the following arrests for Wednesday and Thursday," the article began, and then went on to list the names, ages, and addresses of the men and women who'd been charged with an assortment of crimes ranging through armed burglary, dealing in stolen property, grand theft, possession of marijuana, leaving the scene of an accident, battery on a police officer, possession of cocaine, assault, possession of cocaine again, grand theft again, possession of marijuana again . . . and again . . . and again . . .

Calusa was getting to be a busy little city.

I left the restaurant at eight-thirty. It was already dark as I drove back to the house. I spotted the red Porsche in my driveway when I was still only halfway up the street. *Sunny*, I thought, and remembered what she'd said to me the first time we met—"I'm as mean as a fuckin' tiger, mister"—and wondered if this was an example of the meanness, coming here instead of going home to her mother. And then it occurred to me that the Porsche may have been driven here by Veronica instead. Maybe Sunny *had* gone home after all, and maybe Veronica was here now to tell me the good news. I pulled the Ghia in behind the other car, let myself into the house through the kitchen door, and then turned on the house lights and the pool lights. I pulled open the sliding door then and stepped out onto the terrace, ready to welcome either the lady or the tiger.

It was Sunny, and she was in my pool again.

She wasn't naked this time. She was wearing instead a purple dress that billowed around her like a cloud of ink.

She wasn't swimming, either.

She was lying face downward on the bottom of the pool.

Two police divers wearing scuba tanks, face masks, and wet-suits went down after the body. I did not think the wetsuits were necessary, since the thermometer in the pool registered the water temperature as eighty-eight degrees. But perhaps the Calusa P.D. had its own set of regulations about the proper attire for recovering a dead twenty-three-year-old girl from the bottom of a swimming pool.

Captain Hopper supervised the operation.

The divers brought Sunny to the surface, carried her up the steps at the shallow end, and then placed her down gently on the terrace tiles. The purple dress clung to her. There was a hole in her forehead, and another hole in her left cheek. Bone splinters showed jaggedly behind the hole in the cheek.

"Shot her first," Hopper said at once, and looked at me. "What time did you say you found her?"

"Just before I called the police," I said. "Quarter to nine, something like that."

"And you say you were out having dinner before then?"

"Yes."

"Anybody with you?"

"I was alone."

"And you came back here . . ."

"Yes."

". . . turned on the pool lights . . ."

"Yes."

". . . and spotted the body."

"Yes."

"Why'd you turn on the pool lights?"

"I'd seen the Porsche, I thought someone might be out on the terrace."

"You thought the girl might be out on the terrace?"

"Or her mother. I thought it could be her mother."

"Why'd you think that?"

"I know her mother."

"You know the girl too?"

"Yes, sir, I do."

"Pretty girl," he said, looking down at her. He raised his eyes to mine again. "Anybody else here when you arrived?"

"No."

"Didn't see anybody, hear anybody?"

"No."

"Just turned on the pool lights and saw the girl, right?"

Bloom came out onto the terrace.

"I just phoned the mother," he said. "She'll be here as soon as she can. The ranch vehicles are both gone, she's got to find transportation."

"Gone?" Hopper said. "What do you mean? Stolen?"

"No, sir," Bloom said, "it's just they're being used by the people she's got working for her."

"Why didn't you tell her you'd *send* a car?"

"Be a two-way trip that way, sir, out and back again. I thought we ought to get her here as soon as possible."

"How well do you know her?" Hopper asked me. "The mother."

"We're good friends, you might say."

"Might I?" Hopper said, and stared at me. "How well did you know the *girl*? Was *she* a good friend too?"

"I wouldn't say so. I knew her only casually."

"But not the mother. The mother you know *more* than casually, is that right?"

"Yes, sir."

"Here's the ME," Bloom said.

The medical examiner was wearing a short-sleeved shirt with a wild Hawaiian print. He looked oddly out of place in the company of police officers who were wearing either uniforms or business suits. He was a short man with a very red face that clashed violently with the predominant greens and yellows of his shirt. He looked like a neon sign. He nodded curtly, said, "Captain," and then knelt over the body.

"Plain to see she was carried here and dumped," Hopper said. "Those are gunshot wounds in her face."

"Well, let's see," the ME said.

"I seen enough gunshot wounds to know a gunshot wound when I see one," Hopper said.

The ME didn't answer.

"Criminalistics ain't here yet," Hopper warned. "You want to be careful."

The ME looked up.

"They'll want to see there's anything on that dress. The girl didn't *walk* here, that's for sure. Whoever done this had to've carried her."

"I'm only here to ascertain that she's dead," the ME said dryly.

"Take a genius to ascertain that," Hopper said. "You want to show me around the house, Mr. Hope?"

I showed him around the house. He was very careful not to touch anything. Bloom followed us like a shadow. The Ford Econoline van arrived some five minutes later, and the technicians from the Criminalistics Unit went out to the terrace. By that time the ME was through with the body. He told Hopper the girl was indeed dead and suggested that the cause of death was multiple gunshot wounds. I supposed that in forensic reports, anything more than one was multiple.

"*Gunshot* wounds?" Hopper asked. "No kidding?"

The ME looked as if he'd come straight here from an outdoor barbecue and was eager to get back to it.

"Better take her to Good Samaritan," he said. "Southern Medical's backed up."

"I was there last week," Hopper said. "They've got six stiffs decomposing in the freezer room. Place stinks like a Chinese whorehouse."

The state's attorney—Skye Bannister himself, and not one of his assistants—came into the house a few minutes after the ME had left. He was an exceptionally tall man, perhaps six-four or -five, with the appearance of a basketball player, reedy and pale, with wheat-colored hair and eyes the color of his name.

"Hello, Matthew," he said.

"You know each other?" Hopper asked, surprised.

"Old friends," Bannister said, and shook my hand; I guess Hopper stopped thinking of me as a suspect in that moment. "Three in a row, huh?" Bannister said. "Looks like an epidemic." He turned to Hopper. "Anything I should know, Walter?"

"Two gunshot wounds in the face," Hopper said. "Mr. Hope here found the body at the bottom of his pool. The red Porsche outside is the girl's . . ."

"It's registered to the ranch," Bloom said, correcting him.

"What ranch?" Bannister asked.

"The M.K.," Bloom said. "Out on Timucuan Point. The mother of the two victims, the McKinney boy, and now . . ."

"Right, I remember now," Bannister said. "Gunshot wounds, huh?"

"Like the bean farmer," Hopper said.

"But the boy was stabbed, wasn't he?"

"Fourteen times," Hopper said, and nodded.

"Think we're dealing with the same customer?"

"Ballistics won't even have a shot," Hopper said, making an unintentional pun. "There's exit wounds at the back of the girl's head, so we ain't gonna find no bullets inside her. And if she was carried here and dumped, which it looks like, we won't find no spent cartridges, neither, if it was an automatic weapon."

"Maybe the size of the wounds'll tell us something."

"A long shot, though," Hopper said, making another unintentional pun. "I never yet seen a ballistics make from the size of a wound."

"Any powder burns?" Bannister asked.

"Her face is clean as a whistle," Hopper said. "Pretty girl. It's a damn shame."

"Any blood? From where she was carried? Or dragged?"

"None around the pool. Criminalistics'll be checking the car and the driveway. They just got here a little while ago."

"Any other marks on her?"

"None I could see. Bloom? You see any?"

"No, sir."

"Why'd he carry her *here*?" Bannister asked.

"Dumb," Hopper said, shaking his head. "Maybe he figured Mr. Hope here'd be blamed for it."

He seemed to have forgotten all the questions he'd asked me not twenty minutes ago.

"Pretty risky, though," Bannister said. "Driving here with a stiff in the car."

"Most of the people driving cars down here are half dead already," Hopper said. "Who the hell would notice?"

They all laughed.

"Got away on foot, then, huh?" Bannister said. "If he drove here in the Porsche . . ."

"Way it looks," Hopper said, nodding. "I've got men out can-

vassing the neighborhood now. It's a quiet street, maybe somebody noticed him coming or going."

"You don't think a *woman* could've carried her, huh?"

"I ain't ruling it out, but it's unlikely. She's a big girl."

"You get somebody who just done murder," Bloom said,
"they got the strength of an ox sometimes."

"I'd sure like to get some real meat on this," Bannister said.

"Well, we're working it," Hopper said.

"Three in a row, television'll have a field day."

"If they're related," Bloom said.

"Even if they're not," Bannister said.

"They're brother and sister," Hopper said. "Even if they *ain't*
related, they're related."

They all laughed again.

I had not realized that Hopper had such a superb sense of
humor.

"Well, I want to take a look outside," Bannister said. "Get
me something that'll stick, huh? This thing's been dragging on
too long."

"From your lips to God's ears," Bloom said.

Veronica arrived about twenty minutes later. I was glad the
ambulance had already taken Sunny's body to the morgue. The
Criminalistics Unit was still outside in the Porsche, vacuuming
it, going over it for latents. The car she arrived in was a Cadillac
Seville. The man behind the wheel got out, went around to the
other side of the car, and then opened the door there for her. She
was wearing color for the first time since I'd known her. Blue
slacks, a blue blouse, blue sandals. Her exquisite face looked very
pale against the blue. She came into the house, followed by the
man, and Hopper went to her at once and said, "Ma'am, I'm
sorry about this terrible tragedy."

I had the feeling he had used those words many times before
and was repeating them now by rote.

Veronica nodded.

The man with her looked to be in his late sixties, taller than either Bloom or I, wearing a sports jacket over dark slacks, an open-throat sports shirt, and loafers without socks. His eyes were a blue almost as pale as Veronica's, and his white hair was streaked with strands of yellow that told me he'd been blond when he was younger. He was suntanned and lean, a man with a weathered outdoor look about him. I pegged him at once for a neighboring rancher whom she'd called for a lift here. He seemed entirely at ease in the presence of policemen.

"You made good time," Bloom said.

"Ham's a fast driver," she said. "Excuse me," she said, "this is Dr. Jeffries, my veterinarian." Her eyes met mine for the first time since she'd entered the house. "He was good enough to drive me here."

I was glad it was Bloom, and not Captain Hopper, who began questioning Veronica. In the gymnasium, Bloom had behaved like a thug; in my living room, he behaved like a gentleman. Hopper watched and listened as though he truly appreciated picking up some tips on how it was done up there in Nassau County in the wilds of New York, Bloom's territory before he'd moved to · Florida. Maybe there was yet hope for Captain Walter Hopper.

"Mrs. McKinney," Bloom said, "there are some questions I've got to ask you, and I hope you'll forgive me, but they have to be asked."

"I just want you to find whoever killed her," Veronica said.

"Yes, ma'am, that's what we want, too," Bloom said. "Now, ma'am, the last time I spoke to you, you said you hadn't yet heard from your daughter—this must've been close to five o'clock this afternoon."

"Yes, that's right," Veronica said.

"You didn't hear from her *after* we had that telephone conversation, did you?"

"No, I didn't."

"She didn't come back to the house . . ."

"No."

". . . and as far as you knew, she was still out there some-place."

"Yes."

"Mrs. McKinney, can you tell me how you spent the time between five o'clock, when we talked on the phone . . ."

"Why do you want to know that?" Jeffries asked.

His voice gave away his age. Before I heard him speak, I had to keep reminding myself that he was, in fact, seventy-five years old. But his voice lacked timbre and tone, and I noticed now—clued by the voice—that his neck was leathery and wrinkled and that the backs of his hands were covered with liver spots. Bloom turned to him in surprise, like a stand-up comic unexpectedly heckled from a nightclub floor.

"Sir?" he said.

"Sir," Jeffries said, stressing the word, "why do you want Mrs. McKinney to account for her whereabouts?"

"Routine," Bloom said with a slight shrug, falling back on the timeless police explanation. "Her daughter's been killed, we naturally . . ."

"I see nothing routine about your question," Jeffries said. "It would indicate to me that you consider Mrs. McKinney a suspect, and *that*, of course, is absurd."

I imagined him as a younger man, and I could easily see how he had once swept Veronica off her feet. She seemed, in fact, to respond even now to his spirited defense—a slight nod of her head, a flaring of the pale blue eyes. I felt slightly jealous.

"Ask your questions," Hopper said to Bloom. "And I suggest you answer them, Mrs. McKinney."

"Then *I* suggest she be read her rights," Jeffries said.

"This is a field investigation," Hopper said impatiently. "She's not in custody, Miranda-Escobedo doesn't apply."

"You are nonetheless, by implication . . ."

"We are nonetheless only trying to ask a few questions," Hopper said. "Tell her she isn't in jeopardy, will you, Mr. Hope?"

"I think you ought to answer their questions," I said.

Jeffries looked at me as though discovering a new enemy in the camp. I suddenly wondered how much Veronica had told him about us.

"What is it you want to know?" she asked Bloom.

What he wanted to know was where she'd been and what she'd done between five o'clock this afternoon and nine or thereabouts, when he'd called again to inform her about her daughter. It seemed to me that she accounted for her time believably and with remarkable restraint; however Bloom and Hopper hoped to disguise it, they *were* nonetheless trying to find out whether she'd had the opportunity to murder her own daughter. She told them that she'd taken the Jeep out to Mosquito Jam Hammo... little after Bloom's first call, to check out a cow her hand said might be coming down with something. The hand would verify that she was with him until almost six o'clock. She had gone back to the house then, written out a shopping list, and taken the Jeep to the new mall near the interstate highway, where she'd done her grocery marketing for the week. The supermarket manager would remember her because she'd had to go to his office to get a check okayed. That was a rule at the market; any check over a hundred dollars had to be okayed by the manager. She supposed she had got back to the house shortly after seven. Rafe, the ranch manager, had stopped by at around seven-thirty to ask if he could use the Jeep. She'd made no plans to leave the house tonight, and she told him that would be fine. She remembered mentioning that it was low on gas, and that he should fill the tank before leaving the ranch. The hand came by a little later to ask if he could use the pickup; his wife had been listening to one of Calusa's buy-and-sell call-in radio shows, and a woman had a used porch swing for sale and she wanted to go take a look at it and carry it home with them if it looked all right. Veronica had given him permission to take the pickup. This must have been sometime close to eight o'clock. She was certain that both Rafe and the hand could confirm that she had been there in her own living room between seven-thirty and eight o'clock.

She had mixed herself a martini then, and had gone into the kitchen to prepare dinner, sipping at the drink while she heated some stew left over from the night before. She had already eaten and was clearing away the dishes when Bloom called her from here. That must have been a little after nine. She had phoned both Yellow Cab and Blue Cab, the only two taxi companies in Calusa, but both of them had told her it'd be at least a half hour before they could send anyone out there to get her. She had then called Dr. Jeffries to ask if *he* might be able to drive her here.

That was how she'd spent her time between five o'clock this afternoon and now.

"And you didn't see your daughter at any time today, is that right?" Bloom asked.

"I haven't seen my daughter since Monday," Veronica said, and suddenly burst into tears. I was sure she was thinking she would *never* see her again. Except in a coffin.

Bloom and Hopper stood by awkwardly. Jeffries put his arm around her and consoled her. This was where I lived, but I suddenly felt as if I had no right to be here.

"Well," Hopper said, "we'll get out of your way soon as possible." He seemed suddenly embarrassed. "Boys shouldn't be too much longer. We'll need you to come by the morgue to make a positive identification, but that can wait till . . ."

"I'll identify the body," Jeffries said.

"We usually prefer next of . . ."

"I've known Sunny from the day she was born," he said. "You can at *least* spare Mrs. McKinney the ordeal of . . ."

"I'm sure that'll be all right," Bloom said gently. "Do you know where Good Samaritan is?"

"I know it."

"Will tomorrow morning at nine be too early?"

"I'll be there," Jeffries said.

"Sorry to have bothered you," Hopper said, as if the police were here not to investigate a murder but instead to answer a complaint about someone playing the radio too loudly. "Better see how they're doing out there," he said to Bloom, and they both went out to the driveway, where the technicians were still working on the car.

The police entourage did not leave until almost midnight. The house and the street seemed inordinately silent now that they were gone. Veronica sat in one of the imitation Barcelona chairs, facing the blank screen of the television set. Jeffries hovered about her, waiting for a signal that she was ready to go.

"You'd better tell him," she said abruptly.

"Veronica . . ."

"Tell him," she said.

Jeffries sighed heavily. "I'd like a drink," he said. "Do you have any bourbon? Little water in it?"

I brought him a bourbon and water. I brought Veronica the gin and tonic she asked for. I poured myself a snifter of cognac. Jeffries sipped at his drink. On the street outside, I heard the sound of an automobile, and wondered if the police were coming back. They had roped off the area around my house. They had put up cardboard CRIME SCENE signs. I wondered what Mrs. Martindale was thinking in her house next door. I wondered what she'd have to say to me in the morning. I wondered what Jeffries had to say to me *now*, but he just sat there, sipping silently at his drink. The sound of the automobile engine faded. It had not been the police, after all, unless they were simply cruising the area.

"If *you* won't tell him . . ." Veronica said.

Jeffries took a long swallow of bourbon. He sighed again. "Sunny . . ." he said, and hesitated. "Sunny was staying with me."

"What do you mean?"

"At my house," he said.

"Since when?"

"Tuesday."

"She's been at your house since *Tuesday*?"

"Yes. She left tonight. At six-thirty."

I turned to Veronica. "Did you know this?"

"Not until tonight. Ham told me on the way here."

"But you knew it when Bloom was questioning you."

"Yes."

"And you chose not to reveal it?"

"That's what we decided, Ham and I."

"That's what you *decided*? Your daughter's dead, the police are searching . . ."

"*Our* daughter," Jeffries said.

"What?"

"*Our* daughter, Mr. Hope. Veronica's and mine."

So now I listened.

Now I listened to what I *should* have heard the first time around: Veronica alone on the ranch one starry night, her husband off in Tampa or Tallahassee or Denver or wherever the hell, Dr. Hamilton Jeffries there to minister to a sick cow and to minister to the lonely Mrs. McKinney as well. Their affair had started in September and ended in February, a short season, easy come, easy go, at least for Jeffries, who unilaterally decided that what they were doing was immoral, and dangerous as well. What Jeffries hadn't known, and what Veronica hadn't told him, was that she was already carrying his child. Empirical evidence (*Sunny was an August baby, full of rain*) later proved that she was just entering her fourth month of pregnancy on the February night when Jeffries decided to take his cautious moral stand. The baby, as Veronica later calculated it, had been conceived sometime in November, when their romance was at the height of its passion, a love child for sure, Hamilton Jeffries's bastard daughter by any reasonable surmise, since Drew McKinney was in Dallas for most of that month and chose not to entertain his wife on the few occasions when he was home.

"If I'd *known*, of course," Jeffries said now, "it might have been different."

His words lacked conviction, but I made no comment. What was done was done, all water over the dam and under the bridge, and Jeffries was certainly not the first, nor would he be the last, of the red-hot lovers who abandoned pregnant married women, knowingly or otherwise. *I settled down—isn't that the expression one uses?—and became a faithful wife and mother, not necessarily in that order.* Living proof of her fidelity had been her second child, undeniably Drew's—*same dark hair and dark eyes, a spitting image*—her husband's waning interest apparently rekindled by the birth of a daughter he accepted unquestioningly as his own. Jack was born three years later, at the end of June, which meant that Drew McKinney's passion had reflowered in October sometime; the lady seemed to have a penchant for getting pregnant in the late fall.

I don't know why I was getting angry listening to all this. Maybe it was because I remembered that Veronica hadn't expressed the slightest grief over the death of her husband's son, and that she'd wanted to strangle the crying little girl sired by her lover. Well, they were *both* dead now, those offspring by one mate or another, and I couldn't help wondering how much Veronica had loved either one of them. *Or* her husband. *Or*, for that matter, Hamilton Jeffries. I was also annoyed by their joint decision (*That's what we decided, Ham and I*) to keep from the police the information that Sunny McKinney had been staying at Jeffries's house for the past four days.

"Why'd she come there?" I asked. "Did she know you were her father?"

"No, no," Jeffries said. "We decided it was best to keep that from her, Veronica and I."

"The way you decided it was best to keep from the police . . ."

"We could not afford to open that particular can of peas," Jeffries said.

It occurred to me that they'd opened that particular can of peas twenty-four years ago.

"You saw the way they treated Veronica just now," he said. "I'm certain they *still* feel she's somehow implicated. If we'd told them about Sunny being at my house . . ."

"Then *you* might have become implicated as well, isn't that right?"

"Both of us," he said. "Veronica *and* I."

"I thought Veronica didn't know she was there."

"I didn't!" Veronica said. "Until tonight."

"You didn't call to tell him she was missing?"

"I didn't."

"His own *daughter*? You didn't pick up the phone to . . ."

"I told you I didn't!"

I turned to Jeffries. "Was Sunny in the habit of coming to your house when she was in trouble?"

"Not often. Sometimes. She thought of me as a good friend."

"Some friend. She's hiding from a fucking killer . . ."

"I don't appreciate such language, young man," Jeffries said.

"Did she tell you why she came there?"

"She was frightened. She said she needed a place to stay for the next few days, until she decided what she was going to do next."

"Did she say what she was scared of?"

"Yes. She thought someone might try to kill her."

"Then you *knew* that."

"Yes."

"And you didn't call Veronica? To tell her that her daughter— *your* daughter—was with you?"

"I did not. I felt that would be betraying a confidence."

"It never occurred to you that Veronica might be worried about her?"

"It occurred to me."

"Did it occur to you that Veronica might have notified the police of her daughter's absence?"

"That occurred to me as well."

"But you didn't call her."

"I didn't call her."

"So *she* was there on the M.K., unaware that her daughter was at your house, and *you* were three miles down the road, unaware that her daughter was being sought by the police."

"That's it exactly."

"Didn't Bloom come to see you yesterday?"

"He did."

"Where was the Porsche? Didn't he see the Porsche?"

"It was in my garage."

"Then he *didn't* see it."

"No."

"If Sunny told you she was afraid . . ."

"She did."

". . . told you someone might try to kill her . . ."

"Yes."

"Why didn't you tell Bloom?"

"I felt she'd be safe with me."

"Did you feel she'd be safe when she left tonight?"

"I wasn't there when she left."

"Then how do you know she left at six-thirty?"

"I don't mean I wasn't on the premises . . ."

"What *do* you mean?"

"I was out back, in the kennels. I treat all sorts of animals, not only livestock. People bring dogs to me, cats . . ."

"So you were out in the kennels . . ."

"Yes. The phone rang at—oh, I don't know—it must've been a little before six. Either she answered the phone or it stopped ringing. Either way, the next thing I heard was the Porsche backing out of the garage. By the time I came around front, she was gone."

"At six-thirty."

"Yes, about then."

"You didn't know she was planning to leave?"

"I didn't."

"Before then, did she tell you where she might be going?"

"No."

"All right, what *did* she tell you?"

"Only that she was afraid someone might try to kill her."

"Did she say who?"

"The same person who'd killed her brother and Mr. Burrill."

"*Who?*"

"She didn't say."

"Didn't *say* or didn't *know?*"

"She was afraid to tell me."

"Why?"

"Because she felt she might be placing me in danger as well."

"She comes to you for help, she tells you someone might be after her . . ."

"That's right."

". . . but she doesn't tell you *who?*"

"She would not reveal his identity to me, that's correct."

"*His* identity? Did she say it was a *man?*"

"I gathered from the pronouns she used that she was referring to a man, yes."

"What'd she say about him? Did she describe him?"

"She did not."

"Did she say he had a Spanish accent?"

"She did not mention a Spanish accent."

"What *did* she mention?"

"She said he knew about her brother's scheme."

"What scheme?"

"To buy the farm."

"She called it a *scheme?* How was buying a . . . ?"

"Not the purchase of the land per se," Jeffries said.

"Then what?"

"The use to which he planned to put it."

"And what was that?"

"He was going to plant marijuana on it. He planned to grow and sell marijuana."

And now at least *that* part of it made sense.

I had given Jack McKinney all the facts and figures that should have proved the foolhardiness of trying to revitalize Burrill's moribund snapbean farm. I had explained to him that all he could hope to realize was a net of a hundred and twenty-six dollars an acre if he planted a crop that couldn't possibly turn a profit here on the Central West Coast of Florida. He had turned a deaf ear to my reasoning. Jack McKinney was planning to grow marijuana, which required no spraying and dusting, no harvesting machinery, no pickers or packers, no brokerage fees, and none of the other costs that had proved such a burden to Burrill. Burrill must have gone dancing in the streets the day a sucker like Jack McKinney came along to relieve him of his fifteen acres of snapbean farm.

But McKinney had known all along that you could plant marijuana in soil you wouldn't choose to be buried in, you could plant it in a window box, you could plant it on a bald man's hairpiece, you could plant it on a goddamn *rock*, and it would flourish. I supposed you could even plant it among your rows of snapbean bushes so that from the air it would go undetected; the pilot of a Sheriff's Department helicopter would only wag his head in wonder at the stupidity of yet another fool trying to grow *beans* here.

Some fool, young Jack.

He'd had us all convinced that he was about to trade his mother's cows for a handful of beans.

Instead, he was planning to drop golden nuggets into the soil. I had no idea what the going rate for a bale of marijuana might be; Bloom would know for sure. But I was willing to bet that McKinney's first harvest would have more than quadrupled his investment in the farm.

"How'd Sunny find out about this?" I asked.

"Jack told her," Jeffries said. "They were very close."

"Did he also tell her he'd been stealing his mother's cows?"

"No. She figured that out for herself."

"And this person she was afraid of—how'd *he* find out about Jack's plan?"

"I assume she mentioned it to him."

"When?"

"As soon as she learned of it. Sometime before Jack was . . ."

"Crowell," I said.

Bloom wasn't convinced.

In the car on the way to New Town, he did the same shadow dance he'd earlier performed for me on the telephone, only this time his silent partners included a detective named Cooper Rawles, a huge black man with wide shoulders, a barrel chest, and massive hands. It was not often that you ran into a person as big as Rawles; he made me feel like a Munchkin. It was even less often that you ran into a black cop with the rank of detective on Calusa's police force. Maybe his size had something to do with it. Maybe somebody figured it was better to have him on *their* side than on the bad guys' side. Rawles sat as silent as a mountain in the back seat. I was sitting up front alongside Bloom.

"First of all," Bloom said, "the kid's got an alibi a mile long. The alibi is Sunny McKinney, who says she was with him all night on the night her brother was killed, am I right, Coop? That's what the girl told us, that she was with Crowell all night that night, in the sack with him while her brother was getting slashed. So if this is the guy who actually *killed* her brother, why would she alibi him? That doesn't make sense to me, does it make sense to you, Coop?"

Rawles knew an answer wasn't expected. Bloom was talking to himself out loud, trying to put all the pieces together. Rawles grunted.

"I mean, this is her *brother* we're talking about here—though it turns out now he was only her half-brother. Still and all, she *thought* he was her brother, and you don't go around alibiing somebody who killed your own brother, however great he may be in the sack—it's just not something you do. But that's what she told us, that she was with this Crowell creep from when they got back from McDonald's till the next morning. So that's the *first* thing, the kid's got an alibi, or at least *had* an alibi. His alibi's dead now, same as the brother—why the hell didn't those two *tell* us what they knew?"

He was referring now to Veronica and Jeffries. *I* knew what he meant. I wasn't so sure Rawles did, even though he grunted again.

"Girl's with him four days," Bloom said, "he never dreams of calling the police, even though she tells him somebody may be out to get her. Turns out he's the girl's father, huh? Some father, he doesn't recognize his daughter's in danger, doesn't call the police, lets her stay there without a peep, doesn't even call us when she takes off—six-thirty, is that what Jeffries said?"

"That's what he said."

"And you found her in your pool at a quarter to nine, that means somebody had two hours to shoot her and dump her, that's more time than you need, you can ice somebody and get rid of the body in what, Coop, ten minutes, you're really pressed for time?"

"Five," Rawles said.

It was the first time I had heard him speak.

"So let's say, for the sake of argument, that this Crowell creep *is* the killer, though I can't figure out any motive, can you, Coop? But let's say she heads for his place at six-thirty—I can't figure out why she'd go *there*, either, not if she thinks he's trying to find her and do away with her, but let that pass for a minute. Let's say she goes there, and Crowell pumps two shots into her head and then carries her down to the car and carts her over to your place—why *your* place, that's another thing—but how can he manage that in a place like New Town? You mean to tell me nobody heard shots? You mean to tell me nobody *saw* him carrying down a body and dumping it in a car? They see and hear *everything* in that neighborhood, am I right, Coop?"

"You fart in that neighborhood," Rawles said, "they hear it three blocks away."

"So they don't hear two gunshots, huh?" Bloom said.

"Didn't shoot her in the car, neither," Rawles said. "Criminalistics didn't find no bullets, no expelled cartridge cases."

"Maybe she met him someplace," I suggested. "Maybe she was afraid to go to his apartment."

"Lots of lonely places in Calusa," Bloom said, nodding. "Maybe she phoned him, said meet me at the beach or something, that's a possibility. But why? If she knows the guy is after her, why hand herself over on a silver platter? It doesn't make sense, I don't buy it. And *another* thing," he said to himself. "Let's say Crowell is the killer, okay? Just for the sake of argument. What's his motive? You see any motive, Coop? He knows about the pot farm, terrific—what's the going rate for a bale of marijuana, Coop?"

"You mean the cheap Mexican and Jamaican shit?"

"How much is that running?"

"Five, six hundred bucks a pound. You get your better stuff from Colombia, California, and Hawaii, that'll run you a thousand a pound."

"How many pounds in a bale?"

"Depends whether it's packed loose or tight. A hundred, a hundred and fifty."

"So McKinney was figuring, say, six thousand a bale."

"Nice little cottage industry," Rawles said. "You know how many homegrown plants the DEA destroyed last year?"

"How many?" Bloom asked.

"More than two million. Close to two thousand *tons* of the stuff. Growing right here in the U.S. of A."

I had underestimated Jack McKinney. His first crop of marijuana would have made him an entrepreneur.

"So where's the motive?" Bloom asked, circling back. "McKinney doesn't even *own* the farm yet, he hasn't planted seed one, so what does Crowell hope to get by killing him?"

"Maybe he went there looking for a piece of the action," Rawles said. "Cut him in on the dope scheme, you dig? McKinney tells him to fuck off, and Crowell stabs him."

"Sure," Bloom said. "But you're forgetting Burrill. Why would he kill Burrill?"

"That's a question, all right," Rawles said philosophically.

"Maybe . . ." I shook my head. "No, never mind."

"Let's hear it," Bloom said.

"Well . . . let's say he *did* go to McKinney wanting a piece of the action. McKinney turned him down, so Crowell stabbed him and stole the thirty-six thousand . . ."

"Right, the money," Bloom said.

"We were forgetting all about the money," Rawles said.

"Love or money, those are the only two motives for murder," Bloom said.

"How about hate?" Rawles asked.

"The same as love. The other side of the coin, that's all."

"How about your crazies?" Rawles asked.

"Crazies don't have motives, that's another thing entirely, your crazies."

Shop talk, I thought.

"So he goes to Burrill," Bloom said, "and now he's got thirty-six grand in his hand . . ."

"Possible," Rawles said, but he did not sound convinced.

"And he offers the money to Burrill, tells him McKinney's dead now, and *he* wants to buy the land himself, take over McKinney's brilliant scheme, so to speak, set himself up as a pot farmer. How does that sound, Coop?"

"Too smart," Rawles said. "This Crowell kid is a dummy."

"Einstein he ain't," Bloom said. "But this wouldn't have taken any figuring. McKinney worked it all out already. This would've been a simple takeover."

"Then why kill Burrill?" Rawles asked. "You don't go killing the goose that's about to lay a golden egg."

"Maybe Burrill turned him down, too."

"No," I said, "that isn't likely. He was too eager to sell that farm. He'd have sold it to anybody, believe me."

"So if Crowell went there with thirty-six grand . . ."

"He'd have snapped it up in a minute. The bank was already holding four in escrow, and he was sure of getting at least that in default. If Crowell offered him another thirty-six, he'd be right where he wanted to be."

"Home free," Rawles said.

"So, okay, he wouldn't have turned it down," Bloom said.

"Never."

"So why'd Crowell kill him? *If* he killed him?"

"You're dealing here with an asshole," Rawles said. "Don't forget that. The Crowell kid is a total nerd."

"We're dealing here with an asshole, maybe," Bloom said, "but he's an asshole with an alibi as long as his arm."

We were back to square one. We were also approaching New Town. A former illustrious Vice-President of the United States once remarked that if you'd seen one slum, you'd seen them all. It later turned out that he and his immediate superior were wrong about a lot of things, including their assumptions that the American people would stand still for crooks occupying the highest offices in the land. But he'd been wrong about slums, too. Slums are as different, one from the other, as are warts. You cannot equate the squalor of Soweto with the desolation of New York's South Bronx, you cannot equate the rat-infested brick tenements in Harlem with the clapboard shacks in California's Venice. You can only compare those areas with what exists elsewhere in the same geographical location.

If you told a slum-dweller on Chicago's West Side that you were going to move him into New Town and you described it as a cluster of two-story stuccoed buildings surrounding a grassy compound planted with sabal palms, he'd have thought you were inviting him to a paradise on earth. When he got here, though, he might look around and discover for himself how *other* people were living in Calusa, and he would perhaps notice that more people were packed into the four square miles of New Town than were scattered over all of Calusa's keys, and he might also notice that most of them weren't white. Maybe that's what the former Vice-President had in mind. Maybe he was saying that the *color* of slums was the same.

"I sure wish I was white," Rawles said, as though reading my mind. Bloom pulled the car into the curb outside Crowell's building. "They hate black cops down here," Rawles explained, and Bloom cut the ignition.

"You stay here in the car, Matthew," he said. "This turns out to be real meat, I don't want to lose him on a technicality."

I did not stay in the car. I stepped outside the moment they went into the building, hoping for a breath of fresh air. It was almost two in the morning, but the citizens of New Town were out in force, similarly seeking relief from the contained heat of the day. They sat on their front stoops in shorts and undershirts, shorts and halter tops, and—in at least one instance—a bikini bathing suit. The air was redolent of that peculiar Florida aroma that lingers in the summertime, a mixture of mildew, salt, and blooming tropical plants. The stuccoed cinder-block walls of the buildings had been painted a pink that was already peeling and stained. The windows were wide open to whatever vagrant breeze stirred on the empty hours of the night. Somewhere a phonograph was playing loudly. No one seemed to mind. They sat whispering on their stoops, and the whispers somehow spoke more loudly than the sound of heavy metal.

I was still leaning against the fender of the police sedan when Crowell came out of the building. He came out at a gallop, barefoot and barechested, pushing his way through the handful of people cluttered on the front steps, almost falling over the lap of a woman who sat Haitian-style, her knees open, her dress tented down over her crotch. I heard him swear, and then I saw the gun in his right hand, and my first instinct was to duck behind the car, and then I heard Bloom's voice from inside the building, bellowing out from the darkness of the stairwell—"Stop or I'll shoot!"—and I pushed myself off the fender of the car and moved across the pavement to intercept Crowell, figuring Bloom was right behind him with his own gun, and never once stopping to think about what might happen next.

What happened next was that Crowell shot me.

I had never in my life, before that moment, been shot. I don't think most people have. It was not like in the movies or on television. I did not just fall down peacefully. I yelled like a son of a bitch when the bullet went through the meaty part of my shoulder. I yelled because it hurt. It hurt the way even a pointed stick hurts when it's stuck into your body, but what was stuck into my shoulder was a metal bullet traveling at enormous velocity and trailing fire behind it. The fire hurt, and the force hurt, and the force spun me around and away from Crowell, still yelling, and knocked me flat on my back on the pavement, where I did not lie there quietly so the director could concentrate on his other actors, but instead thrashed and kicked in pain because it hurt, oh God how it hurt.

Bloom burst out of the building like a hand grenade. He shoved his way through the people who were no longer sitting on the stoop but who had jumped to their feet at the sound of the first shot and were still too shocked to scatter. He fired a shot into the air the moment he was clear of the steps, and Crowell must have taken this not as a warning that he was in imminent danger but instead as a signal to do something and do it fast. What he did was turn with his gun-hand extended, and what he did next was fire a shot that missed Bloom by a mile, but that sent everyone rushing off the front stoop of the building, rushing inside, rushing off onto the patchy lawn with its scrubby palm trees, some of them yelling the way I was still yelling, though none of them had been shot.

Crowell fired again, directly at Bloom this time, who swerved on the concrete path and then stopped cold in his tracks and leveled his pistol in both hands, the way they must have taught him at the Police Academy years ago. He could have shot Crowell dead on the spot. He was well within his rights, and his target was motionless now. Instead, he shot him in the leg. I wondered about that, but only for a moment, because somehow I passed out.

9

What had happened was this.

I learned all about it in the hospital.

I was in the hospital for six days, and Bloom came to see me a lot during that time, and told me all about the little visit he and Rawles had made to Crowell's apartment. He also told me that the reason he was coming to see me so often was that he felt guilty as hell about my getting shot, confirming my partner Frank's surmise that Jews and Italians are the most guilt-ridden people on the face of the earth. Bloom said I shouldn't have been there in the first place. In the second place, I should have stayed in the car. In the third place, I shouldn't have tried to intercept Crowell; I should have run in the opposite direction instead. In his eagerness to explain the enormous guilt he was feeling, Bloom made *me* feel guilty. We both sat there feeling guilty in my hospital room. And he told me all about what had happened in the fifteen minutes preceding my "accident," as he insisted on calling it.

He and Rawles had approached suspect's apartment—a bit

of police vernacular crept into Bloom's recital every now and then—had listened outside the door and ascertained that suspect was in the company of another person, most likely female, had announced themselves flanking the door, since, if this *was* a killer inside there, they could possibly expect a fusillade of shots. No shots had come. Through the door, Crowell had asked them to wait a minute, please, and then he had opened the door wearing only a pair of pants, no shirt and no shoes, and he had asked the police what they wanted at this hour of the morning. Bloom—in accordance with regulations—had asked if they could please come in, and Crowell said, "Sure, but like I have company."

The company to whom Crowell referred was the selfsame black woman named Letitia Holmes who'd been there the last time Bloom had paid a nighttime visit, her shower apparently still not repaired. She went into great detail about the inconvenience of having to come here all the time to Jackie's apartment to take a shower, indignantly telling Bloom the police should do something about getting the Housing Authority on the ball instead of knocking on people's doors at two in the morning. She was getting dressed while she talked, seemingly oblivious to the presence of Bloom and Rawles as she stepped into her panties and pulled a striped shift over her head and then slipped into a pair of sandals, and was about to leave the apartment when Rawles said, "Hold it right there, sister," and she told Rawles he was no fucking brother of *hers*, but she sat on the edge of the bed anyway, muttering about her broken shower and about black men who chose to become *cops*, until Rawles told her to shut the fuck up, they were here on business.

Bloom started by asking where Crowell had been between the hours of six-thirty and eight-thirty last night, and Crowell seemed confused at first, wanting to know if Bloom was talking about *last* night between six-thirty and eight-thirty, or *tonight* between six-thirty and eight-thirty. Did Bloom mean *tonight*, Friday night, or did he mean *last* night, Thursday night? Bloom informed him that it was now two o'clock in the morning, which made it *Saturday* already, August the twenty-seventh, to be exact, and he was referring to *last* night, *Friday* night, August the twenty-sixth, between the hours of six-thirty and eight-thirty.

"Oh," Crowell said, and then went on to explain that *last* night, *Friday* night (which of course was when Sunny McKinney had been killed and dumped in my pool), he had been right here in the apartment with Lettie, who'd come over to take a shower since her shower was still busted and all.

"That right?" Rawles asked her. "You been here since six-thirty last night?"

"Right here," Lettie said.

"Long shower," Rawles said.

"Either of you leave the apartment during that time?" Bloom asked.

"We were both here," Crowell said. "Right, Lettie?"

Lettie nodded.

"I wonder if you'd mind we looked around a little," Rawles said.

"What for?" Crowell said.

"Did you know Jack McKinney was buying a snapbean farm?" Bloom asked.

"See we can find anything," Rawles said.

"Like what?" Crowell said. "Sure."

"You *don't* mind if we look around?"

"No, I mean sure, I knew Jack was buying a farm."

"Did you know what he planned to do with it."

"Grow beans on it, I guess."

"How about a little pot?" Rawles said.

"You got some, I wouldn't mind some," Lettie said, making a joke to a cop.

Rawles didn't even smile.

"McKinney was planning to grow marijuana on that land," Bloom said.

"Wow," Crowell said.

"You didn't know that, huh?"

"First I'm hearing of it," Crowell said. "Wow."

Which meant nothing. Either Crowell really *didn't* know a thing about Jack McKinney's plan to grow grass, or else Sunny had told him all about it and he was lying. In either case, Bloom asked, "Where do you think Sunny went?"

"I don't know," Crowell said, and shrugged.

"Who's Sunny?" Lettie asked.

"Girl I used to know," Crowell said.

Rawles had meanwhile begun roaming the premises as if he were searching for something specific, though he didn't dare open a drawer or a closet without a warrant. Crowell watched him from the corners of his eyes. Rawles pretended he didn't know he was being watched. He just kept prowling the place like a suspicious rhinoceros.

"Reason I ask," Bloom said, "is we're really eager to find her."

"I wish I could help you," Crowell said.

Rawles opened the bathroom door and peeked inside. A big bath towel was on the floor; maybe Lettie *had* come here to take a shower, after all. Without turning from the bathroom, Rawles said, "We figure she maybe killed her brother, is why."

"You think so, huh?" Crowell said.

"Nice girls you hung around with," Lettie said.

"'Cause otherwise," Bloom said, "why would she've run?"

"Yeah," Crowell said.

"The way we figure it," Rawles said, and turned from the bathroom door and said, "These your panties in here, miss? On the shower rod?"

"My panties are right here under my dress," Lettie said, and looked at Crowell.

"Wonder whose they are," Rawles said, and shrugged. "The way we figure it is she went to see him that night . . ."

"Sunny," Bloom said. "The night her brother got killed."

"To ask him for a piece of the pot action," Rawles said.

"But he turned her down cold."

"So she knifed him."

Lettie looked at Crowell again.

"White trash," Rawles said to her in explanation. "This girl we're talking about." He winked at her, as though they shared together a great ancient African wisdom that took into account white girls who murdered people and then left their panties on shower rods. Lettie did not wink back. Lettie was listening very hard to everything that was being said, and trying to understand it, but she didn't trust Rawles as far as she could throw him. Rawles knew this. So did Bloom. But she was Crowell's alibi for the hours between six-thirty and eight-thirty last night, and they were doing this soft-shoe dance for her benefit as well as Crowell's.

"She didn't come here yesterday afternoon, did she?" Bloom asked.

"Who do you mean?" Crowell asked.

"Sunny."

"No. I just told you, *Lettie's* been here since six-thirty."

"Who said anything about six-thirty?" Rawles asked.

"You said you wanted to know where I was between . . ."

"Yeah, but who said anything about Sunny coming here at six-thirty?"

"I thought you said . . ."

"What we said was did she come here yesterday *afternoon*, that's what we said."

"You mean *this* afternoon?"

"Take it any way you want," Rawles said. "You want to keep thinking today is yesterday, that's fine with us. We're talking about Friday afternoon, *yesterday* afternoon, August twenty-sixth."

"Today is Saturday," Bloom said. "You think you got that?"

"Yeah, I got it."

"So *did* she come here yesterday afternoon, or *didn't* she?"

"No."

"Not at six-thirty, and not at any time before that, right?"

"Right."

"Then what are her panties doing on the shower rod?" Rawles asked. He didn't know if in fact they were Sunny's panties or even Queen Elizabeth's panties, though he doubted Her Majesty wore

223

lacy black bikinis. As a matter of fact, he didn't care *whose* panties they were. All this bullshit about panties was to put Crowell on the defensive and to alert Lettie to the fact that she wasn't the only woman using his shower.

"Those aren't hers," Crowell said, "Sunny's. She took everything with her when she left the apartment. Except a bathing suit. I think I already told you that."

"And she hasn't been back since, right? Since Tuesday, right?"

"Yeah, Tuesday. I guess that's when it was."

"Then whose you think they might be?" Rawles asked. "You sure they're not yours, honey?" he said to Lettie, and again winked.

"You seen me puttin' mine on," Lettie said. "You want another look at them? Make sure they ain't walked in the bathroom and jumped up on the rod?"

"Maybe later," Rawles said, and grinned at her.

"Must be some other girl's, huh?" Bloom said.

"Well, I know a few girls," Crowell said.

"Did you have another girl in here last night?"

"No, not last night."

"Night before last?"

"When would that've been?"

"Thursday. Two days after Sunny cleared out."

"Yeah, maybe," Crowell said.

"Been partying a lot?" Rawles asked.

"A little."

"Celebrating something?"

"No, just . . . you know."

"*I'd* be celebrating too," Bloom said, "a girl like that walked out on me. Way it looks, she killed both her brother *and* the farmer."

"Only thing," Rawles said, "is the alibi."

"Yeah," Bloom said.

"We ever find her," Bloom said, "we'd nail her for both murders if it wasn't for the alibi."

"You wouldn't know where she was the afternoon that farmer got shot, would you?" Rawles asked.

"When was that?" Crowell asked.

"You have a lot of trouble keeping up with the calendar, don't you?"

"No, but . . ."

"He was shot Monday," Bloom said. "The day before Sunny disappeared. She left here on Tuesday, remember? Packed all her clothes and left. Except for a bathing suit. I was here that same night, remember? Miss Holmes was taking a shower."

"Miss Homes is a very clean person," Rawles said, and grinned at her again.

"Thursday was when I came to see you again, remember?" Bloom said. "At the supermarket. You were spraying cabbages . . ."

"Lettuce."

"Lettuce, right, you *do* remember. That was when you told me again that you and Sunny were together the night her brother was killed. You remember telling me that, don't you?"

"I remember."

"Which is the thing of it," Rawles said, shaking his head. "She didn't have that alibi, man, we'd throw the book at her the minute we get her."

"You're sure you don't know where she is, huh?" Bloom asked.

"Positive."

"Reason we asked about last night," Rawles said, and touched his nose, "is we had her located at six-thirty, she was staying with this friend of her mother's, but she left there at six-thirty. And we had her located again at eight-thirty, in a lounge on the trail; showed a bartender there her picture just a little while ago, he's sure she was the girl. But we don't know where she headed *after* she left the bar, and we thought if she'd come here first, she might have mentioned . . ."

"No, she didn't."

"Or maybe later. *After* she left the bar."

"No, she didn't come here at all."

"*You* didn't see her then, either, right?" Bloom asked Lettie. "At six-thirty. She didn't come here to pick up that bathing suit or anything?"

"I didn't see nobody," Lettie said, and looked at her sandaled feet.

"Well, we'll find her, that's for sure," Rawles said, sighing. "Just take a little time, that's all. Once we get her . . . you're *sure* you were with her all that night?"

They had no way of knowing at this point whether Crowell was buying anything they told him. They were trying to sell three things. First, they wanted Crowell to believe that they did not yet know Sunny's body had been found; as far as they were concerned, she was still alive, and they were still looking for her. Next, they wanted him to believe they were convinced that Sunny had slain both her brother *and* Burrill. And finally, they wanted him to believe that they had enough on her to convict her—if only it weren't for that damn alibi.

Crowell was the alibi.

Crowell was also stupid.

They were counting on his stupidity.

They were also counting on the cleverness most stupid people think they possess. They were hoping that Crowell would cleverly think, *Gee, if I take away her alibi, they'll be* positive *she did both murders*. They were hoping Crowell would not think beyond that, would not wonder what would happen once the police *did* find Sunny's body. A smarter person might have realized at once that the moment Sunny's body was discovered in that swimming pool, she would no longer be suspect in either of the murders; she would instead be a third victim. But Crowell was stupid. And stupid people are incapable of planning very far in advance. They take whatever solution seems expedient, and then worry about the next solution when the next problem presents itself. Or so the detectives were *hoping*.

They had offered Crowell a solution.

Break Sunny's alibi, and we charge her with both murders the minute we catch up with her.

Crowell, if he *was* indeed the murderer and if all of this wasn't just a pointless exercise, had to have known that the police would never be able to charge Sunny with anything; she was already dead on the bottom of my swimming pool. But if he broke her alibi, and they were convinced that she'd killed her brother and Burrill, then wouldn't they think she'd got herself into some *other* kind of trouble afterwards? Something that had led to somebody killing *her*, too? Somebody other than himself, who had Lettie here swearing that she'd been with him from six-thirty on?

He took the bait.

"This alibi," he said, and hesitated.

The detectives waited.

"You mean her saying we were together all that night, don't you?"

"You can't be in two places at the same time," Rawles said. "Either she was here with you, or she was out stabbing her brother."

"Simple," Bloom said.

"Well, I can vouch for her being here with me," Crowell said.

"So that's it," Bloom said. "Sorry to've bothered you, we'll just have to keep . . ."

"*Most* of the time," Crowell said.

The detectives looked at each other.

"She wasn't here *all* that time," Crowell said.

"You hearing this?" Rawles said to Bloom.

"Oh, brother, *am* I?" Bloom said. "Are you saying she left here at some time that night?"

"Yes, sir, that's what I'm saying."

"When? What time?"

"Around nine."

"When did she get back? *Did* she come back?"

"She came back, yes."

"What time?"

"Around ten-thirty."

"Terrific," Rawles said. "Gave her plenty of time to get over to Stone Crab, do the number on her brother, and crawl back here into bed. Did she say where she was going?"

"Said she was hungry, wanted to pick up some burgers."

"Did she come back here with any burgers?"

"No, sir, she did not," Crowell said.

"Why didn't you tell us this earlier?" Bloom asked. "We appreciate your telling us now, believe me, but it would have made a big difference . . ."

"Well, I loved that girl a lot," Crowell said, which was perhaps the biggest lie either detective had ever heard in their combined years of police work. "And I got to tell you, officers, I didn't think she killed her brother, I mean it."

"You just figured she went out for burgers, huh?" Rawles said.

"Yes, sir."

"But didn't bring any back?"

"That's right, sir."

He was "sirring" them to death now. He must have figured he was home free.

"Gone an hour and a half, but didn't come back with the burgers she said she was going for."

"Must've eaten them there," Crowell said, nodding.

"You didn't ask her, though."

"Sir?"

"Whether she'd eaten them there or not?"

"No, sir."

"How about *you*, Jackie?" Rawles said, a clear indication to Bloom that they were ready to close in on him; Rawles had used the suspect's first name, an old police trick designed to make him feel both inferior and intimidated. "Weren't *you* hungry?"

"No, sir, I was not."

"Didn't ask her to bring back any burgers for you?"

"No, sir."

"Even though the last time you'd eaten was . . . what time did you say it was? When you took her to McDonald's?"

"Seven o'clock."

"And came right back here."

"Yes, sir."

"And she left at nine, you say?"

"Yes, sir."

"Gone an hour and a half."

"Yes, sir."

"Jackie," Bloom said, and hesitated. "Where were *you* during that time?"

"Why . . . here, sir."

"All alone?"

"Well . . . yes, sir."

"Nobody with you?"

Crowell looked at Bloom. He looked at Rawles. He must have realized in that instant that breaking Sunny's alibi was the same thing as breaking his own.

"Well . . . I was waiting for Sunny to come back, you see."

"*You* didn't go out during that hour and a half, did you?"

"No, I was right here."

"In bed here, or what?"

"Well . . . yeah. Watching television."

"What show did you watch?"

"I forget."

"You got a *TV Guide*?" Rawles asked.

Lettie, who'd been silent during all this, suddenly said, "There's a bunch of them over on the dresser."

"I don't think they go back that far, though," Crowell said.

Maybe he wasn't as stupid as they thought he was. He had spotted what was coming. They were going to quiz him on the shows he'd seen. The eighth of August was a Monday night. As Rawles went to the dresser, Crowell must have been trying to remember which shows were on every Monday night. There were three or four old *TV Guides* on the dresser, not quite the "bunch" Lettie had advertised. Rawles picked one up, discarded it, picked up a second one, checked the dates on its cover, and said, "We're in luck. August sixth to August twelfth."

Rawles knew, of course, that McKinney had been murdered on a Monday night, the eighth of August. He also knew that the *TV Guide* listings started on a Saturday and ended on a Friday, each and every week of the year. He had been through this particular performance at least a dozen times before with suspects who'd claimed they were watching television. To Rawles, what he was about to do was as routine as strapping on his shoulder holster every day. To Crowell, it was a brand new experience, a test of his memory, a test of his cleverness. But he was stupid. He never asked to check the dates on the cover of the magazine, or he'd have discovered that Rawles was holding in his hands a copy of the August 13–19 issue. Moreover, as Rawles flipped the pages, he assumed that the test was going to be as square and honest as those he'd taken in high school before he'd dropped out to become a clerk in the produce department of a supermarket.

"Monday, Monday," Rawles said out loud, strengthening the impression that this was all on the up-and-up. "August eighth, here we are. Nine o'clock," he said, "that's what time she left, right?"

"Yes, sir," Crowell said.

"Okay, let's see what was on at nine o'clock."

"Tell us if you remember any of these will you?" Bloom said.

"Nine o'clock," Rawles said, and looked at the *eight* o'clock listings for *Tuesday* night, August the *sixteenth*. "Here we go. Channel Three, 'Nova.' Channel Eight, 'A-Team.' Channel Ten, 'Happy Days.' Channel Thirteen . . ."

"'Happy Days,'" Crowell said. "That's what I was watching."

"I like that show," Rawles said, smiling. "That Fonz is hot stuff."

"Yeah," Crowell said, and smiled back. "I like it, too."

"So that's what you were watching," Bloom said. "So that settles that." He, too, had been through this number many times before, with Rawles and also with other detectives on the squad.

He knew that Rawles had fed Crowell false data. He knew that Crowell had identified a show he couldn't possibly have seen on the Monday night McKinney was killed. He had just blown his own alibi for the night of August eighth, and his alibi for *last* night was sitting right there in a striped shift, her legs crossed, jiggling one sandaled foot.

"I don't suppose you watched any television *last* night," Bloom said.

"No, we didn't," Crowell said, and looked at Lettie.

The detectives figured he was playing it safe. As dumb as he was, he was maybe beginning to think they'd somehow pulled a fast one, and he didn't want to take any more chances on television. Better to say he hadn't been watching it at *all* last night. Better to clue Lettie in with a look as obvious as a rivet.

"That right, Lettie?" Bloom said.

"We weren't watching no television, that's right," she said.

"What *were* you doing?" Rawles asked. "You came here to take a shower, didn't you? What time did you take your shower?"

"Soon's I got here."

"At six-thirty? Is that when you got here?"

"Around then."

"And that's when you took your shower."

"That's when I took it."

"Did you take *another* shower later on?"

"What do you mean?"

"You didn't have any clothes on when we got here. Did you take another shower *after* the first shower?"

"Look," Lettie said, "you know what we were doing here, so let's cut the shit about the shower, okay? Far as I know, it ain't no crime, what we were doing."

"Did you take *any* shower at all?" Bloom asked.

"I took a shower, yes. When I got here. I was all sweaty, so I took a shower."

"And that was at six-thirty."

"More or less."

"Which was it? More or less?"

"A little after, I guess. Musta been about twenty to seven, right, Jackie?"

"That's right," Crowell said. "Around then."

"Then it *wasn't* six-thirty," Rawles said.

"What difference does a few minutes make?" Lettie said. "We're talking twenty to seven, a quarter to seven . . ."

"Oh, was it a *quarter* to seven?" Bloom said.

"It was sometime between six-thirty and a quarter to seven," Lettie said.

"You're sure about that? It couldn't have been, say, seven o'clock? Or even eight o'clock?"

"No, it wasn't seven o'clock, it was . . ."

"How about *eight* o'clock?"

"If it wasn't *seven* o'clock, then it couldn'ta been *eight* o'clock, neither."

"Why not?"

" 'Cause I got here at six-thirty, a quarter to seven."

"Where were you before then?"

"My own place."

"Where's that?"

"Across the way."

"You were there at six-thirty, huh?"

"That's where I was."

"How long did it take you to get here from there?"

"Just a few minutes. It's only right across the way, you can see it from the window here if you look out."

"How'd you know Jackie was home?" Rawles asked.

"I seen his car," Lettie said.

"What time did you get home from work?" Bloom asked.

"Me?" Lettie said.

"No. You, Jackie."

"Six o'clock, it must've been," Crowell said.

"And you parked your car outside."

"Right outside. They give these spaces, they assign . . ."

"Where Lettie could see it."

"Well, I didn't know whether she could *see* it or not. I just parked it where I'm *supposed* to park it."

"And that's where you saw it, right, Lettie?"

"That's where I saw it."

"At six-thirty."

"Around then."

"And neither one of you have been out of this apartment since six-thirty last night, right?"

"We both been here," Crowell said, and gave Lettie his pointed look again.

"Both of us," Lettie said.

They were getting nowhere. Bloom sighed. Rawles sighed too, and then touched his nose again, the signal to Bloom that he was about to tell another outrageous lie and he expected Bloom to pick up on it. Bloom didn't know what the lie was going to be. But he was ready for it.

"This man outside," Rawles said, and hesitated. "Sitting on the stoop outside. Black like you and me, Lettie, said he was sitting outside around eight o'clock sometime . . ."

"Little after eight, it must've been," Bloom said.

"Said he saw you coming in the building, Jackie," Rawles said.

Crowell looked at him.

"Said you seemed to be in a hurry, Jackie," Bloom said.

"No," Crowell said, shaking his head.

"No, you *weren't* in a hurry?"

"I wasn't . . ."

"He said . . ."

"I wasn't coming in no *building*!"

"What *were* you doing?"

"I was here in the apartment with Lettie."

"Then how'd this man see you outside? Walking in?" Rawles said.

"In a hurry," Bloom said.

"He was mistaken."

"Not too many white people living here," Rawles said.

"Lettie told you I was here with her from six-thirty . . ."

"Hard for a black man not to know a white man when he sees one."

"Said it was you."

"Said he saw Jackie Crowell . . ."

"No, he didn't," Crowell said.

"Then it couldn't have been you coming back from dumping Sunny in a swimming pool, right?" Rawles said.

"With two bullet holes in her head," Bloom said.

"You told me . . ." Lettie said.

"Shut up!" Crowell said.

"You told me a *dope* bust!"

"I said shut up!"

"Shut up *shit*, man! A thousand bucks don't buy no . . ."

What happened next happened very fast.

Lettie was standing near the dresser when Crowell threw open the top drawer and reached in for the gun. She tried to move away the moment she saw the gun, but he pulled her in against him from behind, his left arm around her waist, the gun in his right hand, flailing the room. Both Rawles and Bloom had drawn their own guns the moment Crowell made his break for the dresser, but neither of them could trigger off a shot because Lettie had been in the line of fire. Now Lettie was being used as a shield, screaming and kicking as Crowell dragged her toward the door, the detectives wedged helplessly in a narrow space on the same side of the bed, each of them hoping Crowell wasn't even dumber than they knew he was. As he backed toward the door, the gun wildly whipping the air, they hoped he wouldn't start spraying the room with .38-caliber bullets, hoped he wouldn't leave yet another dead girl behind him. He shoved her across the room instead, an instant before he reached for the doorknob with his left hand. Lettie collided with Rawles, who bulldozed her aside. She was still on the bed, flat on her back, cursing the entire universe, when the detectives ran out into the hallway after Crowell.

The rest, as they say, is history.

I was the first obstacle Crowell encountered on the street outside.

I was the one he shot, the dumb bastard.

My daughter told me she was a celebrity at school. She told me there was only one other kid in her class who had a father who'd been shot, and that was during the Korean War, which didn't count. She wanted to know how it felt getting shot. I told her I wouldn't recommend it. She kept wanting to know how it *felt*. I told her it felt better than getting stepped on by an elephant, but worse than anything else I could think of. We played a game for the next ten mintues, making up things that might be worse than getting shot. We agreed that getting buried alive in the sand might be worse. We agreed that hanging by the thumbs in a Persian market might also be worse. Joanna suggested that getting shot was probably like breaking off with a boyfriend, all the pain and everything.

Clever daughter, mine.

I told her Dale had been the one who'd wanted to end it. I told her Dale had fallen in love with someone else and she planned to marry him. I told her the man's name was Jim. Joanna said she hated the name Jim. She asked me what I was going to do now.

I didn't know what I was going to do now.

Bloom came to see me again two days before I was to be released from the hospital. He had with him a transcript of the Crowell Q and A.

"I'm not supposed to let it out of my hands," he said, "but who's to say I didn't forget it here while I went downstairs for a cup of coffee? Glance at it, okay? Pretend it fell off the back of a truck."

"The coffee downstairs any good?" I asked.

"Better than the squad room, that's for sure." He tossed the transcript onto the bed. "I'll be back in twenty minutes or so," he said. "Enjoy yourself."

Skye Bannister himself had handled the interrogation for the state's attorney's office. Present had been Captain Walter Hopper and Detectives Cooper Rawles and Morris Bloom. The transcript started with the usual recitation of place, date, and time—in this case the Calusa Public Safety Building at five o'clock on the morning of August twenty-seventh. Bannister read Crowell his rights, and Crowell acknowledged that he understood them and wished no attorney present during the question-and-answer session.

Q: What is your full name, please?
A: Jack Crowell.
Q: No middle name?
A: No.
Q: Where do you live, Mr. Crowell?
A: 1134 Archer Street.
Q: Here in Calusa?
A: Yes.
Q: Can you tell me how old you are?
A: Eighteen.
Q: Mr. Crowell, I want to ask you first about the night of August eighth. Can you recall that night?
A: I can.
Q: Where were you at nine o'clock that night?
A: In the Shore Haven condominium on Stone Crab Key.
Q: Why did you go there?
A: To see Jack.
Q: By Jack . . .
A: Jack McKinney.
Q: Tell me what you did when you got to the condominium. Step by step, please.
A: I parked my car, took the elevator up to the third floor,

236

and walked down the hall to Jack's apartment. I rang the door-bell . . .

Q: Would you remember the number of the apartment?

A: It was apartment 307.

Q: You rang the doorbell . . .

A: Yeah, and Jack opened the door for me. We went in the living room and I told him why I was there.

Q: What was it you told him, Mr. Crowell?

A: I told him his sister had mentioned his plan to me, and I wanted $10,000.

Q: What plan was that?

A: To grow pot on that farm he was buying.

Q: Why did you want $10,000?

A: It seemed like the right amount.

Q: But what made you think Mr. McKinney would give you $10,000?

A: I knew he had it. The farm was costing him forty thousand. That's what Sunny told me.

Q: Yes, but why did you think he would *give* you so much money?

A: To keep me from telling the cops.

Q: Telling them what?

A: That he was planning to grow pot.

Q: What did Mr. McKinney say when you asked him for the $10,000?

A: He told me to go fuck myself. Is it all right to say that . . . with the tape going, I mean?

Q: If it's what he said . . .

A: It's exactly what he said.

Q: What happened then?

A: He told me to get out. I told him I wasn't going noplace till he gave me the ten thousand. One thing led to another . . .

Q: What do you mean by that?

A: He started shoving me, I guess, and I shoved him back . . . and like that.

Q: Like what, Mr. Crowell?

A: I guess I pulled a knife on him.

Q: You went up there with a knife?

A: I always carry a knife.

Q: Is this the knife you had with you that night?

A: Yeah, that's it.

Q: Please have the record indicate that the knife being offered is what is commonly known as a switchblade knife, and that it is equipped with a spring-release button that opens a six-inch-long blade. It was found on the premises at 1134 Archer Street in apartment 202 . . . is that your apartment, by the way, Mr. Crowell?

A: That's my apartment.

Q: By Detectives Rawles and Bloom at 3:10 A.M. this date, August 27, and marked with an evidence tag at that time. What happened next, Mr. Crowell? After you pulled the knife? You said this *is* your knife . . .

A: Yeah, it's my knife, all right. I guess I told Jack I was going to mess him up unless he gave me the money.

Q: What did you mean by "mess him up"?

A: Cut him.

Q: What happened then?

A: He ran in the bedroom. He had a gun in there on the table alongside the bed. He went for the gun.

Q: What did you do?

A: What would *you* do, a guy reaching for a gun?

Q: I'd like to know what *you* did.

A: I stabbed him. His back was still to me, he was getting ready to turn with the gun in his hand. So I stabbed him before he could shoot me. It was self-defense.

Q: You stabbed him in the back?

A: The first couple of times. I kept stabbing him to make sure. He sort of . . . like he turned when he was falling, you know? So I stabbed him in the front too. Wherever. I just kept stabbing him.

Q: What did you do then?

238

A: I looked around for the money.

Q: Did you find it?

A: Yeah. He had it in his toilet tank. In a plastic bag. Like hanging from the plumbing inside there, you know?

Q: How much money was there?

A: I didn't count it till I got home.

Q: How much money did you discover was in the plastic bag?

A: $47,000.

Q: You counted it.

A: I counted it.

Q: And it came to exactly $47,000?

A: And some change.

Q: How much change?

A: Twenty, thirty dollars, something like that.

Q: What did you do then?

A: After I counted the money?

Q: No. Before you left the apartment.

A: Oh. I washed off my knife and where there was some blood on my clothes. I washed my hands too. Before I left. I didn't want to go out of there with blood all over me. Also, I took the gun, tucked it in my belt under my jacket. It was a good piece, no sense leaving it there.

Q: Is there anything else you'd like to tell me about that night?

A: No. That's all that happened that night.

Q: You told the police that you and Miss McKinney were together that night . . .

A: Yeah, but not *all* night. I told her I was hungry, said I wanted to go out for some more burgers. I left her about nine o'clock. It's only ten, fifteen minutes to Stone Crab. That's where I went when I left her. To her brother's apartment. To get my $10,000.

Q: You got a lot more than that, though.

A: Yeah, I was lucky. I almost didn't look in the toilet tank, can you believe it? That was a last-minute idea.

Q: Miss McKinney told the police that you were together *all* night on the night of the murder. Why did she do that?

A: That was my idea.

Q: Did she *know* you had killed her brother?

A: No, no, you think I'm crazy?

Q: Then why did she alibi you?

A: It was the other way around.

Q: I don't understand.

A: I told her the police would think *she* did it.

Q: I still don't understand.

A: I told her if the police knew I'd left her alone there in my apartment, they'd think she ran out to kill her brother.

Q: Why would they think that?

A: Brothers and sisters, you know? The cops always look for that kind of shit. Excuse me.

Q: So you talked her into believing she needed an alibi.

A: Well, I didn't do it *that* way. I mean, I didn't make it sound like I was *conning* her or anything. I made her think I was protecting her, you know? Like I'd lie for her to save her skin, back her up if she said she was there with me all night. That way the police wouldn't try to pin anything on her.

Q: And she believed you.

A: Yeah.

Q: Then why did you kill her?

A: Well, that's another story.

Q: Yes, it is. Maybe we ought to take these in order. Mr. Crowell, are you familiar with a tract of farmland approximately midway between Calusa and Ananburg, what is known as the Burrill farm?

A: I am.

Q: Did you visit the Burrill farm on the afternoon of August twenty-second?

A: I did.

Q: Why did you go there?

A: To see Burrill.

Q: See him about what?

A: Same thing I went to see Jack about.

Q: And what was that?

A: Money.

Q: What money?

A: The $4,000.

Q: What do you mean?

A: Sunny told me her brother gave him a $4,000 deposit on the land.

Q: So you went to see him about this $4,000.

A: Yeah. Same as Jack.

Q: How was it the same as Jack?

A: Well, I *wanted* that money, you see.

Q: You already had the $47,000 you took after you killed . . .

A: Yeah.

Q: But you wanted an *additional* $4,000?

A: Yeah, well, every little bit helps, don't it?

Q: So you went to Burrill's farm to steal it from him?

A: To *ask* him for it, not to *steal* it.

Q: You expected him to *give* you $4,000 . . .

A: Well, I had a gun, you see. The gun I took from Jack's apartment.

Q: Then you *did* plan to steal the money.

A: No, just *ask* for it. 'Cause I figured it belonged to Jack, you see? 'Cause Jack was dead now, and there wouldn't be no deal on the land. That four thousand belonged with the *rest* of the money, you see?

Q: You went in there to commit armed robbery . . .

A: No, just to ask him for the money.

Q: *Did* you, in fact, ask him for it?

A: Sure.

Q: Were you holding a gun on him at the time?

A: Well, I had it in my hand.

Q: Then you *were* committing armed robbery.

A: No, I wasn't threatening him or anything.

Q: Is this the gun you had in your hand?

A: Yeah.

Q: Is this the gun you fired at a man named Matthew Hope earlier today?

A: Yeah.

Q: Let the record indicate that the gun is a .38-caliber Smith & Wesson revolver, and that it was recovered from Mr. Crowell outside the premises at 1134 Archer Street at 2:20 A.M. this date, August 27. What did Burrill say when you asked him for the money?

A: He said he didn't *have* it, even though Sunny told me her brother had given it to him. A deposit of $4,000!

Q: But he said he didn't have it.

A: He said it was in Escrow. I didn't know what that meant. Where the hell is *Escrow*, I asked him. I never heard of noplace in Florida named Escrow.

Q: What happened then?

A: Same thing.

Q: What do you mean?

A: He tried to rush me, and I had to shoot him. Same thing as Jack, if you see what I mean. All I wanted was the money, they shouldn't have tried nothing.

Q: How many times did you shoot him?

A: Three, four times, is all.

Q: Then what?

A: I looked for the money. I tore the place apart.

Q: Did you find it?

A: No. I asked Sunny later where Escrow was. She started laughing.

Q: When was this?

A: When was what?

Q: That you asked her . . .

A: Oh. That same night, I guess. The night before she split. We were laying there in bed, I asked her where the hell Escrow was. I figured maybe it was in Texas someplace. She starts laughing, tells me it's something has to do with lawyers and banks, where they hold money till a deal is settled. I said something like, "So *that's* what he meant," and she asks me what I'm talking about, so I told her about Burrill, about what happened with Burrill. We were drinking a lot, I guess I'd had a little too much. Otherwise I wouldn't have mentioned it. About Burrill, I mean.

Q: You told her you'd killed Burrill?

A: Well, I didn't put it in those words.

Q: How *did* you put it?

A: I mentioned we'd had a little hassle.

Q: She must have heard about Burrill's death by then, wouldn't you think?

A: Well, it was on television and all.

Q: In which case, she'd have *known* what you meant by "a little hassle."

A: Yeah, I guess she knew what I meant.

Q: She knew that you'd *killed* him.

A: Yeah, I guess so.

Q: What was her reaction?

A: Scared.

Q: Did you tell her you'd killed her brother as well?

A: Yeah. Shit, I'd had too much to drink, that's all.

Q: How did she respond to *that* information?

A: She wanted to know why I'd done it. I told her for the money. I told her we could do a lot of things with all that money. I showed her the money. I had it in the toilet tank, same as her brother had it, I got the idea from him. She seemed impressed.

Q: She wasn't scared anymore?

A: I didn't think so. She just said that was a lot of money. No shit? Forty-seven grand? I needed *her* to tell me that was a lot of money?

Q: But she wasn't scared then, is that right? After you told her about her brother?

A: I didn't think so at the time. She must've been, though. She split the very next day, didn't she?

Q: Did that bother you? Her leaving?

A: No, the world is *full* of girls.

Q: But you went looking for her. You went to the M.K. Ranch . . .

A: I wasn't looking for *her*, man.

Q: Then why'd you . . .?

A: I was looking for my *money*, man! She took my *money* with her!

Q: The $47,000?

A: What was left of it, forty-five, something like that. Leaves her purple bikini, takes my money!

Q: So you went looking for her . . .

A: All over town. I told them I was sick down at the market, went looking for Sunny. Staked out the ranch, staked out that lawyer's house—she told me she'd been there once, went swimming naked in his pool, pissed me off, in fact. I figured she might go back there again, take another swim, who the hell knew? Nothing. I finally gave up, went back to work on Thursday. That was when Detective Bloom here came to see me.

Q: How'd you finally locate her?

A: Luck.

Q: Explain that.

A: *Luck*, I just told you. I remembered this old fart veterinarian I used to see at her mother's house every now and then. Guy lives three miles down the road, him and Sunny always seemed very friendly. It occurred to me that maybe she went *there*. I mean, unless she was already in China, she had to be *someplace*, am I right? So I looked up the guy's number—Jeffries is his name, he's in the phone book—and I give him a call, and guess who answers the phone? Little Miss Sunshine herself! I heard her voice, hung up, and hopped in my car.

Q: This was when?

A: Yesterday.

Q: What time?

A: When I called? Musta been a little before six o'clock. I think I spooked her. That's why she ran. I think when I hung up she knew it was me.

Q: What happened then?

A: She was pulling out of the driveway when I got there. Going hellbent for leather, I'm sure I spooked her with my call. I followed her up the road a mile or two till we came to that long stretch where the citrus groves are, you know where I mean? Just before you hit the M.K., if you're coming from Ananburg. There's this long deserted stretch with just orange trees on both sides of the road, not a house in sight. That's where I cut her off. Pulled in right in front of the Porsche, forced it off the road.

Q: What then?

A: I shoved the gun in her face, told her I wanted my money.

Q: Did she give it to you?

A: Not at first. I had to drag her out of the car, whack her around a little.

Q: Whack her around?

A: Hit her. Back and forth across the face.

Q: With the gun?

A: No, not with the *gun*, Jesus! I used my hand. Whap, whap, my hand. She finally forked over the money. It was on the bottom of this purple shoulder bag she always carried, buried on the bottom of it. There was also a little plastic bag of grass in there. I took that, too.

Q: What did you do then?

A: I shot her in the face.

Q: How many times?

A: Twice.

Q: Then what?

A: She fell down on the road near the left front wheel. All I could think of was I wanted to get out of there fast, I didn't want to be nowhere *near* there, all I wanted to do was get home with my money. But I heard a truck coming. From the west. Coming toward us. Not fast, and it was nowhere near close yet, you could hear everything for miles on the road, it was so still on that road with her bleeding near the wheel of the Porsche. So I picked her up and threw her in the car.

Q: Then what?

A: That damn truck! I figured the driver might remember seeing my white car angled in off the road in front of the Porsche. Or maybe he'd seen the blood on the road, it wasn't a *lot* of blood, but it was *blood*, man! I mean, if I left her there dead in the Porsche, that guy in the truck might remember seeing *two* cars, you follow? And *blood* on the road. So I took a rag out of my trunk and wiped up the blood best I could, and then put the rag in the trunk of the Porsche. The road looked okay, I mean a lot of animals get killed on that road, people driving by, I figured if anybody saw the stain, they'd figure an animal got run over. It looked okay, I mean it. So I left my car where it was, and I got in the Porsche and started driving.

Q: Where were you headed?

A: I didn't know *where* to go, I *mean* it. I figured one of the beaches, but it was still light—this was only like seven o'clock, close to seven—there'd still be people on the beaches, you know? So I just kept driving around.

Q: With Miss McKinney on the seat beside you?

A: No, no, she was on the *back* seat.

Q: Nobody saw her there?

A: One guy looked in the car when I stopped for a traffic light, but he must've thought she was asleep or something.

Q: When did you decide to take her to Mr. Hope's house?

A: That came out of the blue.

Q: You thought it would be a good idea to take her there?

A: Yeah. If nobody would see me, it seemed like a good idea. Drop her in his pool, you know? Little present for him. I was still a little pissed about her swimming there naked. So I figured I'd take her there swimming *again*. Provided nobody was home. Otherwise . . . well, I didn't know what I'd do if he was home. But the lights were out, and I just parked the Porsche in his driveway, carried her out, and dumped her. Simple as that.

Q: No one saw you?

A: Did somebody say he saw me?

Q: I'm asking you.

A: I don't think so. It was dark, and I was very quiet and careful.

Q: What did you do after you dropped Miss McKinney's body in the pool?

A: I got out of there. Fast.

Q: Where did you go?

A: I walked to a gas station about ten blocks from the house.

Q: Why'd you go there?

A: To buy a gasoline can and have them fill it for me.

Q: Then what did you do?

A: I called Yellow Cab, told them I'd run out of gas on the Timucuan Point Road, and needed a taxi to take me out there.

Q: What time was this?

A: Nine o'clock? A little after?

Q: Did Yellow Cab, in fact, take you to your car?

A: Yeah. It was already dark when we got out there, you couldn'ta seen the bloodstains even if you were looking for them. I made a big show of putting gas in my tank. The cabbie kept hanging around, wanting to know if I needed a hand. I told him I could take care of it myself. The minute he drove off, I got in the car and headed home.

Q: What did you do when you got back to your apartment?

A: I called Lettie right away, this must've been nine-thirty or so, told her to come over. When she got there, I handed her a thousand dollars in fifties. I told her I'd been in a bar on the Trail and some cops came in and a guy threw a bag of weed on the floor, and I ran out when they started taking names. I told her they may have spotted my license plate. I told her if the cops came around asking questions, she should say she'd been with me since six-thirty. She never saw so much money in her life. She had her clothes off in a minute.

Q: The thousand dollars you gave Miss Holmes—was it part of the money you stole from Jack McKinney?

A: Yeah. Sunny spent about five hundred on clothes, there was forty-four-five in the bag when I counted it. I gave a thousand of that to Lettie.

Q: Did she see you take the money out of the bag?

A: You think I'm crazy? I pulled out the thousand before I called
   her, stuck the bag back in the tank.
Q: Mr. Crowell, I show you this plastic bag containing U.S. cur-
   rency. Is this the plastic bag to which you've been referring?
A: It looks like it. All plastic bags look alike, don't they?
Q: All plastic bags do not have U.S. currency in them.
A: All U.S. currency looks alike, too.
Q: But does this look like the bag of money to which you've been
   referring?
A: It looks like it, yeah. If there's 43,500 bucks in it, then that's
   the bag.
Q: Please have the record indicate that this plastic bag containing
   U.S. currency was recovered by Detectives Bloom and Rawles
   from the toilet tank of apartment 202 at 1134 Archer Street at
   3:40 A.M. this date, August 27, and tagged as evidence at that
   time.
A: You'd better count it. You know cops.

   Bloom came back into the room a few minutes after I'd finished reading the last page. He took the transcript from me,
looked at the blue binder on it for a moment, and then said,
"What do you think?"
   "Nice," I said.
   "Yeah, it'll hold up," Bloom said. He tapped the folder on the
palm of his hand. "Looks like the only one gets out of this with a
profit is the guy with the Spanish accent. We got as much chance
of finding him . . ." He let the sentence trail off. "I guess the
mother'll come out okay, too. The money Crowell stole from
McKinney'll go back to the estate, and she's the only one left,
ain't she? In the family, I mean. The only one left." He shook his
head. He looked sad all at once. "Eighteen years old," he said.
He kept shaking his head. "Damn stupid kid."

   Veronica came to see me on the day before I left the hospital.
She was wearing white. She looked like one of the nurses. Out-

side my window, the winds of September were advertising the full onslaught of the hurricane season. She told me that Bloom had called her on the morning they took Crowell's statement. He had mentioned at that time that I'd been shot. She had not immediately come to the hospital because she wasn't sure whether or not she'd be welcome. She told me she'd been away. She said that on the day after her daughter's funeral, she and Ham Jeffries had driven down to Captiva together. They had only returned yesterday. She had called the hospital late last night to find out if I was still here. She had asked when visiting hours were.

"So here I am," she said.

"I see."

"How are you?"

"Much better."

"Big hero," she said, and smiled her radiant smile.

I nodded.

"So they got him," she said.

"They got him."

There was a long silence.

"I was embarrassed about coming here," she said. "It took a while to work up the nerve."

"Embarrassed about what?"

"Ham. And me. We learned a lot about each other in Captiva. Something like this . . . it draws people together again." She paused. She looked away. "He's asked me to marry him," she said, and turned to look at me again. Her pale eyes reflected the gray of the day outside. The palm trees rattled in the wind. "Do you think I should?"

"That's up to you," I said.

"I loved him very much, you know," she said.

Past tense, I noticed. I said nothing.

"I guess I still do. I guess I've loved him all these years, Matthew."

"Then congratulations," I said.

"Yeah," she said, and nodded.

We chatted about other things then. The fact that hurricanes were now named after men as well as women, which she guessed was a direct result of the feminist movement. The fact that Calusa in September was even worse than Calusa in August. The fact that I'd lost a little weight during my hospital stay. Just before she left, I told her that the money Crowell had stolen from her son would undoubtedly be considered a part of his estate, and since she was his only living heir, would eventually become hers.

"My cows coming home at last," she said somewhat sadly.

I did not think it kind to mention that at last her bull was coming home, too.